Reade

"Johnson weaves her magic into a new tale about life, love, and second chances…a page-turning keeper!" ~Lori Soard

White Eagle's Lady

"Fraught with tension and excitement…Johnson blends historical facts with love…I applaud her skill." ~Romantic Times

"A must read for readers of Native American romance." ~Hope Tarr

Unfinished Dreams

"A debut novel, Pamela Johnson is an author that should not be missed." ~AStoryweavers Reviews

"Burns as hot as Blaze titles…" ~Scribesworld

Cursed Comes Christmas

"Magical, creative, moving, and romantic." ~Rom Reviews

Crumbs in the Keyboard

"Honest and engaging. Please read Crumbs." ~Stella Cameron

"This is wonderful." ~Fern Michaels

"You are phenomenal women!" ~Allison Pogue, Center for Women and Families

WORKS BY PAMELA JOHNSON

NOVELS

Unfinished Dreams
Cursed Comes Christmas
     with Alexis Hart and Blair Wing
White Eagle's Lady
Tides of Autumn

NOVELLAS

Images
Her Captain's Return
Stranded With Children
Love Is Patient
I'll Take Mine in a Kilt
Colin McCarthy's Kiss
A Touch of Heather
Internet Connection
Garden of Dreams

OTHER BOOKS FEATURING PAMELA JOHNSON

Romancing the Holiday, Vol. I
Lovey Dovey; Romance Anthology
Seasons of Romance
Crumbs In the Keyboard (contributor and editor)

Tides of Autumn

PAMELA JOHNSON

Echelon Elite

Echelon Press
Crowley, Texas

Echelon Press
P.O. Box 1084
Crowley, TX 76036

Echelon Elite
First paperback printing: August 2003

Trade paperback ISBN 1-59080-158-X

Printed and bound in the United States of America.

www.echelonpress.com

Dear Reader,

Like Darci, I too fell in love with Mackinac Island from the first time I saw it. Amidst a rich historical background, the island celebrates a more genteel time. Whether its a long evening stroll on the boardwalk, catching the last dredges of a brilliant sunset on the lake, or the heady fragrance of lilacs in bloom, Mackinac's romantic ambiance continues to be a serene spot for the weary heart. My hope is that each of you will have the chance to experience visiting its charm first hand.

~Pamela

Enjoy the island!
Happy reading!
Pamula Johnson
Aug. 2003

$\mathcal{D}$edication

To my Grandmother Stone and my mother for instilling a love of the island through their stories, and to Uncle Sam and Aunt Margaret McIntire for making that love a reality

Prologue

"You're a wealthy woman now, Darci Cunningham, you've got to watch your back."

The words hit her like a sudden gust of wind, causing her to stumble. She fumbled with the cup in her hand, catching it before it crashed to the floor. Exasperated with the bluntness of his words, she straightened and pierced her long time family friend and financial consultant, with a narrow look. "Peter, I didn't realize that you could put a dollar amount on heartache."

He sighed, in the same way Darci had seen him do over the past few months as they worked together to manage her dead husbands last will and testament. They'd only recently begun to dabble in the investments he'd left behind. This was the one area that she'd left to her husband, her attention somehow always on rearing their children and volunteer community efforts.

"Look, I have to be able to see above the emotion."

Peter stood as he loosened his tie and walked to her, removing the coffee cup from her hand. His hands settled all too comfortably on her shoulders. Darci wanted to slip from beneath his captivity, but an uncomfortable gratitude held her gaze to his. As though sensing he wanted more.

"I'm just looking out for you the way I feel Matt would have wanted me to."

His thumbs massaged her skin in concentric circles, his gaze held firmly to hers.

"I need you as a financial advisor, Peter. I doubt Matt would have meant for you to look out for me on any other level."

He shrugged, dropping both hands to his sides. "I've

known the two of you a long time, Darci. Since college, and you know that I would never cross any lines where I wasn't welcome."

"Glad we're clear on that." Darci picked up the cup and walked into the kitchen, a queasy sensation forming in her stomach.

Peter followed, sauntering up to the kitchen sink beside her.

"You know," he chuckled quietly as he stared out the kitchen window. "I used to have a mad crush one you—I mean, before Matt beat me to the punch."

"I *don't* want to talk about this now, please." Darci held the edge of the cabinet, her insides swirling like a tidal pool with decisions that would have to be made for her life. Fighting off a suitor—in particular, one who was her husband's best friend—was the last thing she wanted to deal with.

"Okay, I understand, but you know you can count on me for—anything." He leaned forward, placing a kiss on her temple, the true implication of his offer in the way he lingered near.

She turned her face from his, trying to be polite as possible. Peter was sweet to her, always had been, and was the only Uncle her children had ever known. That meant a lot to both her and Matt, but with Matt gone now, she wasn't sure of how the tide was changing.

Peter hesitated before he sighed once again, and then he left, picking up his briefcase as he headed for the front door.

"Remember what I told you, Darci." The door clicked softly behind him.

𝒞hapter 𝒪ne

It was only a dream. He wasn't supposed to die. Darci once believed that living on Mackinac Island was a simple, lovely spin to her imagination. No more than a cute little joke between she and her husband, Matt. Never in a million years could she have expected she would be living it alone—this whim of hers. It had been left to nothing more than playful thoughts of perhaps how they would live out their twilight years together.

But this—this parasitic, all-consuming silence—this "on-again-off again" feeling of emptiness—was no joke.

Darci stared at the snowy white computer screen, willing some sort of intelligent creativity to come forth from a mind as devoid of life as what she stared at.

Her writer's roadblock had nothing to do with the locale. The intense beauty and history of Mackinac Island had long ago served as inspiration for a dream set aside when she married and bore children.

His life had been hers, by choice. The new journey she now found herself traveling was not meant to be alone.

Her husband, *her* Matt—of twenty-two years had been snatched from her by what the autopsy revealed was a heart attack. Otherwise the pillar of good health, his passing still stumped his colleagues.

She rubbed her palm across the cool, smooth wood of her desk, hoping that somehow its solidarity could be transferred to her spirit. Yet when she shut her eyes the memory of Matt's precious smile taunted her again, reminding her of how unkind fate can be.

The autopsy report revealed genetic make-up and

probably stress related complications, but little other explanation other than apparent heart attack. Thankfully, Peter had gone with her to the morgue and then stayed with her children as they too said their goodbyes. It was Peter who was with Matt at the gym the night of his heart attack.

Not one to question Matt's one night out with the guys, she encouraged that he continue to enjoy the weekly basketball game with his friend since college.

Still, in the months that followed, Darci toyed with the ever-present guilt that maybe there *hadn't* been enough "playtime" in their lives. Perhaps, if there had been, perhaps if she'd been more insistent that he should take the time off—perhaps, Matt would still be here.

"Dammit, Matt," she whispered, glancing up from her laptop to the serene view outside the living room window. A small measure of anger lay buried deep within her, shoved aside during the weeks that followed when she had to make plans, settle insurance papers, and delve laboriously through the pain of a will she never really anticipated she would hear— at least not until she was barely able to shuffle across a room without a walker.

She'd gone to a few of the grief counseling sessions, mostly for Leah and Nathan's benefit. There she realized that the anger she harbored was in the manner in which he'd left her. Without warning, without a chance to prepare for goodbye. One moment he was alive and making promises to her of more time spent together after establishing his practice and the next, she's signing a paper to release him to a funeral home and leave his lifeless body in the company of strangers.

A dull ache of loneliness clung to her heart, making it difficult for her to see all the possibility of the life now before her, in light of what once seemed unimaginable in her recent past.

Wanting to write was a secret longing, a desire buried deep inside her—she'd discovered it long ago. Yet it was only since her honeymoon on the island, that the idea took seed in her soul and somehow she knew, even then, that the island would eventually be her home.

Her passion for words, coupled with her love of books, was as sacred to her as caring for a child. In that respect, she'd already raised two into adulthood, both with Matt's help and guidance.

Now she was alone with a horde of stories and articles she'd dabbled with periodically over the years carefully tucked away in various boxes and binders. Some published in obscure magazines, but most simply collecting dust as they waited their moment in the sun. In the back of her mind, she'd always planned—after all else in her life was in order—that she would then be able to concentrate on her writing. If Matt's unexpected passing had taught her nothing else, its lesson—plain as day—was that life holds no guarantees.

Her desire—as Matt knew and often argued that she should begin—was to write a novel.

She needed some type of outlet that would pull from her all the creativity she longed to share—an avenue to unleash the intensity of emotions within her, and to visualize on paper the stories and characters that had haunted her memory for so long.

For a while, the creativity took form in the rearing of her two children, encouraging them with their own gifts and supporting those endeavors with a full and proud heart. There was always going to be that time when she could pursue her own interests, but those of her children and Matt had come first. Not that she regretted the choices that seemed natural to her at the time, but time was an elusive thing. She mistakenly thought there would always be *time*.

In her mind, she'd assumed that Matt would there beside her when the time came with his ever-present support and quick wit spurring her on.

An icy chill ran down her arms causing her to hug her lightweight, cotton cardigan around her.

The extreme life change, of course, was ludicrous to many who had known she and Matt for years. She—a middle aged woman and a recent widow to boot,—(a year now past, in April)—selling her home and moving everything that was familiar to her Midwestern roots, to an island on the northern border of the country. Best known for it's packed summer days filled with tourists from all over the world and then as foreboding and desolate as an abandoned lighthouse in the winter.

She'd done her research, aware of the penetrating ice and snow that clamped the island each season. Yet even the thought of solitude appealed to her. There she could remember Matt when their love was new. In a way, maybe she thought she could be closer to him as she wrote.

Still, when asked, she couldn't explain her choices to anyone. Their friends thought it was too soon and Matt's colleagues—even Peter, had tried to reason with her. What many people did not see was she could not stay alone in the same house where she'd raised a family with the same man, for twenty-two years. Within those walls, it was impossible for her not to recall his laugh, their talks about everyday things, their heated arguments that ended with warm apologies and passionate nights.

Darci closed her eyes to a wave of bittersweet memories blowing across her mind, and for a brief moment, she allowed herself the luxury of remembering.

"You know I tried to get away, Darci, but there is no one else around this weekend."

Darci's heart sank, as yet another carefully planned romantic weekend evaporated under the responsibilities of Matt's job. She knew he was right and that there was little he could do, *this time*. They'd have to reschedule farther in advance *next time*.

"Okay, fine." She studied the calendar as she tapped a pen to the table. "Two weeks from today. Then I swear, we'll leave Nathan with your folks and just you and I are headed to the cabin. You do remember that little wood hut you spent a fortune to build as a getaway?"

He grabbed her around the waist, pulling her close, giving her an ornery grin. "Fine with me, but Nathan won't like it you know."

"He'll get over it. I'm not leaving a high school kid alone for a weekend."

"Darci, you're a wise woman, I knew that when I married you." He kissed her neck playfully. "Oh, and pack light, you won't need many clothes."

"Promises, promises." She squirmed in his grasp as his lips teased the sensitive spot under her ear. The spot he knew so well turned her to liquid in his arms.

"Obviously, a trial run is in order, to prove my validity." He tugged her towards the bedroom.

Though one child was in college and the other at after school activities, she hesitated, thinking she *should* get supper started. Forever the practical thinker on the outside, as always she assumed there would be more time.

In the end, his persistence wore her down and supper was pizza ordered late and delivered to their home.

That afternoon would stay in etched in her memory.

Muted shards of sunlight peeked through the blowing curtains, dancing across the ceiling in the warmth of the afternoon. The breeze, gentle and cool, brushed over their heated flesh. Darci held him close, perhaps she knew even then that this moment was special. Their lovemaking was slow, gentle, and passionate.

"I've told you that I love you today, right?" His breath whispered warm against her cheek.

Cupping his face, she took note of the roughness of the shadowed hint of a beard he'd been starting. To make him look more distinguished, he'd told her—more handsome.

"You are already more handsome than a person has the right to be." She gave him a grin, but there was truth in her words.

The familiar dark eyes she'd fallen in love with held her gaze as hypnotic as the first time they'd danced. Perhaps it was God giving her that moment to remember as she studied his face and smiled softly. "By the way, do I know you?"

His laugh rumbled deep in his chest. "Maybe not, but in a few moments you won't forget me."

"Egotist."

He had no idea how right he was.

She should have insisted right then that he find someone to else to work so they could escape the tentacles of the schedule that already wrapped itself around his health.

As it was they were never able to find the time to go to the cabin.

With trembling fingers, she brushed away the telltale signs of new tears emitting from older, not-yet-healed wounds. She took a deep breath, retrieving the words of the counselor in the sessions designed to help her deal with both her grief and her guilt.

Numb in her response to the memories, Darci stared at the white caps skipping across the lake under the strength of the late September wind. She wondered when or—*if*—she would ever truly heal.

Oddly, it was her children, now young adults themselves that had ultimately encouraged her to make the move. Coupled with the guidance and help of her aunt and her eccentric cousin, Maevey, she found a small house and a job. Once decided, the initial transition was easier than she'd thought it would be with the exception of their financial consultant's advice against the move.

She sighed again at the blank screen in front of her. However unfortunate, the muse was not going to stop by for a visit today.

Stretching her arms over her head, Darci looked out at the gray sky. More rain would likely fall before the day was out. Generally, she preferred the rain claiming it inspired her to write. Today though, she wished fervently for the sun to warm the cold dampness in her soul.

The shrill ring of the phone echoed through the tiny house, yanking her from her reverie.

"Hello?"

"Weeeell?" Her lovable, but meddling cousin Maevey, stretched the word into one long syllable.

"Well, what?" She mimicked in return, knowing that

Maevey was curious about the story's progress. She'd called Darci every day for the last week and it was beginning to drive her nuts.

She heard a low frustrated growl.

"So, how's the story coming?" Maevey asked, clearly exasperated.

"Oh, well you know," she sighed. "It just *isn't* today." Darci rubbed her hand over the back of her neck attempting to ease the tension. Immediately, she sensed her cousin's disappointment.

"Hey now, something will come to you, not to worry," Maevey replied, her enthusiasm never wavering

And if an idea didn't come to her soon, Maevey undoubtedly would have yet another suggestion to offer.

"How about this—"

Darci shook her head. The woman couldn't be more predictable if she was an egg timer.

Darci smiled. "Go ahead."

"It came to me last night—"

"You need a life," Darci remarked, searching the top of her desk for her hair clip among the clutter of papers and pens.

A short silence followed, then Maevey continued, ignoring the statement. "I was thinking...how about a romance on the island?" The excitement in her voice was as though she'd discovered a Spanish galleon full of treasure.

Darci almost hated to burst her bubble. "You don't think they covered it with *Somewhere In Time*?" Darci teased her cousin.

Another pause.

"Uh, you *do* remember that one with Christopher Reeve?" Darci queried with the quirk of her brow. Twenty some years later, the island still touted the presence of the movie and how it depicted the serenity and romance of the island.

"Well, of course, I remember it. I drooled over that man for weeks." A sigh of contentment emitted from her cousin. "*This* is different."

"You've rewritten the script?" Darci worked at shutting

down her computer, half-listening, half-interested in what Maevey had in mind.

"Listen, you need to be open to your creative side."

Tell me something I don't know. Darci stacked the magnetic mountain of paperclips on her desk. A gift sent to her by her daughter for "down" time, which oddly, there'd been plenty of as of late. "Okay, mind open." Darci smiled at the tsk sound on the opposite end of the phone.

"You could have it set during the winter months." Her voice lowered sounding like those old-time radio show actresses, setting the stage for the surprise twist you know is just around the corner. She had to give the woman credit for having a definite flair for the dramatic.

"You could have two strangers." She paused, no doubt for effect. "Brought together by fate, better yet—*providence*." Her voice squealed with a note of triumph.

Oh, that *all* her writing blocks could be so easily dealt with. Darci envisioned her cousin's gleaming, contagious smile even over the phone.

She watched one of the several catamarans as it bounced along the water—it's nose dipping in and out of the aquamarine blue waves. Their trips becoming less frequent as the summer season spiraled to a close.

"Darci?" Maevey's insistent voice broke her from her reverie.

"Huh? Oh yes, a good idea, thanks." Darci held the phone between her cheek and shoulder as she snapped part of her dark hair into the tortoise hair clip she'd found amidst the chaos of her desk.

Knowing her cousin meant well, Darci simply wasn't sure she was up to writing a romance novel quite yet. Her heart was still in the healing stages. "Let me think about it, ok?" She spoke into the receiver.

Maevey sighed. "Oh, okay." Her disappointment was clearly evident. "Hey, I see you're on tonight. Stop by the desk."

Darci agreed and hung up the phone, grateful for family.

She smiled, thinking of Maevey's impish ways, a dearer cousin, she couldn't hope for. Still she was an incurable romantic, constantly challenging Darci to get on with her personal life. Trouble being, of course, that Darci was not ready to, just yet. Being single was adjustment enough, finding her writing style an even greater obstacle. To add to that a relationship, at this point seemed just this side of absurd—at least in Darci's mind. Not that she'd determined yet to remain a widow the rest of her days, she was after all, a reasonably attractive and healthy woman, but she would not be pushed into anything any sooner than when she felt she was ready. Besides, there had been no one who turned her head a second glance, except on the occasional cover of a magazine.

Peter Beck's words supplied at one of the more vulnerable times in her life, emerged in large bold print in the back of her mind. She'd not spoken to him in well over four months, but his oppressive nature and his words of caution hung over her like a rain cloud threatening any thoughts of romance.

She turned on the light over the bathroom mirror and stared at her reflection. The thought of Maevey's suggestion teased at the corner of her mind. More so, however, the innuendo that she should move forward with her life tugged a little harder at her conscience.

A quick assessment in the mirror made her wonder if she looked old enough to have two grown children in college. Certainly she was not old enough to be a widow.

Outwardly, she'd maintained a healthy figure with her love of walking. What better place to live than an island where the only means of getting from here to there is done by bicycle, carriage, or by foot.

She fished in her sparse supply of cosmetics and applied a hint of mascara to her lashes, and a sweep of plum lipstick to her mouth. The final result of her scant effort intensified the gold in her hazel eyes and her creamy pale complexion.

Darci glanced at her watch, smiling as she thought of when her youngest, nearly a man himself now, had given it to her. As if on cue, it chimed out, "*A Dream is a Wish Your*

Heart Makes", as Mickey's hands pointed out the four o'clock hour.

When did her son begin to know her so well?

Darci peeled off her oversized denim shirt and replaced it with a simple black turtleneck sweater. Her beauty was classic, so Maevey had told her more than once. She possessed a dark Scotch-Irish coloring complete with an acid quick wit, a stubborn streak, and a temper, when provoked. Her greatest asset though was an inner strength that several in her life had come to depend on. All—with the exception of herself—and fate had caused her to learn its value the hard way. It had taken more than a great deal of it to make this life change.

Her aunt had given Darci a hostess/waitress position at the hotel's restaurant, "*The Carriage House*." Through careful planning of Matt and Peter's investments, Matt's passing had afforded the luxury of her not having to work full-time, but she preferred to keep her mind and her hands busy.

The hotel and its staff held a special place in Darci's heart for many reasons. The hospitality and warmth reflected the epitome of the attitude of the entire island, and too, it is where she and Matt spent the first week of the married life. To her the island would always be a romantic place for young newlyweds.

She paused, remembering her first impressions as the ferry shuttled her and Matt across the bay.

The island lay as lush and green as anything she'd ever seen, floating like a great turtle in the vast waters of Lake Huron. Darci stared trance-like, as the island came into full view, feeling a kinship where none had existed before.

In reality, it was her first actual trip to the island. She'd only visited there, through the stories of her mother and her grandmother, but she recalled her mother had said that she was pregnant with Darci the first time she visited the island. After that, Darci always wondered if there was some cosmic connection to why she felt such a deep longing for the island. Her aunt teased her that perhaps it was hereditary, because her uncle had also fallen instantly in love with the island's serene beauty, just before he'd fallen in love with her.

It became to Darci, a magical place and a world of its own, set apart from the chaos of everyday life. It held romance and mystery, and now, with her honeymoon as a backdrop, she would experience it all firsthand.

Her mind wandered to that warm August day, how the sun felt on her face, sprinkled with the occasional spray of water from a passing boat. She remembered the strength of Matt's shoulder against hers and his hand touching her fingers as they leaned over the rail of the catamaran. Effortlessly, a dozen details sharpened in her mind.

Rounding the rocky breakwater, memories of the stories flooded her thoughts and she recognized the very places she had heard of growing up as a young girl. The brilliant blue water, stretched in all directions, as far as the eye could see, freeing her from the realization that she'd never before felt landlocked until that moment.

The catamaran—bustling with the tourists—sidled with a slow, but smooth maneuver beside the long wooden dock, its pier lined with bicycles of all colors and sizes, awaiting the rental of new guests.

Dark green carriages with mahogany doors, their drivers dressed in red waistcoats and black top hats waited at the dock to take its guests to the Grand Hotel.

Children in carriers hoisted on the backs of their parents, their eyes wide with wonder, ate ice cream as their parents walked hand-in-hand along the street eyeing the various artist and specialty shops. Explosive blooms of white, red and pink geranium pots hung from the old-fashioned lampposts lining the main street, their ivy vines trailing bright green tendrils that waved in the breeze, as though in their own way welcoming strangers to the island.

The air on the main street was filled with the thick, rich sweet scent of cooking chocolate and peanut brittle being made as quickly as it was sold in the numerous confectionary shops along the canopied sidewalks.

Though warm from carrying their bags through the

crowded streets, Matt and Darci marveled at the sights. The glimmer of youth shining a bright path on all of their tomorrows—they had nothing but time and each other.

Where did the time go? When had life swallowed them whole?

Thoughts of the papers she'd taken two months ago from Peter Beck crossed her mind and she recalled the last time she spoke with him.

"Are you sure this is what you want?" Peter shifted the stack of papers in his hand and dropped a pen on the table in front of her. "Sign here."

Darci paused a moment choosing her words carefully. She noted, for some odd reason that Peter placed his cup exactly on the worn table ring where Matt's cup had been each and every morning.

"Darci?" Peter's voice was quietly insistent.

"Sorry, Peter." She rubbed her hands over her face to alleviate the numbness in her brain. "I have nothing here to stay for." She picked up the pen and remembered to press hard to get all the carbons beneath the document.

"Well, thanks." He gave her a wry smile.

"Pete, you know what I mean. I need to make a life of my own."

Peter nodded. "Unfortunately, I understand, but do you have to go so far away to do that, Darci? Why can't you do your writing here?"

"There are too many memories. I need to get a fresh start." It's what we talked about. It's what I think Matt would advise me to do."

"And does my advice account for anything?"

The statement though made with a cocky grin, held the slightest edge of bitterness. The implication stunned Darci briefly.

"Sorry, guess I'm used to you heeding my advice."

"Pete, you know I'll always listen to anything you have to say—in matters of our financial security. Matt trusted you implicitly, and so do I."

"Right."

He ran his finger around the rim of his coffee cup as he kept his gaze solidly to hers. It was the one time that Darci could remember feeling uncomfortable being alone with Peter Beck.

"Well." He sighed as he straightened his shoulders and shifted the scattered legal documents in front of him. "The sooner we settle on these few papers, the sooner you can get on with your life."

The finality of his tone left a sinking sensation in the pit of Darci's stomach. "I'd like a little more time to look these over before signing them, if I may?"

She glanced up meeting his icy blue gaze and a shiver ran across her shoulders.

Chapter Two

Prompted impatiently once again by the alarm on her watch she pushed the past into the far corner of her mind. She was becoming a Master at the game.

Wiping her eyes, she made a silent vow that should she ever love that way again, it would not—could not—ever be as deeply. No one could replace Matt. He'd been her rock, her light, and her life. How could she ever commit as deeply to another at the risk of such great loss?

She grabbed her starched tuxedo-style uniform, picked up her book bag, and headed out the front door for the short walk to the hotel. As she gazed out over the choppy waters she decided she would not have to take that risk. She was perfectly fine as a single woman—clarification—make that a single *author*. With that resolved for the moment, she allowed herself to breathe in the cool evening air blowing in from the lake and sensed her muscles relax.

Twilight on the island was one of her favorite times. The deepening indigo sky marbled with magenta and purple hues reflected in the water, making it difficult to discern where the sky ended and the lake started. The phenomenon was unexplainably comforting—it always had been. By this time of the evening, most of the day tourists had fled the island, in favor of the nightlife on the mainland. And with their absence came the peaceful sound of the gentle waves lapping at the nine-mile shoreline accented by the occasional deep-bellied blow of an ore ship passing through the Straits.

Zipping her jacket against the cool breeze, she walked along the white fenced-in Victorian homes, many of them vacant now with the waning summer season.

In her mind, she was transported to the lazy afternoons when she and Matt had walked hand in hand along those very sidewalks. Each yard contained a brilliant variety of gardens, each sporting its own palette of fragrant colors. Massive purple clumps of lilac bushes and pastel pink and blue hollyhocks towering six to eight feet high on sturdy stalks served as backdrop to shorter white and blue delphiniums. Delicate pink and white gladiolas, clustered with various shades of purple Iris gave dimension to the base of welcoming verandas. And fresh-faced white and yellow daisies en masse', their tiny heads swaying in the lake breeze added to the colorful tapestry against the lush green lawns and white picket fences.

Darci glanced at the yards as she walked past. Many of the flowers were already spent with the onset of the cooler weather, but she could still smell the mingled scents in her memory.

"I've never seen anything like this, Matt, isn't it beautiful?" The oft-repeated phrase became somewhat of a joke during their honeymoon, as Darci's only apparent means of describing every new discovery they made on their walks around the island.

Matt would smile his quiet smile and drop his arm on her shoulder, kissing her on the temple as he squeezed her close. "You're going to make a great writer, one day, my love."

Though in her heart, Darci knew, in his teasing way, that he was telling her to follow her dreams.

They spent their days biking, picnicking, exploring the island, and taking dozens of pictures. Photography was a sidelight that Darci had picked up—a hobby really—and an excuse to take scores of pictures to preserve in her mind the memories in as many ways as she could.

Lost amid the crowds of summer tourists, they listened to the street musicians play their hammer dulcimers. They'd not a care in the world and the certainty of tomorrow, in all its glory, lay at their very fingertips.

They sampled every kind of fudge (each known for its famous Mackinac secret recipe) from every shop that drew them in with the sweet aroma of boiling chocolate and sticky saltwater taffy. At night, they would stroll the boardwalk, hand in hand—for the most part penniless, but surviving on love.

She smiled at her thoughts and glanced down the main street, seeing a few last minute shoppers scurrying to meet the late afternoon catamaran at the dock. The sidewalks now virtually empty were quiet in the darkening shadows.

Darci realized as she glanced at the sign hanging over the entrance "*Open May to October*" that no matter how many times she walked up the steps and placed her hand on the screen door, for her, it was like coming home.

She stopped to pluck a dead leaf from the huge pots of double-blossomed red geraniums bursting in colorful protrusion from the clay pots standing sentinel either side of the sidewalk. Darci made a mental note to bring in the pots she had at home.

Climbing the short few steps to the front porch of the hotel, she smiled a hello to a couple seated in the white wicker chairs on the curved front veranda enjoying the serenity of the last dredges of an island sunset.

Swinging open the screen door, she stepped into the lobby of the Iroquois and paused at the desk to say hi to her cousin as requested, before going to change for her evening supper shift.

"Hey," Darci said as she smiled, halfway expecting her cousin to start in on her about one of the guests. Naturally, she did not disappoint her. Maevey was as accurate as a watch.

"That guy I told you about in room three is still here." Maevey's bright eyes sparkled with mischief.

"Thanks, but no thanks. Not looking," she replied good-naturedly as she strolled past the registration desk.

"Hey, but you have to have some inspiration, don't you? Course, maybe older is more your type?" She grinned with the devil in her gaze.

Darci gave her a skeptical glance. "Nice try." She offered a jaunty finger wave as she walked placidly by.

* * *

The panoramic view of the straits from the floor-to-ceiling

windows of the restaurant sparkled under the remaining rays of sunlight. The vista from the dining room was one of the most popular features of the island and yet another reason Darci enjoyed her work.

As the harbor lights began to twinkle along the dark shoreline, Darci found herself taking more time to visit with the dinner guests. With soft standards to classic favorite tunes being played from the piano, the ambience of the room was tranquil and nostalgic, making for a comfortable and relaxing atmosphere.

Most of the patrons, she discovered, were also staying at the hotel. Others were here for the evening and would catch the last catamaran back to the mainland after dinner.

Darci delighted in visiting with guests, discovering, by accident, a new way of researching characters for her writing. While she loved socializing with guests, she was neither afraid of hard work, nor pitching in wherever she was needed. Years of juggling a full-time career, motherhood, and maintaining a home had served to hone her flexibility levels.

As she glanced at the patrons, she spotted a young couple in the far corner of the dining room. They looked younger than her oldest daughter and yet it was evident that whatever they were celebrating was very special. Darci recognized the look on the young man's face and the way he held her hand, pulling it to his lips for a gentle kiss.

"Bridget? What's the celebration over there?" Darci tipped her head toward the couple as she glanced at the young waitress hurrying past.

"Anniversary, I think. Their first," Bridget replied with a quick grin, and then disappeared through the swinging kitchen door.

Darci stared at the couple, her memory jostled back in time to the memory of her and Matt's first anniversary.

"I'm pregnant."

He choked after the first swallow of wine she'd just poured. It was her futile attempt to ease the shock. Apparently it didn't' work.

"You're what?" Matt couldn't hide the look of utter surprise on his face. "I mean—really?"

Darci swallowed the lump quickly rising in her throat. "I take it you aren't happy about this, then?"

"Oh God, sweetheart." Matt pulled her into his embrace, dispelling her fears. "I just hadn't given much thought yet to becoming a dad. I mean to actually *hear* those words, wow—" He hugged her tight, kissing her neck.

"Yeah, and no more prepared than when I saw that little pink plus sign on that stick." She laughed softly, pressing her face to his shoulder, the scent of his cotton shirt, as always, a sense of security for her. "I'm afraid."

"Well, love, that makes two of us." He pulled back and brushed his fingers down her cheek. "But we'll manage, it'll be okay." His eyes were gentle reassuring her that everything would turn out well.

"Promise?" She knew that it was an absurd notion to think a person could have the power over fate itself. Still it was a comfort to Darci to hear him say the words just the same.

"Yes." Matt smiled, and then kissed her gently. "We're going to be great parents."

At the end of a long eight months and twenty-eight days of swollen feet, French fries with plenty of ketchup, and indigestion, came their firstborn daughter, Leah. From the beginning they knew she would be independent and stubborn.

"She gets it from her mother," Matt teased.

Eighteen months later, their sweet-natured but incurably ornery, Nathan arrived, destined to be his older sister's perpetual nightmare.

The sound of an ore ship's blast broke her from her reverie. "I'd like to do something nice for them," Darci spoke quietly thinking no one heard her.

"Great idea, how about a bottle of the house wine?"

Bridget's voice startled her and she turned to see her grinning at the couple in question over Darci's shoulder.

Bridget had chosen to work on the island, instead of going home during the summer between college terms. She'd explained to Darci it was better this way, because it gave her mother the freedom to travel with the friends she'd found since the divorce. Though Darci's heart ached for the young woman and even more for the loss of time her mother would not regain, she could understand her reasoning for staying summers on the island. The hotel's stability and the warmth of its proprietor's had helped to cement her own feelings of security.

"Brilliant idea, Bridget," Darci replied.

The reward of seeing the surprised pleasure on the young couples' faces meant more to Darci than they knew. "To many, more happy celebrations together." She added the last word as she poured the wine, pushing away the bittersweet memories in her mind. "May you have as many fond memories of your stay on the island as I have." She smiled bravely and they thanked her raised glasses and warm smiles.

As she left them to attend to other guests, she could not help but steal periodic glances at the two, noting how very enamored they were with one another. To many, many, more years, she wished them silently.

* * *

Darci moaned quietly as she rubbed her hand over the soles of her feet. There had been little time to sit this evening with the reservations for dinner climbing past the nine o'clock hour. Tomorrow, however, was her day off and she planned to sleep in, provided no one called in sick for the lunch crowd.

She stood, tipping her head from side to side to relieve the muscle tension in her neck. Rummaging through her apron pocket, she pulled out a handful of coins and bills. Tips had been very good tonight, that at least, made up for how tired her feet were. Maybe she'd invest in a new pair of tennis shoes.

Darci tossed her bag over her shoulder and climbed the stairs leading to the front hotel lobby. She figured she might as well stop by and give Maevey one last chance to torture her before she went home.

The lobby itself was empty, except for a few guests watching the late news in the shadows of the adjoining TV room. The night breeze blew cool and even through the front screen door. It was in these tranquil, quiet moments, that she remembered the reason she loved it here. Almost as though fate had brought her home to where she belonged.

Darci stuck her head around the corner of the front desk, to see if her feisty cousin was in the back office. "Maevey?" she called quietly. The soft glow of the stained glass tiffany lamp illuminated the dark mahogany sheen of the registration desk.

Darci reached across the counter to help herself to a complimentary mint, when the shrill ring of the phone made her jump back. She waited through another ring thinking Maevey would surely appear, but no one did. *Where is that girl?*

Another ring peeled through the silent hotel lobby.

Darci picked up the phone gingerly. "Iroquois hotel, may I help you?" She'd heard the phrase so many times coming from Maevey that it was as much second nature to her as well.

"I'd like speak with someone about a reservation." The man's voice on the other end of the connection was soft-spoken, but authoritative. Definitely a man who was used to getting what he wanted.

It caused Darci to straighten and pay closer attention. "I'm sorry sir, it seems we've misplaced our reservations person at the moment."

He responded with a deep, rich laugh. "Misplaced her, huh? Well, I'm calling long distance from Chicago. Is there a better time to call...perhaps after you've sent out the posse? I realize its pretty late, but this trip is sort of last minute. Urgent—boss's orders—I'm sure you know what I'm talking about."

She hadn't a clue, but something inside of her wanted to.

Perhaps it was simply the breeze from the lake, or maybe it was the man's cool, cleansing voice, whatever the case, Darci realized she could have easily gone on talking with him much longer. In the back of her mind, she toyed with what kind of face went with that voice.

Darci glanced up as she heard the sound of footsteps on

the landing above her. Blinking at why she would be so intrigued by this man's voice, she quickly decided it was most likely her frequent thoughts of Matt today.

She caught a movement from the corner of her eye and turned to see her cousin coming down the stairs. Darci motioned for her to hurry and in her impish way, Maevey deliberately slowed her pace.

"The guy in room three needed more towels," she whispered, the dimple in her fair cheek deepening as she shrugged her shoulders and grinned.

Darci raised her brow. There wasn't a single guy in ten counties that had a chance when it came to her red-haired cousin.

"Later, Maevey." Darci held the mouthpiece in her other hand as she stared at her cousin. "It looks like you're in luck, the prodigal has returned." She grinned wickedly as she held out the phone. The sound of his wonderful laugh skittered through her as she passed the receiver to her shocked cousin.

"Night." Darci smiled with a sly grin toward her cousin as she headed for the screen door.

Maevey held up her index finger, halting Darci in her steps. There was a playful sparkle in her gaze. Probably had more to tell her about the guy in room three she thought wearily.

"How can I help you, sir?" she asked the caller, tipping her head as she glanced at Darci.

"Uh huh." Maevey nodded listening, as she opened the registration book.

"You are aware, of course, that we close the hotel in just a few weeks," Maevey explained. Her blue eyes widened as the conversation continued.

"Four months?" Maevey repeated, apparently to make certain she had heard him correctly. "That would be nearly the whole winter season here on the island."

Darci sighed and dropped into one of the padded green wicker chairs in the lobby. Placing her feet on the adjoining chair, she shot a bored glance to her cousin, more interested at the prospect of a soothing shower and her warm bed at the moment.

"I'm sure that once you're here, we can arrange for you to meet with a realtor. Many people sublet their properties during the winter months here on the island." Maevey scribbled notes on the margin of the registration book.

"We'll just need to have your name and time of arrival." Maevey paused momentarily.

Darci half-listened to the conversation as the gentle clang of the breakwater buoy offshore lulled her senses.

"No disrespect sir," Maevey said slowly, "but are you aware of the how brutal it can be in the winter on this island? It can get very isolated to someone not used to being alone. You aren't a real "social" type guy, are you? I mean we have snowmobiles, cross-country, checkers, bingo in the town hall— typical winter activities."

Darci, who'd been half listening, detected the teasing undertone in her cousin's voice. She turned capturing Maevey's devilish grin. Their gazes locked in a battle of wills. Darci stood, facing her. "Checkers?" She mouthed silently.

"Of course, we also have some of the best restaurants around, with staff that will question ever returning to the mainland."

She tipped her head in disbelief to where she suspected her cousin was going with this.

"Okay," Maevey replied into the phone, "we'll be expecting you in a week then. Yes, you have a pleasant evening." She replaced the receiver, looked up, innocence written allover her face. "What is *that* look for?"

Darci shook her head, narrowing a pointed look at this sudden pain in her proverbial backside. "Are you sure there's no Greek blood in our family?"

Maevey shrugged, the light twinkling the mischievous glint in her blue eyes. "Couldn't say." She offered a bright smile.

Darci picked up her bag, heading for the door. She opened it not looking back at what she knew was a smug look on Maevey's face. "Not going to happen, girlfriend."

"Of course not."

"I'm not interested in a relationship." She held her hand on the door handle and stared at the lake through the screen.

"Who said anything about a relationship?"

Darci sighed, there was no use in attempting to quell one of her cousin's ideas. It would die out in due time. "Night, Maevey." She closed the door gently behind her.

From the fort at the peak of the island "Taps" drifted gentle over the breeze, signaling the end of another day. From a block away, Darci could almost here the gears clicking in her cousin's head.

Chapter Three

That darn cousin of hers had been remarkably quiet the past couple of weeks.

Darci's mind raced with the possibilities of what Maevey could possibly have up her sleeve. A skittish paranoia seeped into her mind as she ran the vacuum over her living room rug. She'd not called her since the night the stranger from Chicago phoned in his reservation. Darci fought the urge to call her cousin and ask if he'd happened to check in yet. Purely out of curiosity to match the voice with a face. But it took only a second thought to realize that such a question would only serve to fan the fuel of Maevey's game plan to find her the perfect mate—the perfect replacement for Matt.

She switched off the vacuum and swept up a dust cloth from the nearby cleaning bucket. With frenzied concentration, she polished the silver and glass picture frame of Matt and the kids taken during their last Christmas. What might they have done differently had they known it was to be their last?

She replaced the frame on the mantle, pushing the lump of anxiety lodged in her throat. Grateful they'd been able to have a wonderful family—better than many people have in a lifetime—a part of her soul now wandered aimlessly inside, unable to come to grips with being alone. While still another part of her held onto what they'd had so fierce that no other human being would ever be able to fill the void.

She sighed. What the hell was Maevey up to? Or was it that she secretly hoped that Maevey was planning something and perhaps that it might involve the low-timbered voice of the man en-route to the island?

The wind, blustery and cold had turned over the past

week, straight out of the north. It was a drastic contrast to the perfect mild temperatures of when she'd moved there in the summer and served as a frigid reminder of her new life change. She knew that in the next few months, her choice would again be challenged in more ways than one.

With both of her grown children and in college, and the hotel closing after October, the staff would be off to the company of family and friends away from the island. Leaving her to deal with the absolute solitude.

Darci tossed the disposable cleaning cloth in the wastebasket beside her desk. She sat down in the swivel leather chair and leaned back, feeling the new spring of chair give with a comforting squeak beneath the pressure.

She eyed her creative workspace, reaching out to straighten the pens and pencils in the rough sculpted mug—an art project—that a twelve-year old Leah had given her eons ago for Mothers Day.

The same nervousness that spawned the concern of being alone for the better part of six months had pressed her to stockpile writing supplies, oftentimes receiving a chuckle from the clerk at the office supply store in town.

"Those boxes of computer paper should be in first of next week, Ms. Cunningham. Will you need them before then?"

She caught the glimmer in Burt's eye. "Next week's just fine." Darci paid the man choosing to ignore his joke.

Now as she assessed the six-foot stack of paper tucked into one corner of her small living room, she had to grin. At the rate her writing efficiency, she'd be assured of enough paper to last for the next five years.

Her gaze scanned the now immaculate room satisfied with the progress she'd made. A chenille throw, the soft, pale blue of a clear lake sky, purchased at one of the local shops, added just the right warmth to the yellow floral love seat facing the white fireplace.

Since moving to a new house, she'd discovered that many of her former tastes had changed. Clean whites, powdery blues, and soft yellows now made up the colors of her world and she used them liberally in her decorating.

Darci pushed back, lifting her feet to the desk as a satisfied sigh escaped her lips. She was, for the moment, content that she was as nearly prepared for the winter months ahead and certainly for any unforeseen flood of writing creativity.

She made a mental note to check on who delivered cords of wood and also to contact Abe Fiskas about a new furnace. Her mind winding to a slower, more satisfied speed, she allowed her eyelids to drop for a moment of relaxation.

"I'm calling from Chicago."

Her eyes shot open with a start and she grabbed the desk to keep from tumbling out of the chair. How long had she been dozing? The after burn of the stranger's voice so intimately close to her ear caused a shiver to run down her spine.

In effort to regain control of her senses, she stood up grateful for the firm foundation beneath her feet. She'd only been dozing—that was it, and her mind wandered. Her throat was dry and the guilt of that skipped across her heart, taunting her concerns

Suppressing another shiver across her shoulders, she squeezed her eyes shut in effort to clear her brain of the tingling running through her veins.

Darci searched for her shoes, and finding them stuffed one foot and then the other in each worn leather loafer.

Certain it was only her previous concerns of being alone during the winter months that the re-occurrence of the voice replayed in her subconscious. Moreover, Maevey's constant running dialogue, and not-so-subtle hints of romance, had probably inadvertently taken root somewhere in her brain.

Darci tapped her heel to the floor, emphatic not to let her cousin get to her. In the days ahead, there would be more nights alone and she would have to learn how to cope.

She grabbed her jacket, hoping some of her Aunt's potato chowder and warm bread would help her gain some perspective on her unexplained and rampantly out of control emotions.

* * *

Tyler's eyes stung from the icy spray flying over the bow of the boat. He'd originally thought the pictures at dusk would be an easy beginning to the pictures he planned to include in his book. However, he'd not planned on the water being as frigid as it was, or the Catamaran excursion lasting up to fifteen minutes across the bay to the island.

He pulled his suit jacket collar up and placed a protective hand over the lens of the camera around his neck. It was one of the few times he was glad he wore glasses, they'd at least given him some semblance of protection to the icy spray.

His gaze narrowed as they rounded past the island toward what he assumed was the docking area. In the misty, darkness of twilight he could just make out the pristine grandeur of the Grand Hotel and its six hundred plus-foot pillared veranda set in amongst the lush, dark evergreens.

The catamaran's bow skipped fluidly across the water as if eager to get him to his destination. His hope was that with this final project for his publisher, it would allow him the financial independence to branch out into other areas. At one time, he'd toyed with the idea of a private studio—maybe a gallery of his own. Perhaps he could get a tour of his work to various galleries across the country. Yet it seemed that the moment he finished one project, he'd start another with barely time to make the necessary hotel and travel arrangements.

An ore ship in the distance, coming through from Canada signaled to the passenger ferry skittering atop the indigo blue water. On the horizon, its miniature deck lights twinkled, giving away its presence as it slid through the deepening shadows. He wondered how a vessel of such monstrous size could glide stealth as a shadow through the water, barely a sound audible save the occasional blast of its horn.

Tyler made a note to check out some of the shipping legends and lore on the island before the project was complete.

The boat swung out away from the tip of the rocky breakwater as it approached the Arnold Transit Dock. As it chugged closer to the busy docks, Tyler could see the shadowed silhouettes of those waiting to return to the mainland. A long line of bicycles, of every shape, color, and size were parked side by side in a long line that extended the length of the wharf.

He swung his camera into position clicking off to or three shots of the last rays of sunlight splaying over their brightly shining chrome.

Signaling their arrival, the captain tooted the catamarans horn and the sound echoed in the closed in bay.

Evidence of his lack of enthusiasm, Tyler hung back until most passengers had left the boat. He sauntered down the gangplank, searching for where his luggage was being unloaded.

"May I take these bags for you, sir?" A sturdy young man, wearing khaki shorts and a white polo greeted Tyler, stopping his count of bags holding a multitude of equipment.

"I've got a few here." He was suddenly embarrassed at the number of bags he'd brought. Of the ten, only two were actual clothing. He hadn't given much thought to it until he started loading the bags at the St Ignace dock and the porter there had glanced at him casually asking if he was planning an extended stay. Tyler turned back to the waiting man.

"I'm on assignment. This is mostly camera gear."

"No problem, I've got the hitch. My boss gets these premonitions." The young man grinned as he picked up a bag and slung it over his shoulder.

"Really? And what did she tell you?" Tyler chuckled as he handed another bag to the man.

"That providence was wearing a dark gray suit and would be arriving for a long visit." He shrugged as he stacked another piece of luggage onto the small trailer. He glanced around with a questioning look and followed to where Tyler pointed out another small group of bags. "I took a wild guess that you're the guy she was talking about."

"Good guess. So, I take it your boss is at the Iroquois?"

The porter nodded and placed his hands on his hips checking over Tyler's shoulder for any more pieces of luggage coming from the bowels of the catamaran. "Yep, this is my fourth summer on the island working with her. Maevey's one of those folks you just don't question too often. Her instincts are legendary around here. You single?"

Startled, Tyler looked up. "Who's asking?" He grinned as he adjusted a backpack over his shoulder.

"Just a two-minute warning. Maevey loves to play matchmaker."

Something unexplained popped from Tyler's mouth, "She any good at it?" *Like he was in the market for a long-term relationship.* The thought was absurd, if not miraculous.

The porter shrugged. "Like I said, two-minute warning. Is this it, then?"

"Uh, yeah, thanks." He peered at the man, more than a little curious how he found himself in this conversation.

"Good deal. I'll meet you at the hotel. Just up to the sidewalk and take a left, all the way to the point. You can't miss it." He climbed aboard the three-wheel bike and maneuvered it expertly through the crowd still waiting to board the boat.

He tried to keep his eye on the young man but he disappeared around the corner much faster than Tyler was able to keep up.

Peering up at the evening sky, he took a deep breath of clean air—a marked change from downtown Chicago. He stepped to the edge of the street and assessed his new home for the next few months. No cars—that was the first startling reality—they'd been replaced by people on foot, covered surreys, elegant carriages, and bicycles of every shape and style.

Tyler swerved as a young child and his sister came racing down the street. From a half block away he heard the useless pleas of their parents struggling to peddle as fast. There were times when he wondered what kind of father he might have been had his life turned out differently.

The two skidded to an abrupt halt, turning in unison, much to his surprise. "Sorry." If their unified response hadn't already surprised him, the fact that they bothered to stop at all was an even greater shock. He'd had little chance to see that some kids were still taught manners. "You should wait for your folks." Though they looked at him strange, it was not a moment that passed but he heard an out-of breath, "Thanks" from the female rider beside him. They gave him a short wave as they zeroed in on their children.

A twinge of his childhood sparked like flint in his memory of similar moments with his brothers and then the steward's voice echoed as if mocking his bachelorhood. *"You single?"*

Tyler shook his head to clear his jumbled thoughts and took another deep breath before turning toward the hotel to make his way through the crowd.

The scent of pine mingled with a crisp autumn breeze punctuated by the sticky sweet smell of homemade fudge and peanut brittle made his stomach growl. And he realized that the last full meal he'd had was breakfast that morning back in Chicago.

As always the adventure of a new location inspired the creative juices. He'd get settled first and then research what winter activities were offered on the island. Maybe he'd check out a local pub.

It wasn't so much that he disliked traveling alone, but now and again it was interesting to see what the locals did for excitement and it generally gave him an insiders viewpoint of the location.

He'd learned how to connect over the years of exotic ports, learning bits of foreign languages and participating in unique customs and celebrations. His life—by and large—had been what many people only dream of doing.

Tyler paused in the midst of the crowd and took a closer look at his surroundings. Certainly it was not the white sands of the Jamaican Islands, nor did it hold the colorful history of London.

So what was so special about this place? Unsure yet, he only knew that it was his job to find whatever it was and illuminate it with his subtle photogenic brilliance.

He'd always been prone to travel. Even when his siblings

went off to seek their future in business and law, he chose to travel.

His parents called it and a waste of time.

He called it his choice.

Overhead the shrill cry of the seagulls circled above him, heading toward the rocky beach near the hotel, scavenging for treasured scraps left during the days' picnics in the park.

The gentle clip-clop of horse hooves against the pavement beckoned him to think of slowing down, to return to a simpler time when life was not so hurried.

Tyler dropped his sunglasses into the breast pocket of his suit. In comparison to those around him, he looked like a foreign dignitary.

He glanced up as he approached the Iroquois, just as the steward came bounding down the hotels front steps. "Have all your gear in the lobby. Someone will take it to your room for you."

He brushed his fingers in salute to his baseball cap as Tyler palmed him a generous tip.

A surprised and pleased look shone on the young mans face. "You need anything at all while you're here sir. You ask for Stan." He bowed his head slightly and whistled as he turned the bike around and headed back toward the dock.

"Mr. Landston?" The rich, husky voice of a woman's voice with the mere hint of an Irish brogue greeted him from the shadowed interior beyond the screen door.

Following her voice, he shifted his camera bag and walked carefully up the few steps to the porch. Had he not known better, he'd of thought he was entering a beautiful three-story Victorian home.

"We've been expecting you."

He opened the door and one look into the woman's clear blue eyes spoke to him that this was Maevey.

"Your bags are here, now let's get you settled. The trip isn't long." She turned and her Iris colored broomstick skirt flowed gently, swirling around her legs as she walked. "Still I'm sure you must be famished."

Curiosity pulled his thoughts from the auburn curls as they bounced rhythmically off her shoulders.

He blinked. "I could use a bite to eat."

She grinned over her shoulder. "Well, of course. Anyone who hasn't eaten since breakfast would be starving, I'd think."

Had he told her that?

"Now, let's see what we can do to get you up to your room and out of *those* clothes as quickly as possible."

Her smile held him captive, as did the unusual twinkle in her eye.

"I've arranged a meeting with a realtor for tomorrow." She flipped through a large, old-fashioned leather bound guest book and turned it on the desk, holding out a pen to him.

Holding the pen as steady as his nerves would allow he signed the book. Tyler sensed her intense gaze as he focused on his penmanship. He immediately understood why Stan didn't question the woman. Perhaps he should heed his advice.

* * *

Maevey glanced at her watch. If her instincts were correct—and that was a given—Darci should be arriving for dinner at any moment.

She smiled at the handsome new guest, the one she was certain was the embodiment of Providence come for her lonely cousin. "I'll get your key." If she could only detain him just a few minutes, there was a good chance that fate would take care of the rest.

On purpose, she'd chosen to remain elusive over the past couple of weeks. She knew full well, that by now Darci would be chomping at the bit to find out what she was up to.

Maevey chuckled under her breath. Ever since the night Tyler Landston called from Chicago she'd had her premonitions about Darci in the arms of a tall, dark man.

Though she'd not been able to determine the details of the man's face, it was evident that Mr. Landston was the most likely candidate. "Yes, indeed, my dear cousin," she murmured as she activated the keys. "*Providence* most certainly has arrived for the winter and he looks *damn good* in that gray suit."

Chapter Four

Stray tendrils of mahogany hair danced around Darci's head as she walked with a brisk gate to the hotel, the impact of her recent thoughts pushing her along in a hurried fashion.

She burst through the door of the hotel, her breath shallow from the unplanned rapidness of her walk. Teetering on the tips of her toes she stopped short of falling headlong over a plethora of luggage scattered across the lobby foyer.

By instinct, she had the presence to grab the door handle to regain her balance as she suppressed a giggle given the look of shock on the face of her cousin. Her expression—unseen by the man searching his wallet for his credit card—changed from surprise to a twinkling gleam.

"Thank you, Mr. Landston." Maevey offered a hundred-watt smile to the man as she glanced at Darci. She placed a key on the counter and signaled the young bellhop to help with the bags.

Darci's intuition prickled at the back of her neck. *Maevey... just let me walk through unnoticed.* She held her breath, avoiding eye contact with her cousin.

"Room seven, Stephen."

The boy gathered what he could and seeing his struggle the man slipped one bag from the boys shoulder.

"Here, if you get those, I can get the rest."

Darci briefly registered the conversation, but continued to pick her way through the confusion, keeping her back to the wall as she headed toward her goal of the reaching the dining room unnoticed.

Only a few more feet to the hallway... *Landston? Landston? Where had she heard that name?*

The gentleman, dressed in a handsome dark gray suit turned and reached for the bag at Darci's feet.

Momentarily hindered by his sudden intrusion into her path, she stopped just as the bag slipped from his grasp. Landing with a dull thud upon her left foot.

Sure her eyes bulged from their sockets, only a strangled gasp emitted from her mouth.

His horrified look caught hers. "Excuse me—I—"

Mesmerized by the bold, lightening pace of pain shooting a straight line up her shin, she braced herself for her brain to acknowledge it.

"I'm—I'm so sorry, are you all right? I don't think this is the one with photo equipment—" His hands clenched in midair as his gaze darted from the culprit piece of luggage, to her, and then back as though assessing its contents.

"T—The bag, please?" She spoke between clenched teeth and reached for the bag, clawing to reach the handle.

"Oh, geez, yeah, I'm really sorry." He grasped the handle yanking it free from her foot, dropped the bag behind him without looking, and quickly dropped to his knee.

Though gallant his gesture, the pain pulsating from her foot preoccupied any ability to appreciate his behavior.

"Please, it's fine, really." She wanted only to leave. His immediate familiarity was disconcerting. Truth was, there was something about him—his voice, his manner and the whole scenario that made her uncomfortable, beyond the pain.

"Here now, let me take a look." Lifted her foot in slow motion, carefully inspecting the inside of her ankle.

Still, there was something even stronger that Darci brushed from her mind like an incessant fly. Perhaps it was her whacked out hormones—she'd heard these were the years that women experienced odd sensations and unusual drives, but she refused to believe that was happening yet to her. Odds were it was those thoughts of being alone on the island that made her uncomfortable.

"I'd be happy to take you to see someone." He touched her calf gently as he slid his glasses up the bridge of his nose, inspecting her foot more closely. The course denim encasing her leg did not quell the warmth of his palm.

She stared at the top of his head, mesmerized how he held her foot, studying it with care. Her insides rattled not wanting him to touch her, yet oddly fascinated with the intimacy that, in fact, he was.

"Are you a doctor?" She blinked, glancing briefly at Maevey who, propped casually on an elbow, watched them with a 'cat-who'd-eaten-the-canary' grin. At least the pain was beginning to subside, which probably meant it wasn't broken.

"No, I'm here." He stood slowly and their gazes met again. "On business."

A strange buzzing rang in her ears. It had been a long time certainly, but Darci sensed he was assessing her every bit as much as she was assessing him. Of course, those were ridiculous thoughts for a married woman—or one who'd been and not t*hat* long ago.

Darci swallowed at the sudden dryness that invaded her throat. Those deep green eyes would put a pine forest to shame.

There was the sound of someone else clearing her throat. Her cousin spoke.

"Mr. Landston, this is my cousin Darci."

Her voice was deliberately slow, pacing out the words to stretch the moment. *Bless her conniving little heart.*

"*She* was the one who answered the phone that night. The one that possesses that delightful sense of humor you asked about?" Maevey grinned.

Between the pain in her foot and the fear in her throat, she was only marginally of any introduction. Had Darci not been mentally nursing her toe and physically trying to breathe she would have thrown something at her cousin for being so obvious—like a chair, maybe.

With a well-manicured finger, the stranger pushed his wire-rimmed glasses once again up the bridge of his nose as though to get a better look.

The simple quirk of his dark eyebrow caused Darci's

knees to weaken and she leaned against the wall for support. No doubt it was merely the result of her recent injury; still it was fortunate that her palms were braced firmly to the wall behind her.

"Darci, *this* is the caller from Chicago. You remember your conversation? Something about the prodigal returning, wasn't it?"

Paybacks are hell.

The embarrassment of her catatonic state raised degree by humiliating degree until she sensed her cheeks must be crimson.

She had a gut feeling that in some perverse way her cousin was enjoying her predicament too much and Darci simply was too old to be feeling so nervous. She cleared her throat again, searching for a quirky comeback, but her mind was blank.

He smiled as though he sensed the joke between the two. His presence alone in the tailored Armani was disarming enough, but the way he studied her with a thoughtful gaze caused her reason to scatter like autumn leaves in a strong wind.

She envisioned him on the cover of a *Gentleman's Quarterly*, or as much at ease on the deck of a sailboat—a formidable presence with his dark wavy hair blowing in the wind and a jacket flapping haphazard around his astounding build.

His grin deepened, revealing a well-placed crevice beside his brilliant smile. It appeared he knew of its affect on women.

Darci blinked from her reverie and glanced speechless at her cousin then returned to his consuming gaze.

"You do have a delightful sense of humor." He reached out offering his hand. "I guess I'm lucky, huh?" He nodded toward her foot.

She peeled one hand from the wall and held it out giving him a weak smile in return.

"Hey, I'm truly sorry about your foot. Listen…uh; perhaps to make up for my clumsiness, you'd let me buy you dinner? I mean it's the least I can do." He adjusted his glasses, glancing at first Maevey and then back to Darci. "Unless you already have plans?"

"No, she hasn't," Maevey quickly interjected.

"Yes, I'm afraid I do." Darci shot a stern look of warning toward her cousin.

Darci tugged her hand from his, supremely uncomfortable with the fact that it tucked much too warmly to his grasp. "No, thank you, really, it's not necessary." She shook her head no and glanced at her foot searching for an easy exit line.

An awkward silence followed.

"Maybe a cup of coffee sometime, then?" He tipped his head and gave her one of the more charming grins she'd seen in awhile—at least not since Matt's. *That* thought snapped her back to reality.

"I don't think so. I really have to go. It was nice to meet you. Have a pleasant stay." She stepped gingerly over his luggage—as much as she could with her foot still throbbing. She cast a glance and a tight-lipped smile at Maevey.

"I'm sorry it was under these circumstances, still it was a pleasure."

His voice from the entrance to the hallway, slid over her like a warm bubble bath, but she refused to turn around. Instead, she limped down the hall, mentally shoving him aside for fear it might cause her to forget Matt.

* * *

Tyler leisurely picked up the remainder of his luggage as he took advantage of watching the beautiful stranger—with her pirate-like gait—retreat hurriedly down the long corridor. His interest piqued by the fact that he'd never been quite so graciously rejected by a woman before.

He smiled, marginally confused by her caught in the headlights look mixed with something else, or was that simply nerves in the depths of her eyes? Tyler had made a living reading people's eyes, and that woman held an interesting story, he was sure.

Hoisting his bags over his shoulder, he picked up the one that fell on her foot grimacing at its weight. Guilt assaulted him once again and as he shifted the bag to gain a better grip, he made a promise to find a way to make up for his blunder. The expression on her face flashed again in his mind.

Actually, her resistance was refreshing in retrospect. He was more accustomed to being pursued by beautiful women looking to launch modeling careers than being the one in pursuit. The more he pondered the thought, the greater his urge to follow up with this mysterious woman. Particularly since it seemed his fate to be stranded on this lonely, cold island for the next few weeks.

After all, he needed to find a way to apologize.

His smile deepened lost in his own thoughts as he passed by the registration desk. As he readjusted his bags he caught the steady gaze of the fiery redhead standing behind the desk. He lifted an eyebrow and she responded with the same, adding a subtle curl of the corner at her mouth. Giving a curt nod, he hustled up the stairs.

* * *

Maevey closed her eyes, a futile attempt to recover from the startling mixture of curiosity and determination in the man's dark gaze.

Her Irish instinct told her there was bound to be more than just winter storms brewing on the island over the next few weeks. It might behoove her to find a reason to stay on a bit longer just to watch the festivities.

Darci, my dear cousin, if the look on that man's face had anything to do with you, you are in serious trouble, she mused. A wicked smile slid up her face. What an interesting winter this was shaping up to be.

* * *

Tyler shifted his bags as he stepped into the spacious suite. A king-size bed and small living area met his eye, along with an antique cherry wood desk nestled near the bay window, overlooking the straits. He took a deep breath, feeling as he always did at the beginning of a long-term project. Would this be the place that he could call home? Or would it be another town on a long list of others in the past few years that he'd visited and then moved on from?

The bellhop thanked him for the tip then shut the door quietly as he left.

Tyler dropped his bags on the thick evergreen and mauve colored comforter and walked to the window to take in the view. Weary from his long drive from Chicago and battling a lack of sleep, he shrugged out of his jacket, and tossed it to a nearby chair.

He pulled back gauzy white sheers and gazed at the limitless stretch of water beyond the short span of lawn still green from summer. Below, his view included a portion of the outdoor patio area of the dining room and he wondered if the woman he'd met was still somewhere down there. A quick glance of the area indicated the patio was empty and he turned from the window, letting the curtain drop from his hand. Once again the familiar loneliness assaulted him. His mind filtered back to his response the day his supervisors introduced their idea to him.

"You want a book on islanders? Why don't you run this project during the summer, with the yacht races, and the tourists, when there are scores of people picnicking and sailing. How about when it's *warm*?"

He'd tried to reason with them—the powers that be seated in the lush office of the eighteenth floor overlooking Michigan Avenue. Pleaded might actually have been closer to the truth, but they were certain that a photojournalistic approach to the island, isolated and removed from the world with the backdrop of it's harsh Northern Michigan winters would be their next best-selling pictorial documentary. Naturally, while he was busy snapping those shots on those countless freezing days and nights, *they* would be cocooned, warm, and cozy, in their homes.

Tyler dropped the brochure he'd picked up in the lobby onto the cherry-wood desk surface and gave a short sarcastic laugh. "Hell, they stick Christmas trees in the ice as guideposts for a snowmobile path to the mainland." Not that he didn't like snowmobiles, as long as you knew there was solid land beneath you, and had the promise of a crackling fire, a nice brandy, and interesting company at the end of the ride.

He glanced out the window taking in the view of the reason they called this the Great Lakes and thought about the accounts he'd read of thousands of ships gone down with out a trace. The thought sent a shiver across his shoulders and he decided that tomorrow, he would make a list of everything he might need for his extended stay and make sure he had it *before* the first snow.

Despite his repeated offers to his supervisors to capture the beauty of Northern Michigan in the autumn, the powers that be insisted. They wanted him and they wanted their book.

Tyler Landston had a reputation, not only with women, but also as a "people" photojournalist. His work though now widely known in certain circles including Las Vegas and Chicago was not where he wanted it to be. It had been three years since he'd left Vegas to work for the Chicago based publisher.

He began unpacking his bags, carefully tucking his clothes in dresser drawers, and hanging up the rest. This would have to do until he was able to meet with a realtor.

Having the friendship and connections of Daphne De Marco to bank off of, he'd been able to shoot projects all over the world, setting up for himself a portfolio unmatched by very few. He'd met the DeMarco's while struggling with getting his young life together and they'd invited him to be their personal photographer for a time. When Antonio De Marco died, rumor of Tyler's presence in their home finally precipitated the mutual decision between Daphne and himself that it was time for him to move on.

"You need to get out there and find someone to love, my sweetheart." Daphne called him by the pet name she'd given him. "Find a nice girl and settle down. Have children and take lots of pictures."

"You sound like my mother." Tyler smiled as he gazed over the sun reflecting off the azure water of the kidney shaped pool.

"She is a smart woman, sweetheart. She only wants grandchildren." Daphne shrugged as her chiffon cover-up slipped off her shoulder.

"I'm not sure that's for me, Daphne."

"You'll never know until you try. I can help you get started with your own business. It's the least I can do for all you've done for Antonio and me."

"The rumors are already putting too much pressure on you, Daphne."

"And not on you?" She smiled before sipping her Bloody Mary.

"It's time for me to move on. I can never repay you and Antonio for all you've done."

"You've been like a son to us, Tyler. I hear there's a prestigious publisher in Chicago—a distant cousin—let me make a call—"

"I want to do this one my own." Tyler stood placing his hand on the woman's shoulder.

"Well, of course, you do. I'll get you the appointment, and then you're on your own. Deal?"

Tyler thought for a moment. "Deal."

That seemed a lifetime ago. He began the task of unpacking the lenses and various cameras that had in essence become his family. He wondered if Daphne would be disappointed that he hadn't yet found someone to settle down with.

Surveying the array of equipment strewn across the bed, he unfastened the top button of his dress starched shirt and decided to change into what he really considered his "work" clothes—jeans, a T-shirt, and a comfortable V-neck sweater.

Slipping his sweater over his head, the woman's face appeared behind his closed lids and he stopped a moment as if studying her face yet again. Her eyes were breathtaking, shimmering gold like topaz glittering in the sun. Her deep chestnut colored hair, though pulled back from her face was, he suspected, a glorious mass of curls when set free.

Tyler tugged the sweater around his waist as a shudder

rippled through him. He turned to see if one of the windows had been left open. None had.

He pulled off his glasses, swiping his T-shirt over the lens. Part of him felt bad for having accidentally dropped the bag on her foot, yet there was a part of him that might do it again if it might bring him close to her face.

"What was her name?" He swiped his hand over his mouth in frustration, frantically searching his mind. At one point in that awkward—almost erotic—moment he had heard her cousin introducing them, but the scent of her skin and the hungry, haunted look in her golden eyes obliterated all rational thought.

Tyler shot a look at his reflection in the mirror. *Maybe he was he too old for her?* The disturbing thought popped up out of the blue and Tyler immediately brushed it aside. *You're not that far out to pasture old man.* He smiled at his reflection. *Thirty-nine looks pretty damn good on you buddy.*

He appreciated his health, keeping fit, not for his ego necessarily. Well, not entirely. What red-blooded male doesn't appreciate turning the heads of attractive women now and then? And he'd had his share of heads turn over the years, yet none ever materialized into anything of lasting value.

His lean build and dark features were a rugged contrast to the All-American look of his face, behind the glasses. Often he'd been mistaken for younger than he was. His friends in the advertising realm as a result often begged his services for endorsing men's cologne, sportswear, and tuxedos. Early on in his education the thought of modeling had been tempting—if not just for the travel alone—but in the end it was his chance encounter with Antonio and Daphne De Marco that helped him to finish his college degree. As it turned out, his true passion was to be on the other side of the camera.

Tyler eyed his reflection in the mirror, smoothing a wave of dark hair over his ear, the silver of age, just beginning to thread through it.

He considered going over his outline, but already he was weary of the idea of being isolated miles from the "real" world.

No plays, clubs—no social life.

A little bit like being shipped off to Greenland.

He frowned at the agency's choice in locale. Granted it was not the first time this had happened, but somehow, no matter where they sent him, he'd returned with pictures that had catapulted the agency into a highly sought after business.

Mackinac Island? Tyler stood with his arms crossed in defiance over his chest as he stared at the Straits outside his window—*in the dead of winter?*

He made a mental note to add wool socks to his list as he flipped through his wallet to make sure his credit cards and cash were ample for the next week.

He'd heard of this place. A person couldn't live or work in Chicago very long without hearing of the famous Chicago-Mackinac yacht races. The thought of entering one had tempted him once or twice, but work too often got in the way. He was aware, however, of the great historical significance the island held, having studied extensively on the architecture of the several homes. Plus there was the history of the Great Lakes shipping disasters and the tales of how the lakes could change in an instant in the fall, when the Northern gales began their blustery descent.

Frozen Tundra. It was looking to be a cold, lonely winter.

What he really needed first was to have a nice, quiet dinner. His mind wandered unexpectedly back to the eyes of the beautiful woman in the lobby.

With his stomach beckoning for food and the possibility that his mystery woman might still be in the vicinity—hopefully alone—edged happily into his mind. He quickly slipped into his comfortable loafers and stuffed his wallet in his jeans pocket.

* * *

The sight of the handsome stranger left Darci's toes tingling. She glanced down at her feet in black sandals. Or perhaps it was simply the residual affect of the heavy suitcase landing on her foot.

Still, she could deny the immediate physical attraction

she'd experienced in his presence. There was no mistaking that her body temperature soared into the rafters, flashing all manner of red warning lights as he stooped down to pluck the bag from her foot. The air between them moved just enough to provide a gentle sampling of his provocative cologne—very business, very confident, very sensuous.

A rush of heat radiated in her chest and Darci's hand instinctively went to her throat, to make sure she could swallow.

Hot flashes? Weak knees? Darci paused, catching her image reflected in the shiny stainless steel refrigerator. Maybe she *was* experiencing the onset of early menopause? She held her palm to her cheek.

"You feeling all right this evening, Darci?" Stu, the head chef paused next to her, dropping the back of his hand against her forehead. In his other hand he balanced a tray of peeled cold shrimp on ice.

"Just a little accident with my foot. I'll be fine. Thanks, Stu."

"You look a little green."

Stu had a penchant for telling it like it was. Most of the time, Darci appreciated that.

"Kind of feverish…sort of—"

"I'm fine. Really." Darci brushed an errant wisp of hair from her neck. It clung to the perspiration that beaded all the way to her chest. This was one night she wished that she had another dress besides the v-neck black rayon/ spandex to wear as the restaurant hostess.

Stu eyed her suspiciously and then nodded. "Okay, but if it gets worse, tell me and we'll hunt someone down to cover your shift."

He handed the platter to a nearby waitress. "Party of five, near the piano."

She smiled at him and then disappeared through the swinging door.

"Hey now, I meant what I said. I know what I'm talking about, Darci. When you get our age, things just don't seem to

53

heal as fast as when we were younger, you know?" He gave her a wink and a playful nudge with his elbow before going on his merry way.

Darci stared after the man's departing form. "You've no idea how right you are, Stu."

She emitted a deep, cleansing sigh and closed her eyes to erase her former thoughts. Regardless of how her body reacted, her brain reminded her that she had work to do and more than enough to keep her occupied all night.

Besides, what on earth made her think that she could see another man in the same way she'd known Matt?

Chapter Five

Tyler stepped into the silent hallway, marveling at the quiet. It was then that he realized the warmth of the hotel reminded him of his boyhood home back in rural Illinois.

A lover of design, he studied the woodworking, noting the architecture of the interior hall and the way the rooms connected. He ran his fingers along the scrolled edges of the gleaming white painted railing.

From what he could discern, most likely the main structure of the hotel was in its day nothing more than an oversized three-story Victorian house. Perhaps a summer home of the wealthy elite from the Chicago area who was known to have built many of the grand summer homes on the island during the late 1800's.

The proprietors had obviously expanded over the years creating grand wings that connected to the main house while preserving the simplicity and grandeur of the structure.

With any luck, the success of the hotel would have something to do with its restaurant as well. As much time as he spent on the road, there were times when he longed for a home-like atmosphere. Particularly when the thought of cold winter months alone loomed ahead of him. He made a mental note to ask the realtor about a fireplace.

Tyler paused momentarily as he descended the stairs. In the distance a voice emitted from a television turned low, in the room separated by an arch near the lobby area.

The aroma of home-baked bread wafted up the stairs teasing his senses and for a split second he imagined he was nine and his mother was calling him for supper.

"Tyler Landston! This is the second time I've called you

for supper!

Instead, he caught the curious look of the lovely red-haired desk clerk.

He blinked, pulling himself from his reverie. Those days were a lifetime ago.

"Everything to your liking, Mr. Landston?" There was a slight note of caution in her voice giving way that she'd caught him in his daydream.

"Wonderful thanks." The memory of his mother dissipated with that of his childhood. "This is a very comfortable place." He smiled, stopping at the desk to pull off his glasses and clean them on his sweater.

She smiled as though she'd heard similar comments before. "We like for our guests to feel at home, Mr. Landston. It's been a tradition in my family for years. At one time, the only television in the hotel was the one in the lobby." She pointed to the room behind him. "It's still there, but times change and to make the most for our guests we did make the addition of cable available in each room."

"I don't really watch TV that much."

She nodded, smiling as she arranged a vase of fresh flowers. "It's our policy that those who stay with us have as little distraction as possible." She looked at him with a wry grin. "Distractions of the technological variety at any rate. Do you plan to relax a bit while here on the island, Mr. Landston?"

If he could manage to find out her cousins name, he just might consider it. Tyler replaced his glasses, and leaned his elbow to the counter, giving her a sweet smile that—usually—managed to get him what he wanted. He hoped it would work as well on this feisty desk clerk.

"Speaking of...uh, I didn't catch your name?"

"Maevey," she replied with a pert answer, her chin lifting slightly.

His eyebrow quirked and he continued, seeing the woman's delicate throat move in a gentle swallow. Never let it be said that well-practiced charm didn't work wonders on the opposite sex. "Maevey? Now, would that happen to be Irish?"

She nodded, her gaze never leaving his.

"Listen, Maevey." He leaned in close over the polished registration desk. "May I ask a favor?"

"Depends, but I'll try," she replied not letting down her prim regard of him.

"The woman, the one earlier in the lobby? Did I understand correctly that's she's related to you?"

A smile tugged at her lips as she straightened her shoulders, her gaze brightened to a clear blue. "She's my cousin Mr. Landston, and I would be curious to know why you ask?"

"Please, call me Tyler." He slid his glasses back on, sensing that timing and honesty was everything to this woman. "So I could apologize properly for the mishap earlier."

She paused as though wanting to make it clear that she was carefully weighing her answer, but only after she was sure about him.

His insides squirmed under her intense scrutiny, even though her assessment only took a moment. He sensed she'd stripped him bare and dressed him again.

Her gaze narrowed, then she smiled, one that sent him the message that—for whatever reasons—she approved.

"Her name is Darci." *And I saw the sparks flying between the two of you.* Her twinkling gaze added.

He shifted, remembering the dock porter's words about Maevey's matchmaking abilities. Tyler stepped away from the desk. "Uh, thank you."

She held his gaze with an unblinking stare.

"I've got good intentions, you've no reason for concern." Hopeful he reassured her.

"Well, sure it is that I know where to find you, don't I?" Her smile was pleasant, her meaning crystal clear.

He nodded, not wanting to tangle with this one.

She nodded in return and continued to straighten the brochures on the countertop.

As he walked the short hallway to the dining room, he had the sudden urge to check the days bearded growth on his face.

Pausing in front of the glass front of the phone booth, he winced, wondering if he should have shaved before coming down.

Pretty sure of things, aren't you?" he muttered. From his experience in this line of work, first impressions were sometimes crucial in developing a relationship. Tyler sighed remembering the pained expression of the woman in the lobby. Yeah, well, so much for first impressions.

Ahead in the dining room, he heard the content mumble of dinner conversation, while the aroma of the food and fresh coffee caused his stomach to protest.

He scanned the room, please to discover that his clothes were entirely appropriate for evening. Occupied with searching for the soothing piano music he suddenly felt as though he was being watched.

Glancing to his side, he was pleasantly surprised to be looking again into those enticing topaz eyes. Motionless, he allowed his gaze to absorb the transformation from jeans to the gorgeous creature that stood next to him.

Her gaze remained steady as he took in the sleek, black dress that hugged every curve. Peeking from beneath a sexy slit on the side was a good bit of rather shapely leg.

Tyler smiled upon seeing the faint tinge of pink color her cheeks and suddenly his appetite increased—just not for food.

* * *

"One, sir?" Darci caught the surprised look on his face as he scanned her from head to toe. She drew in her leg, clamping her knees together in an attempt to eliminate the view of her bare leg from the slit in her long skirt.

"Unless you'd care to join me?" he replied, his slightly crooked smile gave his handsome face a charming appeal-one that caused Darci's stomach to lurch. She smoothed her dress hoping to quell the nerves he inspired.

"I'm sorry sir, I'm working, but I'd be happy to seat you." She answered quickly, snatching a menu from the shelf and motioned for him to follow, hoping he wouldn't detect the telltale signs of his effect on her.

Gingerly winding her way through the candlelit tables, she could sense him studying her as before. The thought sent chills up her arms.

She turned brandishing a bright business-like smile. "Will this do?"

His brows arched as his gaze pulled up from where he'd been focused. "Looks great to me."

She placed the menu on the table, catching the subtle curl at the corner of his lip.

"Bridget will be your waitress this evening, Mr. Landston." Darci picked up the extra silverware off the table. His body brushed softly against hers as he walked behind her to be seated.

"I guess that means you won't reconsider?"

He sat down his gaze intent on her face. It would take nothing more than for him to reach out and tug her to his lap.

"But I'm flattered you remembered."

Darci straightened, creating a greater distance between them. She held an extra water goblet in her hand, drawing protectively to her chest. "Remembered what?"

"My name." He grinned, removing his glasses, laying them carefully beside his plate.

Nervous enough by the unsolicited attention he gave her, Darci couldn't will her legs to move.

He slowly looked up with eyes that threatened to pull her into their lush coolness. "I must have made quite an impression on you."

Shaking off her high school fascination, she answered, "That you did, Mr. Landston. Enjoy your dinner."

"I will, Darci."

His voice, smooth and dark, with a hint of mystery followed as she snaked her way back to the hostess' podium. Clearly he was the type of man that was used to being around women. Openly appealing, charming, knowing just what to say, and when to say it. Leah would call him a player.

* * *

It was obvious she was not interested. Maybe she already

59

had someone in her life? Tyler toyed with that thought, distracted that it should bother him. He'd only just met this woman and clearly she'd given him the brush off. Maybe that's what he found so damn appealing.

Then again, wouldn't her cousin have clued him into that fact when he asked about her? Tyler placed his glasses on his face just as a young waitress appeared at his side.

She began reeling off the specials for the evening and after the first couple of sentences, Tyler found himself peering around the bubbly waitress in an attempt to see Darci.

"Sir?" The young women, finished and waiting, gave him a pointed look, accented with a noticeable shift to her other leg. She arched her eyebrow, questioning him.

The women around here spoke a lot with their eyebrows.

Tyler smiled pleasantly. "I'd like to try the whitefish. Make that with a baked potato and salad, blue cheese. No, on second thought—" He glanced at Darci. "No dressing, thank you."

She grinned, his faux pas already forgiven as she accepted the menu back from him.

Now if he could make that charm work as well on the lovely Darci.

"Excellent choice, sir"

He glanced at his slightly limping hostess seating another couple. "I think so."

"The whitefish is the best on the island." Bridget tucked the menus under her arm. "May I get you a beverage?" She stood with her hands folded expectantly in front of her.

Relinquishing the stress of the day to the quite ambiance, Tyler leaned back and focused his attention on the young waitress. "A glass of chardonnay sounds nice. Thank you, Bridget."

"Excellent, I'll be right back." Her smile was inviting.

Tyler sensed the young waitress's interest, but backed away from it. Had he made the time in his life, or had married earlier; he might already have a daughter near her age.

A wave of melancholy drifted over him, and he wondered

how his nieces and nephews were doing. They knew him, of course, but only as the adventurous uncle that sent them gifts from exotic ports.

He smiled as he smoothed out a slight wrinkle in the tablecloth. There had been a couple of times when he'd thought about marriage. Unfortunately, his work and travel had not left him with the time or energy to develop any real ties to anyone or anything.

He chewed at the inner corner of his lip, a habit since early childhood when he was in deep thought. His eyes mesmerized by the flicker of the candle flame.

* * *

Darci stared at his near perfect face, obviously lost in his private thoughts. She wondered if her realized what that gesture did to his already provocative mouth.

He held the votive, staring at it much the same as he had when studying her foot, as though all of his attention was focused solely to that object.

Aside from the fact that he was incredibly the most handsome man she'd seen in a long while, he was, she suspected, a man capable of intense emotion. The creative type, she could see that clearly in his eyes and manner. It stirred thoughts in her that she didn't know she'd been hiding inside.

As though he sensed he was being watched, his gaze lifted and the candlelight danced off his eyes. Mesmerized, she was oblivious that she'd been openly staring until the jolt of his unexpected lazy smile shocked her back to reality. She stumbled backward and caught herself before she fell into the lap of man seated behind her.

Her face aflame with embarrassment, she apologized discreetly, dropping a couple of menus on the table in front of her as she kept her focus glued to the floor.

"Your waitress will be with you momentarily."

She chanced a quick glance toward the stranger in hopes that he'd not had the satisfaction of seeing her mishap, only to find him practicing his charming smile on Bridget.

"Miss?"

For reasons Darci chose not to identify, disappointment reared its ugly head. Heap that atop a steaming plate of feeling foolish, and placed with a side order of being almost forty, and her proverbial "emotional" plate was too full to handle.

"Miss?" The man beside her was insistent.

"Yes?" Her response held some of the frustration she was experiencing at the moment. Darci sighed. "Yes, sir?" Her reply was more professional the second time.

"We've already ordered." The patron gave her a puzzled expression as he waved his hand over the salads he and his wife were eating.

"Well, of course you have." She picked up the menus, grinned, and turned away so they wouldn't see the pink tinge in her cheeks.

Darci took a deep breath, and pulled back her shoulders. She was after all a grown woman and it didn't take a rocket scientist to know when to leave well enough alone.

* * *

The methodical tick, tick, tick of the pewter finished desk clock tapped a frustrating tattoo against Peter's overtaxed system.

He studied the portfolio, his gaze narrowing at the projected results. Over twenty-some years in the making—as long as Matt and Darci were married—hell, before that—he'd meticulously been piecing together a financial portfolio that was destined to make both he and Matt wealthy beyond their wildest dreams.

The sun had long since disappeared over the Kansas City skyline, leaving Peter sitting at his desk with only the garish blue-white cast of the computer screen for light.

He rubbed his eyes with fingers dry and chafed from wading through so much paperwork. Given the circumstances, he knew that the very success of what he'd poured his life into rested on the fact that every detail needed to be covered. There was no room for error. Its what his friend would have wanted.

Their friendship was a perfect combination—Peter's skills

with money and business matters and Matt's money. After they'd met as roommates in their freshman year, they were rarely apart. Over time, Matt learned to trust Peter's judgment in his financial affairs.

Then Darci came along. Sweet, down-to-earth Darci and the three of them were—for awhile—the best of friends, attending college functions together, going on weekend excursions—there was little they didn't do together.

A year or so after undergrad school, they announced their wedding and while it had come as an inevitably that Darci would wind up with one of them, Peter had held out hope that Darci would see his feelings for her.

Matt had that "big heart" thing going for him though, wanting to help people instead of taking care of himself. That's why he trusted Peter to take care of the details of his finances, so he could focus his attention on that "big heart" of his.

Peter blinked as the thumbnail image of the three of them at graduation popped up on the website screen. It was one of the few pictures he had of the three of them. He'd run across it in Matt's papers after the funeral. When he'd requested it from Darci, she simply waved her hand and nodded.

It was unfortunate she knew as little about her husband as she did. Even now, when Peter tried to explain her enormous net worth, she continued to brush it off—in affect, brush him off—again, or perhaps just unwilling to deal with Matt's death

That made it hard on him—to watch her suffer like she did. Perhaps not by outward appearances, but certainly her suffering on the inside. That's what Peter knew—what was inside Darci Cunningham. How she reacted when she was scared or worried. How she had the habit of chewing on her thumbnail when she was troubled.

Peter drew his thumbnail away from his teeth and wiped his hand on the front of his shirt. He reached over and snapped on the small desk lamp as he readjusted his focus on the computer screen.

There were but a few details left, getting Darci to sign over the power of attorney was one of them. If he couldn't convince her of that, he'd have to convince her that he wanted to take care of her, that he had deep feelings for her, and could give her a good life. Of that, he was certain he'd have no trouble accomplishing.

Yes, he could be patient. Just as he had been over the years watching Matt's financial investments grow to maturity, he could be a patient man.

Yes, he would take care of her. She'd see one day that he had only her best interest at heart. It was a promise he'd made to Matt, just before he died.

Chapter Six

Darci stretched under the luxurious down comforter of her queen size mission-style bed. A gift she'd treated herself with as the days grew colder. Though she'd not planned on working last night, she didn't mind. Understanding a mother's plight, she agreed to fill in for Beth when her young son became sick and she needed to go home.

The employees, as a rule, were good to one another and after all, she'd wanted the company of people. Though the unexpected episodes of needing the comfort of crowded rooms were fewer now, than when Matt first died.

Her gaze followed a slender finger of sunlight stretched across her ceiling. In the distance, the muted clang of a buoy caused her thoughts to dawdle.

The mere thought of being alone on the island all winter had spooked her enough last night that she nearly ran to the hotel for the comfort of people. At some point she knew that she would be able to manage the periods of intense loneliness, she just needed to give herself time.

Rubbing her eyes, she yawned, lazily pushing her arms overhead. She checked the clock, discovering it was almost ten and quickly flipped back the covers. The chill in the house hit her full force as her stocking feet touched the floor. Once again, she made a promise to herself to do something soon about her heat situation.

She'd been intending to do so for weeks. Her procrastination had quickly become the brunt of many jokes among her friends at the restaurant. She'd taken many verbal jabs of needing to find "alternative means" of body warmth with a good-natured smile.

While she hated to disappoint the roll they were on, winter was closing in on the island, and she needed to see Abe about fixing the furnace.

She padded into the sunny yellow kitchen, repainted from the deep purple of the previous owners, while she pulled her unruly hair into a ponytail.

Grateful for her spontaneous purchase of the wool blend fisherman socks, she wiggled her toes as she scooped the rich roasted coffee into the pot and flipped its switch, filling the tiny room with a heavenly aroma.

Darci leaned back against the cabinet, and glanced down at the Snoopy Boxer shorts her daughter had purchased for her. Not exactly "Victoria's Secret," but then again—who was she trying to impress?

Thoughts of her daughter's generous support made her wonder briefly what Leah would think if she were to consider dating again.

It had been with her daughter's encouragement to move to the island and pursue her writing—but dating again? What would be her children's reaction to that? Darci hoped if that ever became an issue that Leah's reaction might be as free-spirited as was her reaction to the move to the island. Closing her eyes, Darci remembered her initial conversation with Leah.

"I say you go for it, Mom!" Her daughter's eyes shone bright with enthusiasm. "You've talked about living on *that* island for years."

"But what about you and Nathan? What about being able to come *home* on breaks and at Christmas?" Immediately Darci's thumbnail clicked against her front teeth.

A silence fell between them and then Leah quietly sighed. "Mom." Her daughter's expression changed then from a young woman to one of greater age and wisdom. Even now the look in her eyes was etched in Darci's brain. "Dad would have wanted you to follow your dreams."

From that moment she'd never doubted her choice to move, or her choice a writing career, but the choice of becoming involved with another man? *That* hadn't been part of the equation.

Darci turned grasping one of the two coffee cups on the countertop coffee rack. If she looked at things realistically, of course, what had really changed?

At this point, it wasn't as though hundreds of eligible suitors were lined up on her doorstep. Yet the unexpected encounter with the man in the hotel lobby was enough to elicit sensations she hadn't thought about in a while.

Her concerns were, of course, ludicrous, in that she barely knew Tyler Landston, and Peter—well, Peter had become almost over protective of her in recent weeks. Not exactly stirring anything in her other than frustration over his oftentimes-bossy behavior.

Darci shuddered. Something about Peter's overt friendliness sent up red flags whenever he was around and she'd known him for many years. On the other hand, one encounter with Tyler Landston and she'd pondered for the first time—since Matt's passing—her physical needs as a woman.

Her thoughts turned to Matt and a sudden constriction grabbed her throat. Squeezing her eyes against the tears she forced herself to admit once again the complete absurdity that they had such a short time on earth together. He'd been a part of her strength, loving her simple outlook on life and encouraging her in all she undertook. She truly enjoyed his partnership and their love. What would he tell her if he could speak to her now?

Shaking her head in anger, determined that she would not allow herself to become a maudlin widow, she forced her gaze to the vast blue lake. As always, it's great, tranquil presence touched a part of her she barely understood herself.

In all the years of dirty bottles, tantrums, and financial struggle, it held a place of quiet fortitude in her spirit.

Slipping into a kitchen chair, she drew back the curtain and followed the sight of a great ore ship as it chugged its way through the Straits.

She blew across the top of her coffee and out of habit lay one foot atop the other as she leaned her elbows to the table.

The unconscious act conjured sudden memories of how Matt used to tease her incessantly about it. She smiled softly, the watery images of his face swimming in her mind.

Her thoughts glazed over in her mind as the face wavered, evolving to a set of forest green eyes behind wire-rimmed glasses. His grin, slightly crooked accompanied his gaze as his fingers pressed his glasses up the bridge of his nose.

In her daydream she saw him from across the restaurant, slowly turning the candle in his hands, his study of the flame evoking the kind of solitude she'd in recent days, experienced herself. What kind of man would travel to a remote island in the dead of winter? Darci arched her brow—for that matter, what kind of woman would do the same thing?

Darci's muse frolicked across her mind, gleefully playing various scenarios in her head. Well, if nothing else, certainly his mysterious nature had given her fuel for characters in her writing.

She tipped the cup to take a sip of her coffee and missed, sending the scorching coffee down the front of her shirt. Jumping up from the table, her daydream vanished and she hissed as the hot liquid soaked through her shirt. Holding the cloth away from her skin, she cursed herself for being an idiot.

As if a guy like that doesn't have a platoon of women at his whim!

Better to be realistic rather than to face the desire his outward appearance conjured up. Good Lord in heaven, it wasn't as though she was ready for a new relationship, but there had been moments, off and on, when she missed the scent of a man's skin and a set of strong arms to hold her at night. Fresh guilt, much stronger in intensity washed over her, causing her cheeks to burn.

She needed to channel this energy.

She showered, using more cold water than usual and then slipped into a pair of jeans and an oversized sweatshirt. Armed with a fresh cup of coffee and a renewed determination, she wandered to her laptop to write.

Today, the ideas flowed. Her muse was generous. Some

thoughts came in succinct rapid-fire clarity, while others remained elusive, looking for just the right place to land on the paper. Darci seized the moment, knowing that whatever else, these images needed to be in front of her—something tangible that she could hold onto.

For her this was like breathing, shoved aside for her entire life, it now consumed her.

With no consideration of time, she worked her fingers relentlessly for hours, until finally her stomach protesting for sustenance signaled how long she'd been writing.

Appeased by a piece of bread and a slice of cheese, she labored furiously on. Her drive was high today, she felt strong. The passion of her writing was intense, causing her to sit back and stare at the words she'd just poured onto her computer.

It empowered her to see that such a fire existed within her.

She had to admit, she liked the way the storyline was developing. Perhaps Maevey's not-so-subtle hints had taken seed.

Darci read the words aloud on the screen.

"I can't keep myself from you, God knows I've tried." The *stranger's lips covered hers with a passion she'd long since forgotten could be produced by two people.*

She covered her mouth, stunned by what she'd written.

Just three weeks before, Maevey had given her this exact storyline.

And she'd refused the idea.

At what point had she gone from reluctance to driven?

Surprised at what had come out of her frenzied emotions. She considered it might have been the incident in the hotel lobby the night before—her brief, albeit intense encounter with *Mr. I.M. Gorgeous.*

Darci flushed from the memory alone.

Damn pre-menopausal symptoms.

He was after all just another man.

Even now her palms sweat as she recalled the gentleness in holding her ankle and the scent of the lake and wind lingering on his skin.

She winced recalling the entire incident. Crystal clear it replayed in her mind in slow motion. Her face warmed at the sensations of his face close to hers...his smile...those eyes. Her breasts unhampered under the loose sweatshirt, tingled with the memory.

Yet, despite her clumsiness, despite the fact that she could barely speak, he'd come down to the restaurant.

A tiny voice tweaked at her thoughts. *He has to eat. Of course, he'd go to the restaurant.*

Then there was the way he smiled at me—

"He smiled at Bridget just the same," the voice taunted.

Darci groaned and put her face in her hands.

The voice of reason won that round.

She stared at the computer screen and sighed. No doubt he had a great deal of practice emitting that charm.

It was so much easier, albeit wiser, to place him in the category of the consummate player than to deal with her nagging curiosity.

Darci reached for her coffee, only to find the cup cold and empty. She glanced at the clock on the mantle, realizing that it was already time to get ready for work.

She was a grown woman. A grown *widow* woman and she had no business dealing with thoughts that could turn her life and the lives of her children upside down.

Snapping down the lid to her laptop, she scurried to the bedroom to get ready for work. Part of her trying to convince the other part that she didn't want to run into Tyler Landston again.

Darci pressed her uniform, swaying to the rhythm of the 80's station playing on her radio. "You might as well face it you're addicted to love," she sang the words of the popular *Robert Palmer* tune as she shut off the iron.

Above the blare of the radio, purposely turned loud to distract her thoughts, the phone rang.

She reached across the bed to turn down the volume as she grabbed the receiver with her free hand.

"Hello?"

"Darci? How's my girl?" Peter's familiar voice was pleasant to hear, but his possessive connotation left little to be desired.

"I'm fine, Peter, but I wish you'd not refer to me as your "girl.""

"Sorry, force of habit after all this time. Not trying to make you feel uncomfortable, Darci."

A short silence followed. She heard the sound of shuffling paper.

"I hadn't talked with you in a while, so I thought I'd call and see if you'd had a chance to look over those papers and get your *Jane Doe* on them?" He laughed at his own joke.

"Not yet, Peter."

There was another brief silence.

"Now we talked about this, Darci. This would free up some of the profits of the stocks that Matt tucked away. More importantly, it would leave you and the kids sitting quite comfortable for the rest of your lives. We don't want to miss this opportunity, do we? Don't you trust me, sweetheart?"

Uncomfortable—that described exactly what she felt like at the moment. Something prickled at the back of her neck. "Then why not leave it alone and sell them off later when we could really use them—like for retirement or creating a trust fund for my grandchildren."

"Is there something about the kids that you're not telling me, Darci?"

"No, Peter, I'm just offering another option."

He laughed again. "Well that's a relief, I thought you'd forgotten to share some good news with your best friend. Listen, sweetheart, these stock issues sometimes get sticky. Right now they look good. It would be wise to sell them when the market is high. Stuff like Enron happens all the time. Matt would understand this Darci. He'd have jumped on this."

Her lips formed a straight line, not liking particularly where the conversation was headed. "I'll think about it, Peter."

"That's fine, but don't wait too long."

"Certainly, Peter. I'll contact you the minute I've looked

them over."

"Listen Darci," his voice softened, "I was thinking, I could come up for a weekend. You know go over those papers and explain the possible benefits of this venture with you."

Darci's mouth dropped open in shock. "Peter Beck, are you trying to—?" She could not say the words that stuck in her throat.

"Oh God, Darci. No, no. I just thought you could use a familiar face up there." His nervous chuckle emitted through the phone. "You're kind of up there in the middle of nowhere."

"Surrounded by my family."

"Sure, but…I miss him too, Darci. The three of us used to be close, remember?"

"And you'd like for that arrangement to continue, I assume, right, Peter?" Bile crept into her throat and she clamped her hand over her neck.

"Now I've gone and upset you. That was the last thing I wanted to do, Darci. Don't you think Matt would want me looking out for his best girl?"

Best Girl?

"You're a wealthy woman, sweetheart. Downsizing by selling your house and the investments Matt made at my suggestions. I'm only looking out for your welfare. Just concerned that you're okay up there."

"You think Matt would appreciate how you've been hitting on me these last few weeks, Peter?" Anger built inside her.

"Okay, okay, simmer down. Let's pretend this conversation never happened. You're turning things around here and I understand that your emotions are a little raw around the edges. So, you take a look at those papers and get back to me soon."

"I will and thank you for your concern." Darci forced the lie through her lips. She leaned her head against the kitchen cupboard and closed her eyes.

"Just be careful, Darci. There's all kinds of people out there and some of them aren't above conning a widow woman out of her money."

"Point taken, Peter." Darci held her palm to her forehead.

"I'll be in touch. Meantime, I'd advise you not to speak to anyone about your financial matters, except me."

For the first time in twenty-some years, Darci wished that Matt had not been so damn fruitful with his money.

"Okay Pete, I need to run."

"Take care, honey."

"I'm n—" The phone clicked, disconnecting the conversation before she could remind him that she wasn't his "honey."

Determined not to let Peter's phone call affect her she slipped on her uniform and checked her minimum of makeup. A quick sweep of her favorite plum color to her lips and pulling her hair back in the tortoise hairclip and she was ready.

Staring at the face in the mirror, she saw a reasonably attractive, reasonably wise woman. Confident in her abilities and yet afraid that no man might ever see past the wealth she'd acquired through heart wrenching circumstances.

More confused, Darci grabbed her house keys and headed out the door.

* * *

Tyler had wandered the streets of Mackinac most of the day, taking pictures of the main street buildings, St. Anne's Church, and the boats bobbing in the harbor, some already being pulled out for the winter storage.

The crisp bite of the wind in the clear blue sky gave an exhilarating preview of the days to come.

He captured the faces of several hardy souls who prefer the island after the hubbub of the summer tourist season, still tourists, but more in tune with the quiet, reflective mood of the fall season.

He'd been to the Fort, taking great strides to make it up the long path to the top, and getting there, discovered the breathtaking view it provided of the straits. Winded from the walk, he caught a carriage back down the hill where it stopped near the blacksmith's shop. There he'd visited with the proprietor and snapped a few shots of him shoeing the horses.

It was at the pub that he'd learned the inside tracks about the island. By lunching with a group of older men, he'd learned that the summer tourists were called "*fudgies*" a name given to them due to the sweet confection acting as a siren to those unable to stay away from its allure.

He explained to them why he was there and they chuckled though they told him they thought it sounded like a great idea, they were a little dubious that being a "city slicker" from Chicago, he would last the winter on the island.

Nonetheless, they'd been polite to listen to him anyway.

The various stores and boutiques satiated some of his restlessness and reading up on the history of the island appeased his curiosity. Some-thirty odd rolls of film later, he still could not push the thought of his chance meeting with this woman from his mind.

He tried to reason to himself that it was because she'd rejected his attention. He'd dated scores of women in his lifetime, sleek, exotic, and well traveled.

It was just plain unreasonable he should be attracted to her; she was nothing at all like any of the women he dated.

Yet despite his logic, her lovely face persisted in his mind and he found himself wondering how her hair would feel through his fingers. How her mouth would taste against his.

Tyler attempted to swallow, but a constriction of desire held his throat at bay.

With a frustrated sigh, he leaned against a white picket fence to clean his camera lens and ponder why this woman, in particular, should grab him like a fish on a hook.

Loneliness?

Yeah, maybe, but he'd been lonely before. He could handle that.

Curious?

Certainly. It was part of his nature to be so.

Perhaps it was the idea of being in effect "trapped" all winter on an island with this beautiful and desirable woman?

He clicked the snap on his camera bag and headed back to the hotel. There was the logic—due to close proximity and nothing more.

Satisfied with his conclusion, he moved on to deciding that he would need to make up his mind about which house he would sublet for the winter. He'd looked at two. One that sat on the far side of the island from Main Street and the other that was a mere three doors down the block from one Darci Cunningham.

His thoughts betrayed him as he positioned himself to capture a few shots of the brilliant fireball of the setting sun behind the Mackinac Bridge.

A tiny house with a crackling fire popped into his mind and he was snuggled under a cozy blanket with a woman with honey-colored eyes. In the back, off the porch, there was a tiny dark room—

Tyler straightened, blinking at the glare from the sun.

Hallucinations. That was all—nothing that a great dinner wouldn't cure.

He turned and bound up the hotel stairs like a kid coming home from school.

* * *

Maevey watched the handsome stranger as he stood on the porch staring out over the water.

She recognized the pensive look. He had all the markings of a man in search of something missing in his life.

Or perhaps the look of a man who had recently found what he was searching for and didn't know it yet?

Maevey smiled as she dusted the registration desk countertop, her Irish eyes twinkling.

* * *

"The place is packed tonight huh, Darci?" Bridget remarked as she carried empty plates through the kitchen door.

Though there was a difference in their ages, the two had quickly become friends. Bridget was open and friendly. Darci was steady and strong. It made for a good friendship.

"Sure is and my feet already know it!" Darci replied as the full tray she was holding above her head tilted precariously.

The furious pace they'd kept all evening had held thoughts

of the handsome stranger at bay and the fact that he'd not shown yet for supper gave her reason to believe that he'd chosen elsewhere for his evening meal. That alone helped Darci breath a little easier. She had no desire to morph into what she perceived she'd been behaving like—a gawking teen with a crush on the coolest guy in the school.

"I'm getting the hang of this tray thing." She shifted the glimmering silver tray heaped with steaming pasta to the flat tips of her fingers. "Watch this!"

She grinned at Bridget and wiggled her brows as she hit the door with her backside.

Chapter Seven

Tyler admitted that he hoped Darci was working tonight. He could as easily chosen a half dozen other places to eat, but the truth was plain. He wanted to see her again. Not to appreciate her beauty, or the grace of her smile, but to take an objective look at this ordinary woman and once and for all— wash her from his system.

The same method had worked in the past and inevitably it turned up something that he'd previously missed. He'd become a master at ending relationships. It was obvious the life he'd chosen did not involve "settling down." His life was full of international adventure and exotic beauty and for years it had served him well.

For starters, this woman represented none of those things. She just happened to be here on this God-forsaken island and— well, he'd have to make sure this infatuation of his was nipped in the bud.

He was waiting in line to be seated when his golden opportunity came swinging through the door, with a full tray of steaming pastas about to be hoisted above her head.

He was not able to react fast enough.

Her eyes grew wide as she realized what was about to happen.

The entire contents of the tray laden with pastas and red sauce splattered down the front of the creamy white fisherman's knit sweater he'd just bought earlier in the day.

The expression on her face mirrored his own surprise and for a moment, everything came to a standstill.

Then as though someone ethereal force pushed the "play" button, life resumed in a rush of waiters and waitresses scurrying to placate the customers who'd had the unfortunate fate of being seated in the circumference of the disaster.

Darci grabbed the napkin from the lap of the man next to her and dabbed the cloth into his white wine. The patron's mouth dropped open and he stared at Darci as though she'd gone crazy, which from Tyler's standpoint, was a definite possibility. She attacked his sweater with the damp cloth, tugging, sliding her hand beneath his clothing, as though oblivious of his presence.

Tyler was very much aware, however, and fought to keep his gaze averted from where her face hovered just inches from his crotch.

Bridget covered Darci's exuberant behavior, smiling weakly at the confused customer as she handed him a clean napkin. "Uh, maybe you should just take him into the kitchen." The young waitress smiled nervously at Tyler as she glanced around the room, now grown still in watching the trio.

Darci glanced up at Bridget and realization of the spectacle they'd created crossed her face.

She dropped her hand from under his sweater and the wet fabric slapped against his T-shirt underneath.

No doubt, she'd probably ruined one of the more expensive sweaters he'd purchased in a long time. So why did he want to draw her into his arms and give *her* comfort?

If she'd given him a better reason to find her presence distasteful, he couldn't think of one. She'd handed a great excuse not to be interested in her and on a platter, no less.

"Darci, isn't it?" This was not in his original game plan. Dammit. His thoughts were jumbled between her pained expression and the brush of her hand against his stomach. Maybe he could pretend that he didn't remember who she was, even if she had popped into his mind more than a dozen times during the day.

She grabbed his arm and he found himself being hustled through the kitchen door. "Uh…really, this is not necessary—" He sidestepped another waitress avoiding another catastrophe.

The woman hadn't heard a word he'd said. The

devastation of what she'd done was clearly etched on her face as she tugged him toward the sink.

"I am so very sorry." Her words were punctuated as she wove through the kitchen, dodging kitchen staff in effort to get to the sink. "I should have been watching. It's been like Grand Central in and out of that door tonight. I'm afraid I get so used to the pace that I forget to pay attention."

Her sincerity made it difficult to remain upset about the incident. Hell, it was only a sweater.

He pulled the heavy, wet, knit fabric from his chest, suppressing a shiver.

He didn't want her to feel any worse than she obviously did.

"Really, don't worry about it." He held out his sweater, sighing quietly as he stared at the smeared blotch of orange stain like a target on his chest.

He caught her silence and glanced up slowly, unable to pass lightly over how well she fit into the pristine black and white uniform. He licked his lips forcing his gaze to her face, fortunately turned away from his gawking stare. "It's just a sweater." His voice seemed stuck in his throat.

"Excuse me?" She blinked from her reverie.

Obviously, she was less aware of him, and more aware of his sweater. "Really, don't worry about it. It's just a sweater." Tyler attempted to keep the mood light, fighting the tension building in his gut.

She was slightly shorter than he remembered, coming just to his shoulder, but it was her hands he remembered as her nails raking lightly across his stomach in a furious attempt to fight the stain.

Tyler doubted she was even aware of touching him, but he'd felt the jolt and even now it lingered way too much for his curiosity.

"Guess this makes us even." He held out his hand in a gesture of truce.

She looked at him trying to muster dignified, but falling short with little more than an expression of humiliation and embarrassment.

She accepted his hand, closing her eyes as she spoke. "I insist you send me the cleaning bill or at the very least allow me to purchase another sweater to replace this one."

Tyler allowed a moment to pass, for no other reason than to hold her hand. This was not going remotely close to where he'd intended. He waited until she looked at him.

"It's the least I can do." Her soft eyes pleaded with him to agree. Making things right was obviously very important to this woman. *Making it* with this woman suddenly seemed vital. It was a torrid, sleazy thought and he should feel horrible for thinking such things—but he didn't. He had to find a way to get to know her. It was the only way to appease the aura of mystery around her.

He couldn't let go. His hand still held hers when the sudden swoosh of the kitchen door grabbed their attention.

* * *

Maevey stuck her head through the door with a bright smile on her face. "Everything going well in here?" She glanced at Tyler and then at Darci.

There was no mistaking the glitter in her mischievous eyes.

Darci cast a humiliated look toward her cousin, but before she could offer explanation, Maevey spoke.

"The hotel will be happy to pick up the tab for dry cleaning, Mr. Landston."

"I've already offered, Maevey. It was completely my fault."

"Accidents happen, Darci. Thanks to my quick thinking crew, hardly anyone noticed.

"She's right. You were right on top of that stain."

Tyler grinned, his dark and teasing gaze held hers. Gravity grabbed Darci's equilibrium and she reached for the counter for support.

"Honey, you look a little pale. Perhaps you should take the rest of the evening off? You filled for Beth last night and haven't had a night off in several days."

Her smile was genuine, but Darci sensed there was a more to her generosity.

Maevey offered a pleasant smile to the recipient of Darci's recent faux pas. "And Mr. Landston, dinner this evening—" She paused to suppress a laugh. "Is on the house." She held her hand up as he started to protest. "No, we insist, I'll see to your table myself."

Maevey hesitated as if checking for a response. "I'll just go see to that table, then." She turned to leave, her hand shoving open the door.

"Maevey, I'm sorry, I'm afraid I can't accept your generous offer."

From the moment she watched the pasta slither down the front of his sweater, Darci felt as though she'd been dropped into an episode of *The Twilight Zone. What now?*

"Why ever not, Mr. Landston?" She held the door ajar, staring at him with a curious expression. "Are you not pleased with our menu?"

"No, it's wonderful." He grinned.

Darci caught Stu's curious gaze, he'd been eavesdropping on the conversation and she saw his relieved smile. The entire staff, though pretending to be busy, had all been eavesdropping—she was pretty sure of that.

"I can only accept your kind offer on one condition." Tyler glanced at Darci and then leisurely turned his attention to Maevey. "That this lovely woman would join me for dinner." He brought her hand to his lips and kissed the back of her hand in a charming gesture.

Her shocked gaze watched in amazement as he straightened and smiled down at her. "That's very generous, Mr. Landston, but I simply couldn't impose on you—how, why?" Words of reason stay lodged in her throat. This was not the reaction she would expect from someone whose sweater she'd ruined. "I just couldn't—thank you, but I...can't."

He grinned and turned to Maevey.

Who of course, ignored Darci's presence entirely.

She nodded her approval. "What a wonderful idea. Table

for two, coming right up."

Darci opened her mouth to speak, but Maevey had already disappeared.

The clang of pots and pans combined with the sizzle of the griddle echoed in the wake of Maevey's' departure.

They'd not even asked her thoughts on this idea.

Darci's mouth gapped open at the sudden turn in the tide. She stared at the door, wanting to say a few choice words to her cousin—were she still in the room, instead of setting up a cozy table for two.

She glanced at Tyler's disarming smile and let her hand drop from his.

"Well, how about it?" He said, letting go of his sweater, apparently satisfied with the outcome. "Shall we?"

Any other time, she'd have jumped in his arms with a willing, rebel "Yes!"

"Mr. Landston—" How was she to explain that she wasn't ready to date yet?

"Don't think of it as a date, Darci."

Her gaze shot to his, stunned that he should read her mind.

He smiled, shrugging his shoulder. "I had a feeling." He nodded toward her hand, the indentation of the band still white from where her wedding ring once was.

Maevey had talked her into finally putting it away, hoping that it would allow her more freedom. The outward gesture, however, did little to eliminate the self-imposed wall she'd erected around her.

She stared at her hand, debating what type of game providence was playing with her heart.

"We can talk about it over dinner." His voice was gentle, in a way that lulled a person to wonder why they wouldn't follow him to the ends of the earth.

"I'd rather not just yet."

"Have dinner?"

"Talk about it."

"I can do that." He raised her chin with his finger. "Have you had dinner?"

She shook her head no, though she honestly wondered if she could eat anything with the jitters playing havoc in her stomach.

"If I promise not to retaliate with a food fight? Will you have dinner with me?" His face broke into a grin.

"Do you mind if I change out of this uniform?" She swallowed, stalling for time. *Maybe he was in a hurry—*

"Nope, not if you don't mind—" His words muffled as he pulled the stained sweater over his head, revealing a black T-shirt that rode part way up his taut stomach.

Darci stared, remembering that Matt had started to develop a slight paunch to his middle. So had she, after children. Though she'd finally managed to whittle back down to her original weight. Still, there were changes that time and childbearing could not erase—*and why in God's Name was she concerned about this?*

"I'll be right back." She skirted around him, careful not to touch her body to his for fear she might ignite in flames.

Darci ripped off her apron and it landed with a thud to the floor. Holding a hand to her stomach, she took a deep breath and shook her head, then reached down and plucked the tips from her apron, shoving them into her book bag.

With trembling fingers, she unbuttoned her black blouse, only then did she notice that she too, was covered with marinara sauce. The broader scope of the accident suddenly hit home and she realized she had two choices. One, she could go back out into that room full of patrons who'd witnessed the incident, or she could feign she didn't feel well, skip dinner with this handsome stranger, and run like a mad woman to the safety of her home.

Darci weighed the possibilities as she stepped from her short black skirt. She caught the sight of her in the reflection of the wall mirror the staff had hung in the changing room. With greater scrutiny, she assessed the wisdom of what she was doing.

The man was a well-seasoned traveler, gorgeous, and charming and he wanted to take her to dinner, because she'd ruined his sweater with pasta sauce. Made perfect sense.

Her cheeks flushed at the memory of the edge of glittering awareness in his eyes as he looked down at her a few moments ago.

Darci tugged at the straps of her bra, hoping to perform emergency "lift and separate" to her breasts. "This is not a date." She reminded herself.

* * *

Tyler was no fool, nor was he blind. He knew she was hesitant about dinner, but he'd also seen the hungry look in her eyes when he took off his sweater in front of her. It was the look of a woman who missed the sight of a man. Generally that would signal to him that, given a bit more charm, he'd have the offer of a warm bed to rest his head.

Tyler wadded up his sweater as he watched Darci scurry down a short hallway and duck into—what he presumed—were the staff quarters.

Something about her was different than the women he was used to. There was a depth, an unmistakable strength that implied when she made choices, they were not made lightly. This was not the type of woman prone to one-night stands—that was clear.

He stepped just inside the shadow of the hall and leaned back against the wall, cradling the sweater balled at his waist.

"Sir?"

Tyler followed the voice. It was Bridget.

"I'm to come get this, so we can have it sent out to clean."

"Really, that's not—'

"Maevey insists," she demanded as she held out her hand. "You might as well not fight her, Mr. Landston."

Darci's voice, nearer than he realized, voiced opinion from around the corner. Something about the familiarity of her speaking to him as she changed her clothes formed a tight knot in his gut.

"She does seem to have a reputation, doesn't she?" Tyler handed the sweater to Bridget. He glanced toward where Darci's voice had come from and realized that he could see her reflection in the mirror.

Good lord in heaven. Tyler's mouth went dry, unable to pull his gaze from the sight of her in peach lace panties and what the heck was she doing with that matching bra?

He turned away attempting to swallow as he forced his gaze back to the kitchen, his brain leaping over his options like a man stepping on hot coals.

The muscle in his jaw clenched. Maybe it'd been longer than he thought since going out with a woman. Then again, he couldn't recall ever going out with someone with as sincere of a combination of personality and natural beauty that this woman possessed.

Nervously, he tapped his fingers against the wall, trying to stay interested in the hustle and bustle of the kitchen, while his memory taunted him with the image of her luscious curves.

"Pervert," he mumbled under his breath.

Stu, the head chef paused, glancing sideways at him, then moved past him.

Technically, he should move to the other side and thereby resolve any temptation— Sweat broke out on his upper lip.

"Are you still there, Mr. Landston?"

Darci called to him and his heart leapt as he was pulled from his daydream.

He opened his mouth to speak and no sound came forth. It was like puberty all over again.

"A glass of Chardonnay, Mr. Landston?"

Tyler's head felt as though it was on a swivel. "Thanks." He accepted the glass from the smiling Bridget and quaffed it in a single gulp. "Great year." Tyler handed the glass back to her, averting his eyes from her shocked expression.

What the hell was wrong with him?

* * *

You're an attractive woman Darci. "Inside and out," she muttered to herself as she pulled off the thick-soled waitress shoes.

You're interesting, funny...a mother—almost forty years old.

"This is ludicrous," she reprimanded herself. "It's only dinner."

She tugged a chocolate brown turtleneck over her head, opting to twist her tangle of curls up into a hairclip.

Searching through other clothing, she discovered her long denim skirt and slipped it on, checking her image in the mirror.

She spotted a russet scarf with dark brown, cream, and purple swirls on the countertop, recognizing it as one of Bridget's, and she hoped her friend wouldn't mind her borrowing it.

Tying it loose around the neck of the sweater, she gazed at her reflection, realizing that her thumbnail clicked nervously against her front tooth.

"It's only dinner, Darci." She turned to the side, holding her palm flat against her tummy and threw her shoulders back to stand straight.

Matt had always liked her body, often telling her that it fit him perfectly.

Tears pricked at the back of her eyes and she frowned, not wanting maudlin thoughts to interfere with this evening. Part of her was lonely for male companionship. Perhaps Tyler Landston needed the same in a female counterpart? These days it seemed odd if a man and a woman exchanged conversation over dinner and didn't wind up in bed.

The thought sent a shiver up her spine.

She missed *that*, too. There'd been no one else since Matt's passing. That part of her she'd locked away, assuming that she would not utilize those emotional or physical needs for a long time—if ever.

Darci knew she was stalling. She carefully hung up her uniform and meticulously folded the white starched apron, placing it on the rack with the other uniforms to be cleaned.

She wondered what cologne Tyler wore and how it mingled with the unique scent of his skin.

"You're lonely, face it. Or you're just horn—" She stopped, slapping her hand over her mouth, realizing he very well be within earshot.

"Darci, did you say something?"

His voice sounded strange, a little strained.

"I'll be right out." She gave an equally strained laugh in response.

A quick check of her blush revealed she had no need of any more; her nerves took care of that. So she freshened her lipstick and stepped back to assess the finished product.

The man was used to svelte women with long legs and breasts that never, ever lost their perkiness. Good Lord, I'm not even in his league. Her shoulders pulled up as she took a fortifying breath.

Well, if nothing else, she would have a nice dinner and pleasant conversation out of the deal. Maybe she could ask him about exotic places to obtain writer's information.

Or study his handsome face and derive the hero for future novel ideas.

Darci stepped into the dimly lit hall and Tyler pushed from the wall like it was on fire. Unsure of his skittish behavior, she assumed he was tired of waiting.

"Sorry for the wait. That uniform isn't the most comfortable thing in the world."

He smiled as he stepped aside ushering her ahead. "Maybe not, but I have to tell you, it looks pretty hot on you."

"Hot, huh?" She went along with his teasing familiar with the term having heard it enough from her eldest son. What harm could it do? Maybe it was one of the terms he was used to from the circles he ran in.

Darci tucked a stray corkscrew of hair back into the clip.

His breath blew warm across the back of her neck as he stepped close enough for her ears only. "Very *hot*."

Darci turned to face Tyler and nearly ran into Bridget carrying a full tray.

He grabbed her waist and pulled her from harm's way.

"Seems you have a tendency to be accident-prone, Darci Cunningham. Or is that just around me?"

The heat from his chest seared through Darci's thin turtleneck sweater. His hand clamped on her waist held in firmly in place. Maybe he was right.

"Our table is probably ready." She smiled at Stu who stood across the room, holding a headless salmon in midair. He tipped his head with a faint smile as his brows disappeared beneath his chef's hat.

"Bridget came for my sweater," he said quietly.

She appreciated that he'd not announced it too loud, still the intimate whisper next to her ear caused emotions she was not yet prepared to deal with.

Darci pulled out of his arms and headed with greater purpose for the dining room.

"Leave it to, Maevey," she called over her shoulder. "She'll have it to you by morning, even if it means getting the dry cleaning owner out of bed."

"Really? Is she *that* aggressive?" Tyler appeared quickly beside her and held up his hand, peeked through the porthole window, and then opened the door for her.

Darci threw him a wry look before she walked through the door, though she herself made a quick assessment, getting her bearings. It was clear she did not have all of her senses about her this evening.

"Is the spaghetti any good?" he whispered in her ear as he seated her.

Chapter Eight

To Tyler's surprise, the dinner conversation had relatively few pauses, the definite sign of impending disaster on any date. Of course, he had the feeling that it may have had more to do with the glass of wine Darci inhaled just after they were seated.

He was already one up on her. Still, he found the fact that she appeared a bit nervous charming—in a "watch-out-for-flying-trays" sort of way.

Tyler was taken by her easy laugh, and the intensity by which she listened to his every word. She was certainly good for his ego at any rate, though she hadn't made him feel as though her strokes were superficial. That alone, set her apart from the other women he'd known.

"More wine?" He held up the bottle, watching her eyes as she tried to decide if two glasses was too much.

"I'm walking home, sure." She grinned, lifting her glass as he filled it. "Thanks."

She took a sip and concentrated on sawing her small steak. "So tell me how you got started in the photography business, Mr. Landston." She was busy cutting her meat into tiny bite-sized pieces.

He eyed her efforts thinking old habits are hard to break, and wondered how old her children were now.

"Did I mention to you that I was a photographer?" He grinned realizing suddenly that he'd not told her his profession.

"You mentioned photo equipment when you dropped the bag on my foot." She gave him a pleasant smile.

"I really did make an impression on you, didn't I?"

"I figure we're even now." Her smile was genuine as she

took a sip of a wine.

"I'm really sorry about that, sort of. Though if my luggage hadn't attacked you, then who knows if we'd gotten together?" He tipped his head, waiting for her reaction. "How is your foot?"

"It's fine, thank you." She placed her knife and fork on the plate and folded her hands under her chin. "Look, this is awfully nice of you to offer me dinner, but I have to tell you, Mr. Landston, up front that—" She pressed her lips together, a hesitant look of great quandary evident on her face.

He mirrored her stance, keeping his gaze to hers when he spoke. The message she was attempting to convey was more than clear. "For the record, I am not trying to pick you up, Ms. Cunningham and as I recall, we already established this wasn't a date." He arched a brow to end his point.

"I'm a little skittish about *that* word." She grinned. "Date."

He'd nodded realizing that suddenly the conversation had turned the corner from a light banter to serious. "You want to talk about it?"

She glanced down, picking up her fork and toyed with the sweet peas on her plate. An obvious stall technique—he knew—he'd used it before. "If you'd rather not." Whatever it was affected her deeply to the core. Though he suspected to delve too far into this woman's personality was setting himself up for wanting to know more, and hence become more involved—well, it just wasn't a wise choice to make—for him, or for her.

"I'm a widow."

The news hit Tyler like a jumping into the icy waters of Lake Huron in October. *A widow?*

She didn't look old enough to be a widow, not any widows he'd seen recently anyway.

"I'm sorry, please accept my condolences. No wonder you aren't comfortable." He pushed up from the table, preparing to leave. Perhaps she was right, this was not a good idea.

She caught his forearm. "Does the fact that I'm a widow

make you uncomfortable?"

Tyler stared into those warm honey eyes rimmed with dark lashes. *Uncomfortable?* Plenty, but not in the way she thought.

"Of course not, some of my best friends—" He cringed, knowing that didn't come out like it was supposed to. Still he didn't feel like now was the right time to talk about his own experience with widows.

"Please sit down and let's try to just have a simple conversation between two adults." She smiled then, the creases showing at the corners of her eyes. Lines created by years of laughter. "It's not as though we're teenagers on a first date, right?"

"Right," he chuckled his response as he eased back into his seat. Nope, this was much worse.

"Thank you, now you were going to tell me how you got started taking pictures." She picked up her fork and gestured toward his plate. "You better eat before it gets cold. Stu will have your head on a platter."

"No more platters, please."

She laughed and the sound carried him to someplace familiar, he just couldn't put his finger on it. He found himself grinning.

"Okay." He scratched his chin searching for the right words. "I was always that kid in school, a little—I guess— removed from the rest. Always wanted to be different than the rest, go my own way. It drove my parents nuts."

"A rebel?"

"Not quite James Dean." He grinned.

"A geek?"

"Close, only with long hair and an attitude."

"Ah, I know the type." She smiled. "What do they think of you now?"

Tyler wished he knew. After the last call several years ago, the relationship between him and his parents had been severed. They had two sons who they felt made something of their lives. He was in essence, their disappointment, though they hadn't verbalized it, he felt it as much as if they had. In their eyes, his only goal was to travel the world and be a playboy and they just could not support that. Now if he wanted to come home and help out on the farm or go to college and get a "real" job, then they would talk.

Tyler took a long swallow of wine and averted his eyes from her steady gaze. "Not sure." He directed his attention back to her, hoping the look on his face indicated that she not ask any more questions in that area.

Her smile faded and something close to pity flashed in her eyes. He didn't want that either.

"It's okay." He shrugged, and for all it was worth, he'd gotten past the initial sting of their abandonment many years ago. "These things happen. I'm sure I'm not the only man to come from a dysfunctional family." He polished off the remnant of his wine.

"On the contrary, I think, given that array of camera equipment in all those bags, the way you dress, and your impeccable manners, that you've done very well, in spite of their lack of faith in you."

Tyler stared at her as he lowered his glass to the table. The woman surprised him yet again. It felt as though he'd been on the receiving end of a mules kick.

He knew she was not saying these things to impress him; she'd made it crystal clear she was not searching for a relationship.

That she so effortlessly pinpointed and eradicated something that had gnawed at him for years shocked him. "I guess that's true, though I never really thought about it."

She shrugged one shoulder and went back to her steak.

"What about you? What brings you all the way up here?" He'd opened up—unintentionally—a part of him kept secret from most of the world, now he had the sudden urge to want to know details of her life.

She lifted the bottle and without asking, filled his glass, then hers.

"Well, I am a writer. Actually, an author, if you want to

92

count my magazine articles that have been published." She lifted the glass to her lips.

"A kindred spirit, then?" He raised his glass and tapped the stem to her glass.

"How so?"

"You write what you feel, thereby—hopefully—making readers feel what you write." He relaxed his shoulders realizing they'd been tense. "And I take pictures in order to evoke passions and feelings. Kind of the same thing."

Maybe it was the wine, or her gentle smile, but something stirred inside Tyler, something dangerously close to wanting to know this woman more intimately.

"And so you've some here to write. You have your own place here, then?" He held up his hand. "*That*—was not a proposition, by the way."

She laughed. "Understood, and yes I do. Though there is a problem with my slacker way of preparing my house for the winter."

He loved watching her eyes smile as she spoke. More than once he'd suppressed the urge to reach out and tuck one of her soft mahogany curls behind her ear, to feel its silkiness through his fingers.

"Uh, why's that?" He couldn't fathom this woman being any more regimented than she appeared to be.

"I haven't had my furnace checked since I moved in. I keep meaning to do it, but between writing and work, it hasn't been a priority."

"Maybe I could take a look at it sometime?" He shrugged, hoping the offer wouldn't send her running the opposite direction. Funny thing is that he had no idea why he made the offer, he knew damn little about the intricacies of being a homeowner.

"Look at the time!" Darci exclaimed, showing him her watch.

"A Mickey Mouse fan, I see?" He chose to let the remark about the furnace slide and a part of him was glad she apparently had.

Her eyes held his and for a moment he had to admit, he didn't want the evening to end.

"It was a gift from my son," she spoke quietly as she lovingly touched the clock's face. "He gave it to me before I moved here. See, it plays—"

She offered her watch-clad wrist for his viewing and pushed the small button the side. The tiny chip played "*A Dream Is A Wish Your Heart Makes*", as Darci gazed at her wrist.

He gaze lifted to hers, her eyes shone with soft admiration and pride. *Lucky kid.* "Must be a very special young man"

"Not so young anymore." The tone in her voice was wistful as she clicked off the tune.

A long silence followed and Tyler wished he knew what she was thinking. This woman showed enormous courage coming alone to this island to pursue her dream.

"I guess I better get home." She slid out of her chair, adjusting her sweater around her waist. The image of what she wore underneath flashed in his mind.

"I'll walk you, it's late."

"That's not necessary, really."

"Please?" Tyler held out his hand, hoping she wouldn't refuse him.

She searched the room, now empty except for the lone waitress setting the tables for the next morning. "Well, I guess it wouldn't hurt. It is late." She placed her hand in his.

* * *

The lobby was deserted as they approached the front door.

"Here let me help you with that." They paused at the front door of the hotel long enough to put on their coats.

Tyler held her coat, sliding it up her arms. His hands paused briefly on her shoulders and then he gently lifted the tendrils of her hair from her collar. The tips of his fingers brushed against the flesh of her neck and she tingled from his touch.

"Good night, cousin." Maevey appeared behind the registration desk, her silhouette outlined by the back light of the office behind her.

"Night," Darci responded, a luxurious fog settling comfortably in her brain. She wasn't certain if it was the wine or the company, causing the warmth penetrating her body.

The walk home was more subdued than the dinner conversation. Darci could not deny the fact that she was physically attracted to him and she sensed he had some interest in her, though on what level she didn't wish to venture.

"So, how long were you married, if I may ask?" He stuffed his hands in his pockets as they walked past the dark shop windows.

Darci took a deep breath, the chilly night air swirled in her lungs. They hadn't broached the subject of age yet, though she noted a smattering of silver in his dark hair during dinner. "Twenty-two years, we have two children, they're both in college now."

He nodded.

Is he thinking I'm too old? Well, turnabout is fair play.

"How about you?" she asked as she fished her gloves out of her pockets.

"Married?" He glanced at her and grinned, looking much sexier than she would have liked him to. "A couple...okay, one—moderately serious girlfriend." He held his hand out, wavering it to make his point.

"Forever the bachelor, huh?"

He shrugged. "It just didn't work out."

They walked a few moments in silence. It had been a long time since she'd tried to discern what a man was thinking when he was quiet.

"This place is beautiful at night." Tyler stopped in the middle of the street, his focus on the landscaped park that ushered tourists to the enormous embankment leading to the entrance of Fort Mackinac.

"I walked that hill the other day." He laughed, pointing to the pin dots of light coming from the Fort atop the great hill. "It made me realize that I'm not as young as I used to be."

"It's quite a jaunt, if you're not used to it. There are some lovely trails up behind the Fort. You should hike up there and get some pictures." Darci stopped beside him letting her gaze take in the view.

Beside them she heard the gentle lap of water against the array of fishing boats, sailboats, and yachts as they bobbed in their berths. Many now empty with the oncoming season. The light of the newly restored Round Island Lighthouse flickered offshore and in the distance, she heard the gentle clip-clop of a carriage taxiing someone to their destination after a full evening. She lifted her face to the night sky and took in the carpet of brilliant twinkling stars.

"Hey, but they gave me a button for making it to the top." He laughed. "Maybe you could take me on a tour sometime?"

She'd almost forgotten she was with someone. The island, at times, seemed to call to the very core of her, enveloping her with a serenity she never wanted to lose.

"Sure. I'd be happy to. There's all the usual tourist stuff, which is wonderful, but aside from the tours, you can experience the island a lot on your own."

"A native's perspective?"

Darci looked at Tyler and shook her head. "Not yet, haven't proven myself through the winter."

"Yeah, the boys at the pub were a little skeptical the guy from the city could survive." He smiled holding her gaze briefly before continuing. "So what insider tips of the island would you recommend?"

Darci pointed down the street dimly lit by the islands charming, old-fashioned lampposts. "I'll think as we walk, its getting cold." She laughed and sniffed needing a Kleenex.

Tyler pulled out a folded navy bandana and handed it to her. "It's clean, I promise."

Her brow rose at his gallant gesture, she'd not seen such displays often in men—not since Matt.

She laughed. "Thank you. I didn't think men carried handkerchiefs any more." Darci drew the cloth beneath her nose catching the combination scent of Tyler's cologne and the leather jacket he wore. "I'll take this home and launder it."

"I'll let you." He grinned and once again held her gaze for a moment.

Clearing her throat, Darci searched for where their conversation had left off.

"You were going to give me some insider places to discover on the island."

"Right, thanks." She held up the hankie before she stuffed it in her coat pocket. "There's the old cemetery, which is fascinating to walk through. Then there's the lookout point."

"Higher up than the Fort?" Tyler asked with a surprised tone.

"Just a little, short hike, really."

"People up here have a different sense of short," he muttered.

"The real test is walking around the entire island." Darci was enjoying the banter so much she didn't realize they'd walked past her home until she saw the lights for the Mission Point Resort.

"Oh wait." She turned around and saw the silhouette of her little house surrounded by its cape cod white picket fence. "I'm back there."

Tyler laughed and cupped her elbow in a gentlemanly manner. "No more wine for you."

He walked her to the front porch and stood on the bottom step as she unlocked her door.

Darci turned around to find him staring at her.

"I had a great time this evening."

"Well, you've been a good sport about the—you know, the sweater thing." She tipped her head, the affect of the wine giving cause to her giddiness. "I think you're a very nice man."

He lowered his gaze to the ground, and walked up the two steps, that brought him in front of her. That close, he appeared taller, his broad shoulders blocking out the streetlight behind him. She could smell the damp leather of his coat.

Darci dug her hands deep into her pockets, balling her hands in her knit gloves, her palms sweating. The gentle ding of a buoy in the distant blackness was the only sound, save that of his quite sigh. Something in the expression on his face made her want to pull him close and dispel whatever concerned him.

"At the risk of sounding really cliché'—where have you been all of my life, Darci Cunningham?" His fingers barely touched her cheek.

Making a life. She wanted to answer him, but something stopped her. She'd only just met this man, why did it feel like she'd known him forever? Maybe she'd had too much wine.

"I'm sorry about the sweater." She wasn't ready for a relationship. She didn't want to risk giving her heart again.

He tipped her chin to meet his eyes. "I can be at the same place tomorrow night if it means you'd have dinner with me again."

Her laugh was light as she held his magnetic gaze. Only one other man had ever been able to capture her undivided attention.

"You have—just a terrific voice, has anyone ever tell you that?" *How much more awkward was this going to get?*

The corner of his mouth curled upward, followed by an inviting grin. "No one."

Her heart raced wild, thudding against her chest, her body suddenly warm against the autumn chill.

"You have a terrific laugh, anyone ever told you that?"

Somewhere in the misty fog that was formerly her memory she remembered someone had once commented on that, but it didn't seem to matter at the moment. His fingers held her chin, and just as he'd studied her ankle, he gave the same careful attention to her face.

"You told me I had a great sense of humor, does that count?" Somewhere along the way, she knew that neither of them cared about laughter, or for that matter any other attributes at the moment.

His gaze dropped to her mouth as his palm slowly cupped her cheek.

"How about your mouth?"

Darci swallowed, her insides skittering like marbles over a polished floor. "I—I don't think—" she stammered. "Unless you mean my attitude, sometimes I can get a little—"

His gaze lifted to hers and she swallowed again at the hunger present in his the depths of his eyes.

She knew what was happening was not rational, nor wise, but the part of her that longed to feel as a woman again blocked out reason.

"You have a beautiful mouth."

The subtle fragrance of wine fanned softly across her face, causing her to speculate how he would taste.

Darci's breath caught as the soft pad of his thumb brushed across her bottom lip. It was an intimate gesture that Matt was prone to do when he wanted to be alone with her. She closed her eyes against the thoughts reeling in her mind, but she could not quell the beating of her heart.

Subtle as a soft morning breeze, his lips touched hers— tentative, cautious.

Her eyes opened in reaction, her brain screaming to tell him she wasn't interested in forming any relationships. His mouth lifted from hers and he stared at her as though gauging her reaction.

When she made no attempt to move, she knew she was lying to herself. She'd wanted this from the moment he touched her face—maybe sooner.

Her mouth met his, greater urgency to freefall into her curiosity taking over as she opened to him, savoring the heady combination of wine and the crystal clarity of lake air.

His hands tugged at the collar of her coat, holding her firm against him. If ever a man could spawn images of his lovemaking technique, Tyler Landston was succeeding in seducing her thoughts and enticing her to want more.

Then it was over and he stepped back clearing his throat and blinking as though realizing what he'd done. One fist still held her collar, its grip less feverish than before and more as though to steady himself. His labored breathing matched hers.

I didn't mean to—"

Darci held up her hand, careful not to touch him again. She didn't trust the lethal combination of loneliness and wine in her system. "Don't tell me you're sorry."

"I should," he said quietly as he returned his gaze to hers, "but I'd be lying."

For a moment, Darci thought he would kiss her again; instead he pulled his hand from its grip on her coat, swiping his fingers across his lips as though unsure of the reality of what just happened.

"If it makes any difference, I'm not sorry that it happened." Her comment was impulsive, if not dangerous, made to a man—a total stranger—in the dead quiet of this late hour.

His heated gaze shot immediately to hers and she could see the struggle in his eyes. He wanted to kiss her again.

And God help her, she wanted him to.

"I should go." He licked his lips.

She held his gaze unable to bring herself to agree for the desire that heated her insides. Still, she knew it was too soon, even for consenting adults.

"Tell me I should go." His voice was deep and, tinged with a raspy plea.

Flowing away like the ebb tide—the passion moments ago that rushed over her, drowning her reason—left in its wake a quiet reality. She closed her eyes and nodded. "You should."

"Yeah." He took a step back, his foot slipping off the top step.

She reached for him and he grabbed the railing, tossing her a smile that he had everything in control. Darci held her feet in place, unsure of her equilibrium. She tucked her hands in her pockets to prevent from pulling him back. The thought of her cold, lonely bed waiting inside warred with her better sense.

"I'll see you tomorrow, then?"

"Tomorrow?" She blinked trying to remember when they'd planned that.

"I was hoping maybe you'd take me on that tour." He backed down another step, glancing first where his foot was before continuing.

For some reason she found it comforting—if not a little flattering—that his nerves were not entirely steeled against the unexpected power of their kiss.

"Um, well, I don't work until evening, I suppose that would work."

He took a deep breath and nodded. "Great. Okay then—tomorrow?"

"Tomorrow." She smiled feeling as though she was on her first date; reminding herself quickly that this was *not* a date.

He loitered on the sidewalk; his hands stuffed in his jeans pockets. "We could go to that place to eat or I could get the hotel to make up a picnic lunch, which would you prefer? I hear the picnic baskets are pretty good."

To that comment, Darci's laugh was easy. "Don't let Stu hear you refer to them as "pretty good. It would hurt his culinary pride. I vote for the picnic lunch."

"Sounds like a plan."

Her heart faltered at Matt's favorite saying. "What did you say?"

He stopped and there was a hesitation before he answered. "Sounds like a plan?" He shrugged. "If tomorrow's not a good day, you know—we can do this another time."

A stiff wind whisked the strands of hair off her neck, chasing a chill up her spine. *Providence looks damn good in a gray suit*, Maevey had told her.

Just maybe he looks good in a leather jacket as well.

"Tomorrow is fine. Ten?"

"Ten is perfect. I'll pick you up."

"Wear comfortable shoes," she cautioned as he headed down the deserted dark street.

He paused under a lamppost and turned. "Promise to be nice to me, I'm an old man and for God sakes woman, go inside, it's cold!"

She waved as she sauntered to her door. Once inside, she leaned against it and closed her eyes, her lips still tingling with the electricity of their kiss.

"Thank you, Providence," she whispered as she touched

her lips. "You are good to me." Darci shoved from the door sighing as she tossed her coat to the couch. For now, it seemed that fate was shining down on her, giving her a little bit of happiness.

Sometimes the ways of Providence are not our own.

Chapter Nine

"Well that went exactly the opposite of how you'd planned," Tyler muttered to himself as he pulled his coat collar up against the chilly night air. A plastic bag caught on a gust of wind rattled past him reminding him of how their shared kiss had sent his system out of control. God knows he hadn't planned it and he strongly suspected that she hadn't either, given the stunned and confused expression in her eyes. But she didn't hold back either and that had him wanting to push her inside, off the street to find out what they both seemed to be searching for.

The sound of his shoes against the pavement echoed in the silent street with only the occasional whistle of the wind through the trees to accompany his thoughts.

A blast of wind blew across his face and above him came the sound of screeching metal. He couldn't read the signpost, so he stepped out into the street to get a better glimpse.

"You've got to be kidding me." He stared up at the green and yellow sign swaying in the breeze. It read "*Ty's Restaurant.*"

He looked up at the last minute as the sound of clopping hooves intruded his thoughts and missed just being brushed by the side of one of the elite Grand Hotel carriages.

"You okay, mister?" The driver peered down at Tyler from his perch high atop the carriage and the passengers inside gave him a puzzled look. No doubt they mistakenly concluded alcohol the reason for his odd behavior. Little did they suspect a reason bordering on a daydream.

"Sorry, fine. Just wasn't looking." He waited as the carriage pulled forward on its trek and then stuffed his hands in his pockets, crossing the now empty street toward the Iroquois.

True that while he hadn't planned on kissing Darci, he also hadn't planned on getting spaghetti dumped all over him either. And just as he hadn't planned on accidentally seeing her scantily clad image in the mirror, he hadn't planned on making a date to see her again—even if that's what they agreed they weren't doing.

Tyler wondered what else he hadn't planned that he could look forward to with as much anticipation.

* * *

"Good morning, Mr. Landston."

Maevey's songbird greeting came with an overly generous smile. His feet as though filled with lead plodded down the stairway to the front desk.

After a restless night where the only image scampering through his mind was Darci in her peach lace underwear he was hard pressed to comment just yet on the day. "Thank God it's you, Maevey." Tyler squelched his thoughts before they got started again. He squinted through tired and probably bloodshot eyes at her glowing face. "Where can I find coffee, its an emergency."

He slipped off his glasses, rubbing his eyes for the billionth time since awakening. Somewhere, in the wee hours of dawn, he'd finally dozed. Then his alarm blared reveille at six-thirty a.m. hoping to get a bright start on his day. He grabbed the same clothes he'd discarded on the floor and headed out in search of caffeine.

Noting suddenly the chill of the polished wood floor, he glanced down realizing he was barefoot.

"Are you well, Mr. Landston? Perhaps some tea and dry toast might be better suited for the way you look this morning. Or maybe a hair of the dog that bit you?" She smiled, but the twinkle of mischief was in her eye—best as he could determine.

"This can't be resolved with tea," he muttered, thinking she wouldn't hear him.

"Ah, I see. It's like *that*, is it then?"

A cup of steaming black coffee appeared on the counter before him.

"Maevey—that's Gaelic for "angel," isn't it?" He placed his glasses on his face and wrapped his fingers around the warm ironstone mug inhaling deep its rich, invigorating aroma. He had no idea if it was true, but in his mind at that moment, her offering made her his angel.

"You'd think more people would notice." She grinned. "Come on, let's go sit down a bit. It's nice and quiet and we can talk." Maevey picked up her cup of tea and ushered him to a pair of spacious wicker chairs tucked away off the lobby in a small alcove surrounded by windows.

Tyler eased back into the geranium and ivy print cushions, feeling much older than his age.

Maevey took the seat across from him, and leaned forward with her hands cupping her tea. She offered him a mysterious smile. "Now then, how was your dinner last night, Mr. Landston?"

It was all too easy to assimilate why she had the matchmaking reputation she did. Unfortunately, while he was attracted to her cousin, he didn't think she'd be none too pleased to hear that while in his mode of sleeplessness, he'd deduced the attraction was most likely of a purely physical nature. Darci Cunningham was an attractive, woman, with warm eyes and a caring heart. And yes, while it was true, she also possessed great strength and courage to face the adversities life had tossed at her, the fact she had a smile that could light up a room was all he really knew about her. Definitely the woman had a great set of teeth. He wasn't about to go into her other attributes, considering that Maevey might toss him out on the front lawn should he share those findings with her.

"The food was excellent, even better when served on a plate." He hoped to detour the inquisitive look in her eye. Tyler sipped his coffee knowing full well she was not interested in what he ate, but only in what happened between him and Darci.

Trouble was, he was yet engaged in struggling with the

myriad of questions in his own head and was nowhere near able to sit and chat with Maevey about them, no matter what her track record in making successful matches.

"A pleasant evening was had by all." Recharged by the caffeine, and needing a reason to escape Maevey's inquisition, Tyler straightened and purposely changed the subject. "Who do I see about putting together a picnic lunch?"

Her brows arched, disappearing into her flame red curls scattered across her forehead. She turned in her chair, peering at the hazy, overcast sky. On a good day the view offered a spectacular vista of the boardwalk with the Mackinac Bridge in the distance, a breathtaking panorama of brilliant blue water kissing an endless azure sky. Today, however—

Tyler followed Maevey's questioning gaze.

"You want to add a couple of ponchos to that picnic lunch?"

"Doesn't really look like much of a day for a picnic, does it?" Still, it would be a perfect day to get some great pictures of the gray mist-laden skies over those churning, murky gray-green waters.

"Well." She slapped her knee. "It could very well clear up by mid morning. The lake has a mind that is hers to change in a moments notice." She turned her attention back to him. "You still want that lunch?"

Tyler considered that if worse came to worse they could always picnic on the floor in front of a toasty fire back at Darci's place. On the other hand, staying in the public eye might prove to be the wiser of choices for the both of them. "Go ahead, I'm going to run up and grab a shower. I've got to pick up Darci at ten." He headed with purpose towards the stairway, turning on his heel when he realized he still had her cup.

He nearly ran headlong into Maevey, not more than a few inches behind him.

"Uh, here's my cup. Thanks for the coffee." Tyler handed her the mug.

"My pleasure." She grinned as she tipped her head. "So,

it's my dear cousin you'll be taking out on a picnic this fine and glorious day?"

"As if you didn't know." Tyler smiled and gave Maevey a quick peck on the cheek. Rain or no rain—with the coffee energizing his brain and the prospect of a hot shower—there was very little that could ruin his day.

* * *

He was ten minutes late having to stand in line to secure a carriage. He'd have guessed that by early October that most tourists would have gone in search of warmer weather. Still, the more time he spent here, the more the islands history and slower pace took root in him. A dangerous thing for someone who'd built an entire career around travel.

Tyler took the two steps to her porch in a single bound and rapped his knuckles to the freshly painted white screen door.

He surveyed the house's exterior in the light of day, impressed at its quaint simplicity. The white picket fence made him wonder if she had a dog, but by now surely he'd have heard evidence of that. He walked to the end of the front porch and leaned over the railing searching for signs of life in the backyard, but only the gentle lap of waves on shore beyond a stretch of lawn met his curiosity.

At the farthest end of the residential street, her house stood next to a large empty space, probably owned by the luxurious resort just around the corner. Pairs of weathered white Adirondack chairs all facing the lake view dotted the span of dying grass, offering remembrance of sunlit, warm summer days.

Tyler pulled up the zipper of his leather jacket against the bite in the air, glad he'd decided on the turtle neck instead of a long sleeve t-shirt. He checked the sky searching for any sign that the misty gloom would clear off.

Finding himself at her front door again, he'd heard nothing from inside. Perhaps she'd forgotten the plans they'd made? He raised his hand and the door swung open tentatively.

"Hi." With her face shrouded by the shadow of the screen he could not detect if she had a smile or not. There was, however, no doubt to the tone—it was a benign 'don't-even-think-about-that-kiss-last-night' greeting. But it was too little, too late—at least for him.

"Come on in, I'm almost ready." She pushed the screen open enough for him to catch his hand on the edge and then she disappeared inside.

Taking liberty of her invitation, he stepped inside and scanned the room, pleased in thinking that her sunny, warm décor fit her personality.

Though small—smaller in scale at least than his warehouse apartment in Chicago—she'd arranged her furnishings so that it held a welcome respite from the world. The thought occurred to him that this aspect was also in Darci's persona. That's why he'd been so comfortable around her from the start. There was little frivolous about her, simple, grounded in who she was, what she wanted, that's what he saw. And at that moment, it was that quality that appealed to him. Being around her was familiar, comfortable as his favorite jeans.

He peeked around the heavy wood door storm door and took note of an ornately carved antique hat tree with brass captain's hooks and a bench for changing shoes.

She had a style that was uncluttered and Tyler found that refreshing.

"Make yourself comfortable, I'm just finishing here," Darci called from the kitchen.

Tyler signaled to the driver to wait and closed the door. He glanced toward the kitchen as he started to sit down in one of the navy and white check wing back chairs that flanked the fireplace. A buttery yellow floral love seat dotted with geranium, white and navy accents sat opposite the fireplace and a small oval coffee table served as the piece that completed the uncomplicated arrangement.

But what caught his eye was the array of framed photographs displayed prominently from one end of the fireplace mantle to the other.

He checked the kitchen door once more, hoping she wouldn't think he was snooping. "Take your time, we're in no hurry."

He stood, taking one of the pictures off the mantle and with an artist's eye focused on the faces staring back at him. It was the four of them—Darci and her family, including her husband. Oddly he found his gaze narrowing as if trying to dissect the expressions on their faces—particularly Darci's. Surprised at the direction of his thoughts, he returned the picture to the mantle and stuffed his hands in his jean pockets.

Left to his own devices, he considered that perhaps her cool behavior was directly related to the kiss that he'd spent the greater share of his night trying to forget. He had to face that in the stark light of day, there was a chance she'd seen it as a mistake.

He didn't want to think about that.

Tyler brushed his hand through his hair in frustration. Granted they'd both had enough wine last evening, but they both seemed to want the same thing at the time. Her response was as intense as his, but apparently the aftershock hadn't affected her in remotely the same way.

Darci appeared at the kitchen door, her expression sullen. Dark circles shadowed her lovely eyes and his concern was immediate. Loneliness that he'd not seen before now showed on her face. It made him feel like a fool for thinking what he had about the kiss. Obviously, something of much greater concern was bothering her.

"Darci?" He held out his hand, surprised, yet pleased, when she reached for it.

She stepped around the edge of the couch and dropped her book bag to the floor. Reaching out, she plucked the picture of her family from the mantle. "It's my son." She sat on the edge of the couch, her thoughts appearing a million miles away as she gazed at the picture.

"Is he all right?"

"He's fine. Really I shouldn't let this ruin our plans for the day." She placed the picture in its spot.

It was one of the single most odd feelings Tyler had standing there watching her. He glanced at the picture.

Technically, he had no right to pry into her personal life, yet he couldn't stand by and watch her be miserable.

He sat beside her, careful to keep his distance. "I don't mean to pry, and god knows, I'm not qualified to be a parent, but I'm here if you want to talk about it." If nothing else, Tyler could bank off his own experiences of college life—could things have changed that much?

She sighed placing her palm over her eyes. "I must look horrid."

"Not to me." His hand hesitated in reaching out to touch her shoulder. "Darci, I would understand if you'd rather not go through with our plans today."

Tyler waited as a moment clicked by and then stood ready to excuse himself and leave her to her privacy.

"Wait." She reached for his sleeve. "I'd really like to keep our plans. I had such a great time last night."

He considered whether it was safer to cut his losses and decline, but he'd already paid for the carriage, and the truth was, he wanted to see her smile.

Tyler smiled as he patted her hand. "Okay then. If you're ready, I've got a surprise for you, come on." He grabbed her hand and tugged her from the couch.

"I'm ready if you think this polar fleece is enough." She reached for her bag, shifting it over her shoulder.

Tyler laughed. "Maevey packed us plastic ponchos with our lunch."

"That's my thoughtful cousin." She glanced at him and a glimmer of brightness had returned to her eyes.

"Who, by the way, thinks we're nuts for picnicking in this weather." Tyler opened the door and stood back waiting for her reaction.

The thrill on her face when she saw the horse-drawn carriage gave a jolt of pleasure to his system. Seeing her smile was worth every uncertain thought moments before.

"M'lady you carriage awaits." He grinned as he bowed, ushering her from the house.

* * *

"Here I thought we were going to do that eight point two miles around the island." She glanced at him as she closed her door and followed him down the steps.

"We will. Just in the carriage." He grinned. "The way I have it figured you'd have me hiking those back trails the rest of the afternoon. Starting out the morning in the carriage, you can point out some of the sites without getting ahead of me."

"Concerned for your athletic prowess, Mr. Landston?" She climbed in the waiting buggy, the warmth of his hand around her waist not going unnoticed.

"Is that a challenge, Ms. Cunningham?" He pulled his camera from the bag at his feet, signaling the driver. "I'll have you know, that I go to the gym at least five times a week and swim forty laps every morning."

"Really?" She was not surprised given his physique.

He grinned. "Nah, I'm lucky to make it to the gym. Heck. I'm lucky to sleep in my own bed once a week."

She raised an impervious brow.

"Meaning I travel a lot."

A smile tugged on her lips.

"I have to tell you that seeing that beautiful smile on your has made my day." He worked at the lens, testing the view, adjusting an odd array of buttons and levers.

She'd forgotten how it felt to receive a compliment from a man, particularly one that she liked. Her cheeks heated from the realization that she did enjoy Tyler Landston's company, but to what end their relationship would progress she chose not to think about.

"So listen, why don't you tell me what was bothering you this morning. Sometimes it helps to just talk to someone."

The carriage lurched as a bicyclist whirred by, not heeding to keep their distance from the horses. Darci grabbed Tyler's sleeve to keep from pitching forward.

"Sorry folks, the weather's got Molly and Buttercup a bit skittish this morning."

The driver spoke over his shoulder, and then snapped the reins setting the steeds back on track.

Darci still clung to Tyler's coat. Carefully letting her fingers slide from her grasp, she tucked them in her lap.

"Well, it's obvious I didn't get much sleep, isn't it?" Her admission would certainly validate why she looked like death warmed over this morning. What was more of a shock was Tyler's response.

"I didn't sleep well either." He peered through his lens pointing it towards the lake. "But not for the same reason, I'm guessing, as yours."

She saw him grin, though he didn't look at her just then.

Unwilling to venture into that statement she chose to continue, "My son called me late. He was calling from a frat party."

"Always a worry for a mom."

"Well, he handles that part pretty well. It was that he wanted to thank me for putting money into his account."

Somewhere in the back of Darci's head, Peter's voice cautioned her again about discussing her finances with strangers. She hesitated, faltering between fear of Peter's warning and the need to get another perspective on the situation. These were the times she missed Matt most, but what was odd that even as close as Peter was to the family, she'd never felt as though she could lean on him emotionally. Even as much as she suspected he would like for it to be different.

"Well, maybe his timing was off, but the intent was good, don't you think?" Tyler grinned, the breeze lifting his dark locks from his forehead. Had she noticed the length of dark lashes framing his deep-set green eyes?

Forcing her gaze from his face, she pointed to the houses lined high atop the bluffs ahead. "Did you know that many of these old Victorian homes were built back in the 1890's by wealthy Mid-westerners? Some of them right out of Chicago; industrialists and meat packers, like the Cudahy and Armour families."

Tyler peered up at the bluff. "That's a lot of hot dogs."

She laughed. "Most of them have more than a dozen

bedrooms and were built as summer homes for the elite."

He turned to her with a grin. "Doesn't it make you wonder what they ate for supper?" He shrugged and returned his focus to the hills. "Now they tell you hot dogs are bad for you, but I challenge anyone to badmouth the Smoky links at Wrigley Field. Excuse me." He dropped to his knees and leaned over the seat in front of him, snapping pictures in rapid succession.

Darci delighted in watching him move, switching positions, and even at one point asking the driver to stop so he could run toward the lake for yet a different angle. It was as though he was in a bubble and she wasn't there.

He hopped back in the carriage. "So you never told me why your son offering his gratitude for this money disturbed you."

Surprised he was still plugged in to their previous conversation she hesitated. "Are you sure you want to hear this?"

"I'm here and I'm not going anywhere." He touched her cheek briefly, his fingers barely brushing her skin and then he dropped his hand, focusing on changing to another lens.

"I guess I'm concerned about nothing really. It's just that I didn't make that deposit to his account."

Tyler frowned. "A grandparent overstepping the line?"

Darci sighed, realizing that Tyler was right—he was a good listener. "No, it was our—my financial advisor." She glanced at his puzzled expression. "He also happens to be an old friend of the family."

His brows lifted and he shrugged. "I still don't see the problem."

"Well, it bothers me because he didn't ask me first. He just did it."

"Ah, and I take it you hadn't given him this much liberty before with your finances?"

"Not like this. Matt always trusted Peter with our money." Darci paused, collecting her scattered thoughts.

"Peter?"

Darci nodded, her desire to explain, greater than her

patience. "That's our consultant, Peter."

"Okay, go ahead."

"Nathan told me that Peter called him to check to see how he was doing. He asked what he was going to do over Christmas break and when Nathan told him he was coming to the island, Peter asked if the guys from the Frat were doing anything together."

Tyler sat the lens on the seat and leaned back, draping his arm over the back of the seat, his gaze intent on listening to her.

"Nathan told me that he was reluctant to tell him, but he did finally admit that the guys were going on a ski trip and that he felt he should be with me." She stopped in her rambling tirade. "Is this making sense?"

Tyler's brows pressed together. "You better keep going, I'm sure it will."

Her frustration close now to the surface, she pushed on hoping to expel it from her system before she spoke to Peter.

"Peter told him that I would want him to go with his college friends on this trip. Its what guys did on breaks. Further, he suggested to Nathan that he could join *us* on the island after his trip." Darci stared at Tyler, waiting for a response.

He tipped his head as if waiting for her to finish.

"Nathan said that he told him he really couldn't afford it and that it was okay, but Peter brought up the fact that his dad would have wanted Nathan to have this experience. He told him about some kickbacks of investments that were lying around and he needed to do something with them before the end of the year. He told him he was going to talk to me and that maybe it could be an early Christmas present."

"But he never talked to you."

Darci shook her head no. "Nathan said when he was checking his account online, he saw the deposit and figured that Peter had gotten approval from me. That's bad enough, but not the only thing bothering me."

The gray clouds of the chilly morning had given way to

the sun as the chestnut mares clip-clopped at an unhurried pace around the island.

"I'm sorry, I didn't mean to drag you into the drama known as my life." She smiled, but her heart wasn't in it. "It's not that I mind Nathan receiving the money he needed. Peter happened to have called as they were making reservations and I probably would have done the same thing if Nathan had called me."

Tyler shook his head. "So, what—about all of this is *really* bothering you? Have you talked to this Peter, yet?"

"Not yet, I spent most of the night awake wondering what to say to him." Darci pointed out the street leading up the back way to the Fort. "We should hop out here and walk."

The carriage slowed to a stop and Darci stepped down, lifting the picnic basket from the back of the buggy as Tyler gathered his camera equipment.

They walked a short way in silence before Darci turned to Tyler. "I'm sorry you got the rambling side of me, thanks for listening, I appreciate it."

Something in his quiet manner reminded her of Matt and she scolded herself for it. One day she would be able to look at other men and not constantly compare them with Matt.

He smiled gently. "You'll handle it, Darci. I've no doubt about that." Tyler brushed a curl from her temple and tucked it behind her ear, letting his fingers drift down her jaw. "What else bothers you about this?"

"I didn't invite Peter for the holidays."

His penetrating gaze, much the same as just before he kissed her, seeped the air from her lungs. A part of her wanted him to do so again, instead he stepped away, shifting the basket to his other hand. "Shall we?"

Chapter Ten

Tyler was willing to let any further discussion about this Peter Beck fellow slide. Though he wasn't sure of where things were going between him and Darci, he had a bad feeling in his gut about the guy.

They walked in companionable silence up the empty road canopied by great cedar and birch trees. The dreary morning had kept the usual numbers of hikers in the back trails at bay this morning and Tyler was just as happy to have the time alone with Darci.

Peter Beck? It wasn't like he was jealous of the guy or his obvious closeness to her family—no matter how misguided his intent at the present. It's just that he wasn't sure of the tone in Darci's voice when she said his name. Not that that should bother him at all.

He stopped suddenly, gently sitting the basket at his feet and swung his camera lens to a squirrel perched atop a birch log, a shaft of brilliant sunlight sliced through the trees illuminating the sheen of his black coat of fur.

"That will be beautiful," she whispered at his shoulder.

His furry subject nibbled on a piece of dry corn, twitching his tail and poking his nose into the air as though offering various poses for Tyler.

The subtle scent of Darci's perfume clouded his thoughts and for a moment he simply held the lens to his eye, not wishing to move from that spot.

"Are you going to take the picture?" her voice whispered against his cheek.

"I'm waiting for the right moment." It was a blatant lie. He waited a second or two, and then snapped the picture.

Facing her, he was gifted with a knowing smile.

Nope, kissing a woman once did not give him any claim whatsoever. She had the freedom to date as many men as she pleased, but something nudged at him deep inside and he secretly hoped Peter Beck would not be her choice.

"Okay, you promised to show me the highest point on the island." He picked up the basket, swinging it ahead as he ushered her forward.

"We'll follow this road past the cemetery, and then there's a fork where we'll go on up to Fort Holmes."

"Up?" Tyler queried as he caught up to her side.

"You hardly notice the climb." She smiled as she glanced at him, keeping her stride long and full of purpose.

"That's what the guy at the bottom of hill to Fort Mackinac said," Tyler muttered.

A brilliant blue fall sky emerged through the dissipating gray clouds, allowing a dazzling autumn morning sun to beat down overhead. The effect caused the dew on the grassy hillside to shimmer like a carpet of diamonds.

Taking in the breathtaking clarity of the scenery around him, his gaze fell on the sunlight reflecting the rich mahogany hues of Darci's hair. Several tendrils had escaped from the clip she wore and bounced in time with her rapid gait.

Tyler smiled, musing what it would be like to brush those curls aside and kiss the soft skin underneath. He cleared his throat, if he was going to spend the entire day with her, he'd be wise to put such thoughts aside.

"Tell me about your kids." That had to be a safe topic. Certainly one that would get his mind off how great she looked in running tights.

"Leah is a junior down at The University of Iowa. She would like to be an elementary teacher one day. If we can get her through school."

"Is it tough for her?" he asked, unsure why it interested him to want to know.

"Oh no, the grades are easy. It's adjusting to everything. Matt's death, my move—" Darci looked at him. "Though she was the first to suggest that I make this move." She smiled. "Gotta be a pretty together kid to make that selfless of a suggestion to your mom, don't you think?"

Tyler nodded thinking Leah came from good genes in that respect.

"And then there's my Nathan." She sighed as she focused her gaze to the road before them.

"Handful?" Tyler grinned remembering his own youth.

"Now understand, this is a mom talking. But this boy is handsome as all get out. I mean...there are days I wonder where he came from." She laughed. "And don't you think he doesn't know it." She jabbed her finger in the air.

"Every time I call down there, he's telling me about a different girl he's met. No one has made enough of impression yet to snag him though."

"Is he in a frat house?" Tyler asked, but he suspected he already knew the answer.

"Yeah, I think it's helped him to have the support during this last year. He never really showed it like Leah, but I'm sure he is dealing with his grief in his own way."

"What's he studying?"

"Currently he's in Engineering. We'll see. It's tough, but he would really like to help design more efficient ocean rigs for drilling."

"Those are—very good aspirations."

"Must've been all the *Legos*," she replied, laughing.

They walked the wrought–iron parameter of the old cemetery, taking note of the dates on some of the headstones.

"Why are they grouped liked this?" Tyler asked, noting the odd, small group rectangular formations of the stones.

"I believe they're family plots."

Tyler stared at the several clusters dotting the large area of land, unable to comprehend people being *that* connected to one another.

A cool northerly breeze brought the scent of cedar and the damp moist earth as they continued up the road. His stomach growling, Tyler kept his eye out for a good place they could stop and eat lunch, but the road seemed to stretch forever in front and behind them, and forests flanked them on either side. It was amazing to him that there should be so much untouched land on such a small island.

Darci's pace picked up as they left the cemetery. "So tell me about your family, Landston."

Tyler found he had to push himself to stay beside her. "Not much to tell." He shrugged. "I grew up in Illinois on a farm. Two brothers."

"You have siblings? You didn't mention that." She glanced at him, but kept her pace.

"One's in law, the other has taken over the farm by now, I guess."

She stopped and reached for his arm. "You guess?"

"Long story." He pushed his glasses up and squinted at her in the bright sunlight.

"We have time." She gave him a wry smile.

Unsure if he wanted to reveal this much of himself to someone, he decided that to do so with her in the name of communication was probably easier since they were not involved on any other level.

"Well, long story—short." He walked ahead, waiting for her to catch up to his side. "My folks didn't share my vision for what I wanted to do. Taking pictures was *not* their idea of *making a living*. So basically, they cut me off, saying if I insisted on pursuing this—" He paused. "What was it—oh yeah, *fruitless obsession* of mine, that I would have to do it on my own."

"That's terrible, Tyler."

He shrugged. "Those were my parents."

"So what did you do?"

"I took off, I had a little in savings of my own and one day I packed my stuff and got in my beater of a car and took off."

"That had to have been difficult."

He took a deep breath and raised his brows. "It was hard to leave my younger brothers."

"Do you hear from them?"

"Once or twice. My parents sent them to school, because they were pursuing *sensible* careers." He grinned as he turned to her, but she wasn't smiling. "Oh Darci, don't get maudlin on me. I'm way past the stage of being abandoned."

"I know you're a big boy now. But I was just thinking of doing something like that to my own kids."

"You'd never do that to your kids."

"You wouldn't either."

"I don't have kids." He was quick to point out.

"You're still young. Things could happen."

"Unless I have a heart attack first, do you mind if we slow down a bit?"

Darci's gaze shot to his and she immediately slowed. "Are you okay? Do you need to sit down?" Her hand rested on his back.

A window to all that she'd been through opened up for Tyler and he saw a woman who had a great deal of caring about others. Her husband had been one lucky man.

"I'm fine. You just go at this walking thing like you're running to a fire."

"Well, why didn't you say something?"

He hesitated, considering her question. Truth was, he wasn't sure of his reason for keeping with her rapid pace, other than the fact that there was the possibility that if they slowed down, they might have to deal with the impact of that kiss last night.

Tyler glanced at her sweet, inquisitive expression forcing himself to keep his feet planted where they were.

"I didn't want you to think I couldn't keep up. Besides—" He tossed her the picnic basket. "This has weighed me down."

She caught it taking a step back before finding her balance. "Well that's *terribly* manly of you, Mr. Landston."

He laughed at her exaggerated imitation of a southern belle. "Race you to the top, *Miss Scarlet.*"

Her amber eyes flashed with amused excitement and she tucked the basket under her arm like a football and was three feet ahead of him before he realized she was gone.

Not far ahead, she dropped to her knees, shrugging off her backpack as he fell to the grass beside her. He rolled to his back and stared up at the cloudless sky and for a brief moment, everything inside of him was centered. He glanced at Darci; already busy flipping the small tablecloth in the air, trying to lay it on the ground without it blowing hither-skither across the grass.

Drawing to his knees, he secured one end with his camera bag and tried to ignore her face within a breath of his own. Pulling free from temptation, he pushed to his feet, camera in hand. "Good lord, this is magnificent." He turned full circle scanning the panoramic vista around them.

"Three hundred twenty feet above sea level."

"Incredible." And as it always did, the world became his through his lens. Clicking the shutter, he captured an ore ship lumbering through the Straits like some ancient, metal dinosaur. The vivid contrast of the autumn colors against the blue palette of the endless sky became the canvas by which he created his pictures. For him, it was the exhilaration of seizing a specific moment in time or capturing forever a precious thing of unsurpassed beauty.

"Simply fabulous," he muttered, as he swung his focus to where Darci was busy emptying the contents of the picnic basket.

"Grapes!" She held them up like a prize trout. "Maevey knows I love grapes, aren't you starving?" She held the deep purple cluster in her hand and grinned. "What are you doing?"

He snapped the shutter. "What I do best."

"Please, don't waste your film taking pictures of me." She laughed as she popped a grape into her mouth.

"Well it's my film, but let's say I'm curious. Why do you think that's a waste?"

She dropped the grapes to the napkin and stretched out her hand dangling a stem of the purple fruit to him. "I take terrible pictures."

He sat down across from her. She was the first woman he'd been out with that didn't want her picture taken. Tyler found that not only a curious thing, but also refreshing from the usual begging he received from women wanting to find and easy way to break into the cover model business.

"How do you know I wasn't going for the grapes?" He grinned, snapping off another grape and tossed it in his mouth.

She blushed then and he found it delightful, if not downright sexy. "I'm kidding."

Her hands stilled on the sandwich she was unwrapping. The pink hue in her cheeks deepened.

"Hey, I wasn't trying to make you uncomfortable." He searched her face wanting their light banter back. "Its just that I've been in this business a long time."

She kept her focus on the task of unwrapping the sandwich.

What he wanted to say, he had a feeling would be met with a dubious look. He made no excuses for the kind of lifestyle he led, but that did not negate the sincerity of his thoughts. "I think you're quite beautiful, Darci."

As he guessed, there was the look, and in a way he was glad he'd been able to predict it. "You are." He shrugged, searching for a way to explain to her what he saw—the strength, courage, humor, her face when she smiled, and those fascinating eyes.

"Didn't you tell me the other night that you'd once worked on a *Sports Illustrated* swimsuit issue?" Her wry smile challenged him as she handed him the sandwich.

"Yeah, a few years back." He wasn't sure where she was going with this, but he had a pretty good idea.

"Surrounded by all those beautiful bikini clad women—now *that's* beauty for picture taking." She jabbed an apple slice in his direction for emphasis.

He couldn't deny that, she'd know he was lying. "Well, sure they *are* beautiful. He decided the truth was best at this point. "However, much of that is only surface." He counter-pointed with his sandwich. "That's different than true beauty."

She laughed out loud at that and shook her head.

"What? What's so funny?" He grinned as he stretched out

on the grass, leaning back on his elbow.

"True beauty." She glanced at him as she unscrewed the lid on a ball jar filled with what Maevey reported was Stu's special recipe lemonade. "Guy's mark their calendars for that issue. Are there any men left out there looking for *true* beauty?"

"So you think I'm the same way. And because I travel, what you think is in the "*fast lane*," I'm not capable of seeing true beauty?" *Damn.* He hadn't meant for it to come out in such an accusatory tone. What did it matter what she thought of him anyway? He wasn't going to be sticking around for very long.

"I'm sorry, I didn't mean to suggest—"

He held up his palm. "It's okay. I guess that's probably what most people think about someone whose never settled down and done the normal things that most people do."

"Normal things?"

Her brows pressed together giving a dark intensity to her expression. Tyler had to pull his gaze from hers. "You know—go to college, meet someone, date, fall in love, graduate, get a job, get married, have a house in the burbs, and two point five children."

"I've never figured that one out." Her forehead wrinkled, as did her pert nose.

"Yeah, me neither." Despite the loneliness gnawing at his insides for all the years that felt lost some days, he grinned when she grinned at him.

And for some reason it made him think of their kiss.

"I guess I might have mistakenly seen you as the playboy type." She shrugged as she wiped the crumbs from her lap.

"Might have?" He raised a doubtful brow.

She smiled openly, thereby absolving her from any and all error in judgment on her part.

The gesture spurred the need to for him to ask her what he'd wanted to all day. "You know I didn't sleep well last night either."

He sat up, closing the distance between them, though the

basket and the array of food still provided a safe barrier.

Darci rocked back on her heels, purposely averting his gaze as she did.

More nervous as to her answer than he'd thought he'd be, he realized he was gnawing on the corner of his lip.

"We haven't even talked about it." He kept his distance though every part of him wanted to reach out and connect to her—to understand why she affected him the way she did. She possessed an intriguing blend of independence and vulnerability that caused a stirring need in him to be comforted by one and protective of the other.

"Perhaps, because there is nothing to talk about?" She shrugged and pushed to her feet, taking a deep breath. "This is not the original structure you know." She pointed toward the flat roofed fort, with its small squared opening used as the stockades during the American Revolution.

He had to give her credit, if the woman did not want to discuss a subject; she just damn well ignored it. He could be as stubborn, particularly when the subject matter was important to him. That part, he would analyze later, but what interested him now was her total avoidance of that kiss.

Tyler pushed to his feet and followed her to the historical marker, standing quietly beside her as she read the plaque.

"This says the British acquired the land after the French and Indian war—"

"You're avoiding the issue." He kept his focus on the words she was reading.

"In 1812, the British built the blockhouse and stockade, naming it Fort George—"

A brisk wind caught her hair, causing her hairclip to tumble to the ground, and her thick hair, now unbridled, whipped haphazard in the breeze.

"I want to kiss you again, this time without the benefit of the wine." He turned to her, resting his hand on top of marker. She would not look at him.

"After the war, the island was acquired again by Americans and the Fort was—"

They were alone, save the occasional squawk of a seagull and the ghosts of the past lingering through time.

He touched her jaw, and she lifted her face to his.

"Renamed Fort Holmes after a young soldier who died—"

He knew her misgivings and confusion. Tyler had them himself reeling around inside him but stronger than these things was a desire to see if kissing her without wine as the catalyst would be as powerful. At least if it didn't turn out well, he'd sleep better tonight, knowing it was only the wine.

"A young soldier—American?" Tyler brushed a strand of hair that had blown across her face.

"Yes." Her voice was barely audible over the wind dancing around them.

He rubbed the back of his hand down her cheek, watching her eyes soften beneath his touch. In his mind he searched for a logical reason to stop.

Her gaze dropped to his mouth and he kissed her then, careful to keep it brief, tender.

And his world rocked from its axis.

The taste of her was more potent without the wine. He pulled back searching her face, ludicrously wanting to see the desire to kiss him again in her eyes.

Darci's palm lay soft against his chest, her warmth seeping through his sweater. Gently, her fingers twisted the material in her fist and she lifted a deliberate gaze to his. There was no doubt what she wanted and Tyler was all too happy to oblige.

He captured her mouth, taking greater liberty, his tongue delving to meet hers, still sweet from the grapes. Caught in a vortex of passion and logic, Tyler felt as though he was drowning, being pulled under so deep he couldn't breath—

His sweater pulled tight against his chest and Tyler knew in a moment they would be tearing at each other's clothes. With great fortitude, he took a step back and broke the kiss.

Scrambling to regain control of his senses, he studied her face. "I guess that answers that question." He swallowed hard.

Regardless of the smile that played on her just kissed lips, it occurred to him that he had not anticipated the residual affect of her kiss on him. It had been an experiment, of sorts; one designed to rule out, rather than pull him in deeper.

He strode back to the picnic area and began the task of cleaning up, chuckling at the fact that his hands were trembling.

When she joined him at his side, neither one chose to speak of the re-enactment of the *1812 Overture* canons that had just thundered between them.

In retrospect, Tyler considered that his little experiment was not as innocent as he'd have liked for it to be. It stirred something inside him—between his heart and his logic, a battle raged, and he had no clue as to which would be victor. He only knew this for sure—she touched him on a level that eased his mind, giving him an odd sense of comfort, and an odd sense of belonging.

* * *

The kiss did not come up the rest of the day and Darci was just as glad. She sensed that it had touched Tyler more than he wanted to admit as evidenced by his purposeful distance from her physically for the rest of the afternoon. Still, their time together lapsed into a shared interest in the sites and history of the island and that was to be their common ground, perhaps, Darci thought, for the rest of his stay here.

Oddly, it bothered her less than she'd thought it might. Tyler Landston was a serendipitous addition to her new life and she was not yet ready to succumb to the idea of settling down with one man again. The cost was simply too high and just now when she was only at the threshold of finding a new life for herself; she could not afford the emotional entanglements of a serious relationship. Better to keep things light and though there was a combustible attraction whenever they kissed, she had to remind herself that she had her life to lead and so did he.

So it was awkward when finally the as the sun was begin to set on the western horizon, Tyler walked her to her front door.

"It's been a wonderful day, Tyler." He walked beside her, his hands tucked in the pockets of his leather jacket. His hair was tousled from the wind, his cheeks ruddy from the chill of being outdoors all day. To say he was a handsome man was an understatement.

Darci averted her eyes from his and concentrated instead on working at the lock of her door.

"Maybe we can get together sometime—later."

There was no mistaking the hesitancy in his voice and some part of her wondered if the woes she'd saddled him with earlier in the day was simply too much for him to handle. Anyone with a shred of intelligence should be able to figure out that a self-proclaimed bachelor was not interested in her family problems.

"I'd like to hear some more stories about the island. For someone who isn't a native, you seem to know an awful lot about this place." He grinned, scratching the spot below where his glasses rested on his cheek.

For some reason, she found the gesture intriguingly innocent, if not idiotically sexy. It gave her the gumption to suggest her idea before she had opportunity to talk herself out of it. "Why not Friday night? I'll fix us a home-cooked meal." She pushed open the screen door, holding it with her hip. "I have lots of books on the lakes and—well, I haven't cooked for anyone but myself for a long time. Think of it as helping me to brush up on my cooking skills."

He studied her a moment as though debating his answer. Finally, he smiled. "Okay. Sounds good, I'd like that."

"Great, then I'll see you Friday, around six?" Why her lips tingled as she held his gaze, she didn't know.

"Six is great."

She held his silent gaze.

"Well, you have a good evening at work." Tyler gave her a brief smile.

Darci snapped a look at her wrist, realizing she'd left her watch on the dresser. "Oh, lord, what time is it?"

"What time do you go in?" He pushed up his sleeve revealing a gold Rolex.

Impressed that the photography business must be going

well for him, she grinned. "Six."

"Well, you have an hour." He leaned forward unexpectedly placing a chaste kiss on her cheek. "See you Friday."

"You're not coming down for dinner later?"

He shook his head and patted his camera bag. "Probably not. I want to get these pictures developed. I've rented the back room of one of those empty shops downtown from a guy who'd tried a couple of years ago to start his own studio. It just didn't go over and he had to shut down. Word got out that I was in town and he approached me about the idea of renting his equipment while I'm here." He started down the sidewalk, calling out over his shoulder, "I'll be in touch later this week. Looking forward to Friday."

And he waved goodbye, leaving Darci staring after him.

She stepped inside uncertain of the odd emotions skittering around inside her. Dropping her bag by the door, she shrugged off her coat and wished for the first time in a long time that she could be alone.

The shrill ring of the phone caught her attention and she tossed her coat to a hook and reached for the phone on her desk. As tired as she was, she hoped it was Maevey telling her she had the night off.

"Hi sweetheart, you're a difficult woman to get hold of."

Peter's voice raked across her otherwise peaceful day.

"Hello, Peter."

"Hmm…you sound like you're busy. Did I interrupt anything?"

She heard the shuffling of papers and assumed her was probably using the business line after hours. "I just have to get ready to go into work." She sat down on the arm of her wingback.

He sighed. "You know you wouldn't have to work, Darci, if you'd get those papers signed and unlock my hands to handle things the way Matt and I had planned."

Surprised at his audacity, she braced her hand on the chair and chose her words carefully. "I wasn't aware that I was keeping you from your progress."

"Now don't go putting words in my mouth, Darci. Damn it, you know that my primary concern is you and the kids. When are you going to accept that?"

For reasons she could not immediately identify, her gut told her to placate him for the time being. Meantime, perhaps she needed to speak to her lawyer about how to remove Peter from having so much interest in their financial affairs.

"Of course, Peter. I'm just a little tired, it's been a long day." Her fatigue was not a direct result of being with Tyler all day, but simply being outdoors. She knew if she mentioned Tyler, Peter would start in on his warnings to be cautious of gold-digging men.

"Yeah, when I couldn't get you at home, I called the hotel. Maevey said you were out." There was a pause. "You have a good time?"

At that, Darci chewed her lip, wondering how much Maevey had chosen to tell Peter. There hadn't been adequate time to speak to her cousin where Peter was concerned

"Yes, I did a little hiking." She didn't like feeling as though she had to answer to him about what she did. At one time, she'd liked that Peter always seemed to be there even before she needed him. Lately though, his manner had bordered on possessive.

Darci glanced on the wall, noting the time, but she had one last thing she needed to clear the air about with Peter.

"Peter, I would appreciate if you would ask me before you deposit money into Nathan's or Leah's accounts."

"Ohhh…that's what's bothering you." He sighed heavily in to the phone, its sound condescending. "I could tell that something was bugging you. Listen, Darci. It was one of those times between guys, you know. His buddies were there and they were all excited about making their reservations. I felt bad for the kid and besides, I knew if he called and asked you the same thing, you'd have let him go, right?"

"That's beside the point, Peter." Still she knew he was right and maybe she was making more of this than was necessary.

"Look, I'm sorry. Next time, we'll make sure it all goes through the proper channels. And honestly, I'd planned to call you that night, but I was called out of town and my cell phone went on the blink—"

"Okay fine, just *ask*—next time." Darci rubbed her throat feeling it close.

"So, you didn't mention if you hiked alone today?"

Darci's jaw clenched. "I have to get ready for work, Peter. I hope you have a nice week."

"Oh, and it's a busy one at that. I'll be in touch. Let me know if there is any explanations you need on those papers."

"Sure thing." Darci just wanted to disconnect with the feeling that the wires in the phone were beginning to snake up around her arm holding her to his voice. "Take care, Peter."

"Good bye sweet—"

She clicked the button, not wanting to hear him call her sweetheart again. For some people, the term was nothing more than that—a term. She had the distinct impression that for Peter, it meant something more. The sooner she contacted her lawyer, the better.

"So, you liked the lunch?" Maevey sauntered up beside her, as Darci was busy folding linen napkins into precise little crowns

"Lunch was wonderful and thanks for the grapes." She kept her focus on the task at hand.

""Did you have any time to write then later on your day off?"

Darci glanced at her cousin who'd dropped in beside her folding napkins. "Do I have to tell you everything going on in my life?"

Maevey held a hand to her chest in mock surprise. "Me? Of course not."

"Good." Darci went back to the napkins patiently aware that her cousin would not give up so easily.

"So did he try anything?"

"Maevey." Darci's cheeks warmed as she glanced the area they stood, hoping that none of the customers overheard their conversation.

"It's okay." She leaned close to Darci. "You see Mr. Childs. He's a little hard of hearing and his wife is about as bad. You haven't heard them hollering across the table at each other?" She chuckled and as if on cue, Mrs. Child's held up her fork and shook it at her ageing husband.

"I told you that the fish would give you gas!"

Turning away from the couple to hide their laughter, Darci looked up and her gaze slammed headlong into Tyler Landston at the opposite end of the bar paying for what appeared to be a take out dinner. Maevey jabbed her in the ribs.

She ducked back to work, hoping he'd not heard any of their conversation.

Before he said a word, she sensed his presence as he passed by the bussing station where she and Maevey stood.

"Ms. Cunningham. Ms. Stone." His tone was polite, congenial, but nothing more registered in his expression. Not the fact that they'd spent the day together or that they'd shared anything else of "heated" value for that matter.

"My gawd something *did* happen." Maevey's head swiveled from Tyler's departing form to Darci.

"Nothing happened." She was beginning to believe that more and more as time went by.

"Oh no." Maevey wagged her finger in front of Darci's nose. "A man doesn't use Ms. unless he's trying to hide something."

"He used Ms. on you as well and he didn't kiss—" *Dammit.* Darci gritted her teeth.

Maevey's eyes widened as she filled in the remaining letters of the word Darci had tried to cut off—just not in time for her astute cousin's radar.

"Kiss?"

"You did that on purpose." She frowned at her grinning cousin.

The familiar Irish twinkle sparkled in Maevey's eye. "He

kissed you?"

Darci's brows pressed together. "It was nothing. It was just the—moment."

"Sure." She nodded. "Where was this—*moment*?"

"Up at Fort Holmes." Darci sorted the clean forks from the knives, depositing them into the proper carriers.

Maevey let out a tsk, the one that Darci was so fond of. "And on your first date too. Fort Holmes has always affected folks in that way."

"It was just a kiss."

"Which is why you're ten shades of crimson at the moment." Maevey shrugged. "No big deal though, right?"

"Right."

"Who got kissed?" Bridget leaned over the partition with a wide grin

Darci covered her face and groaned.

* * *

Her feet were killing her and her pride was badly bruised as well. By the time Darci left the restaurant at eleven, almost the entire staff had found out about the heated kiss at Fort Holmes.

It was humiliating, particularly since she wasn't completely sure that Tyler Landston himself remembered the kiss.

Stuffing her key into the lock, Darci could hear the phone ringing from inside. She dove inside and grabbed the receiver. One of these days she was going to have to invest in an answering machine.

"Hello?"

"Hi mom, how's it going?" Leah's voice brought a smile to Darci's heart.

"Hi love, everything is great here. I just got home from work."

"Yeah Maevey said earlier that you'd gone out."

She rolled her gaze to the ceiling. How many other people did her dear cousin brief about her outing?

"She mentioned something about a picnic?"

Darci's hand stayed on the button she'd been unfastening. "What did she tell you?"

"That you'd gone on a tour of the island with a professional photographer."

Darci knew that Maevey would not have stopped there. "What else?"

"That you took a picnic lunch from the hotel." Another pause.

She hoped that her daughter wasn't concerned that she'd been with another man all day—not like it was a date or anything.

"It wasn't a date." She emphasized the fact more for her own benefit than for her daughter's.

She tossed the uniform to her bed as she spoke into the remote phone receiver.

"I didn't say it was," Leah responded.

She heard a teasing lilt in her daughter's voice and chose to cast it aside.

"Okay, good, because it wasn't. He needed someone to—you know, tell him about the island."

"Oh, really?"

"Yes."

"Maevey said it was to get ideas for a cover for your book."

Darci closed her eyes. Bless her cousin. She'd maim her for life first thing in the morning. "She must have meant pictures for *his* book."

"He's a writer then?"

"No, he does pictures for books, like those big hardbound coffee table books with the great pictures."

"Uh huh." There was a hesitation. "So, why would you be along and how did you meet this guy?"

"It's a long story, but I spilled a platter of pasta sauce on him."

"Smooth move, mom, I'll have to jot that one down."

"He needed someone familiar with the island to show him some good picture taking spots." As she listened to herself try to justify her time with Tyler, the worse she began to think it sounded.

"So, where'd you go?"

"We took a carriage ride up to the back trails and hiked to the look-out."

She supposed at this point that she could be glad that she'd not made her phone call to the hotel this evening. "What else did Maevey have to say?" Darci cradled the phone on her shoulder, bracing it with her cheek as she rolled off her pantyhose.

"Just that he's hot."

The receiver slipped from her grasp and clamored to the floor.

"Mom? Mom? Are you all right?" She could hear Leah's evil grin in her tone.

"I'm fine. The phone dropped." She readjusted the receiver on her shoulder. "I hadn't noticed."

"Noticed that he was hot?" Leah's tone was incredulous. "Mom, please you aren't blind."

"Leah."

"Mom."

Darci emitted a long-suffering sigh.

"Mom, it's okay."

"What's okay?" Darci flopped back on her bed, staring at the plaster ceiling above her.

"You don't need my permission, or Nathan's to start dating."

The phone fell from Darci's hand and she lay in stunned silence at her daughter's admonishing words.

She placed the phone back to her ear. "Leah." Using her authoritative "mom" voice. God knows she'd had enough experience honing it to an instrument of cold steel. "I am not and have not, started dating."

"Okay, mom."

Her apathetic tone only heightened her guilt.

"When I start I'll let you know."

"Okay, mom."

Darci sat up struggling with the zipper at the side of her skirt.

"Is there anything else?" She stood and the skirt pooled at her feet.

There was a moments' pause before Leah spoke. "Only what you'd tell me in this situation."

"Which is?" Darci straightened, grasping the receiver in her hand.

"Be careful."

She was too tired and too confused to deal with this conversation and so decided the better part of valor was to concede for the evening. "I will. I'll call you later in the week."

"I love you, mom."

"I love you, too."

As she stood at her dresser, rummaging for a nightgown, Darci caught her half-naked reflection in the mirror. The image that stared back at her was not the same one that had moved to the island, of that she was sure. At the moment, it was about all she was sure of.

Chapter Eleven

Why she was nervous about having Tyler for dinner hinged on two possibilities Darci could readily think of.

"Looks like a nice dinner you have planned, Darci." Russ, the clerk at Doud's Mercantile smiled. "You need any help finishing off those steaks?"

Darci smiled, a bit of warmth climbing into her cheeks, aware suddenly as she precariously balanced the two overstuffed grocery sacks that she'd probably bought enough for a small army. "Thanks Russ, but I have company coming."

"So I heard." He grinned and waved as he started checking out the next customer.

Darci grinned, wondering if she would ever truly have any privacy again. Still, the thought of people talking about Tyler coming to her house for dinner could not shake the jitters she'd had all week at the simple thought.

She hurried home as best as she could amid the blustery wind, already spitting a mist as the day approached dusk. For days the weather had steadily deteriorated to the point where it became of greater discussion value than she and the handsome photographer's dinner date.

Icy pelts stung her cheeks as she made the short walk from downtown to her home and she was glad she'd gone ahead and bought extra batteries for her weather radio. If there was something she'd learned from listening to the locals, the weather on and around the island could change in an instant. It was that very aspect that gave cause for the many shipwrecks along the submerged jagged shoals where ships tried valiantly to escape the monstrous waves of the Great Lakes.

She hoped that Tyler's aerial photo shoot of the island was over and his plane back safe on the ground. Casting a pensive look to the darkening sky, she made a mental note to call Maevey and see if Tyler had returned to the hotel.

She shifted the bags in her arms and stuck the key in the lock, surprised to find the door opened easily without need for her key.

Cautiously, she peered inside to find the lights blazing in her living room and to her greater surprise—Leah and Peter involved in a game of Chinese checkers.

"Hi Mom!" Leah jumped from the couch with a wide grin, bounding to her with all the glee of a newborn puppy. "Surprise!"

The bags in Darci's arms slid to her feet as Leah grabbed her in a bone-crushing hug. She looked over Leah's shoulder catching the unmistakable satisfaction on Peter's face.

"Hi Darci." He pointed to the checker game. "I forgot how much you love this game."

"What a lovely surprise—" Darci shrugged off her coat as though unfazed by the unplanned arrival. She was more than happy to see Leah, but she wondered what it was that Peter was up to.

"Is everything all right, Leah?" Darci held her daughter's chin, studying her face with the slim glimmer of hope that Peter had brought her there under real reasons concerning her health.

"I'm fine, mom." When Uncle Peter called the other day, I was feeling really homesick and this morning when he called to say he had the weekend free, he suggested we buzz up here and see you." Leah glanced over her shoulder beaming at Peter.

"How thoughtful." Darci captured Peter's gleaming smile to her daughter and bent down to get her groceries.

"Oh here, let me help." Leah reached for the bags and her eyes widened as she lifted one into her arms. "Good lord, mom, were you expecting an army?" She smiled as she vanished into the kitchen and Darci grabbed the other sack, only to have it snatched from her hands by a smiling Peter.

"Here allow me." He scooped the bag from her arms with a grin.

She followed him into the kitchen, her mind unable to grasp just yet how to approach telling them about her dinner date.

"So I thought bringing Leah up would be good for both of you. It's been since—when—? The beginning of school that you've seen each other?" Peter sat the bag on the table glancing first Leah and then to Darci "Of course, I'll just wanted to say hello and then I'm off to the hotel to find a room, so you all can have a nice weekend together."

Leah shot him a look, jabbing her hands to her hips. "You don't have to do that, does he mom? We have plenty of room here, if I sleep with you. Uncle Peter can sleep in the guest room."

Peter's slow and steady gaze lifted to Darci's. There was very little she could do. To suggest any alternative in front of Leah would be to open up a great many suspicions and she was not yet ready to deal with them and certainly not in front of her daughter.

"Of course, you can stay here. In the guest room."

"Great, this will be fun! Let's go get some wood and start a fire." Leah grabbed Peter's arm and drug him from the room.

"The weather doesn't look real great mom," Leah called from the next room. "It looks like there could be ice or snow. They said it depended on the lake and ground temperatures."

Her voice held the enthusiasm of youth preparing for a great adventure, secure in being indoors with those that she loved.

Darci wished she felt the same. Spying the phone on the kitchen wall, she snatched up the receiver to call Maevey. With any luck he'd be there and she could explain that they'd have to cancel their plans for the evening. "Hotel Iroquois. May I help you?"

"Hi Maevey, have you seen Tyler? He was supposed to have been with a pilot today taking aerial shots of the island. I was hoping maybe you might have seen him?"

"Haven't seen him yet, would you like to leave a message?" The tone in her voice was teasing.

On any other day, she might have been able to handle it. "Just tell him to give me a call when he gets in, okay?"

"Will do," she replied. "I have another call coming in, people are already booking for the lilac festival. I'll pass on your message if you promise me that one of these days you fix me dinner and tell me all about that tour you gave our hot guest. Later, hon."

As usual, Darci was not able to get in a word edgewise. She snapped the phone back to its cradle and shrugged. Things being what they were on this island, Tyler would hear the news of Peter and Leah's arrival before she had the chance to talk to him.

"Wow, looks like you knew we were coming." Leah breezed into the kitchen. "Uncle Peter told me to come inside and help you." She dug into the first sack and started pulling out the groceries. "Steaks, salad—crusty bread?"

Darci occupied herself with emptying the other sack, unsure of what her daughter would think of her cooking dinner for a strange man in her home. Yet in the time she'd spent with him, she'd experienced a connection to him. One that she could not deny gave her every bit of satisfaction, in most ways, as the camaraderie she and Matt had shared.

She and Leah worked in silence putting away groceries.

"Oh, keep that out for dinner." She pointed to her angel hair pasta Leah was getting ready to put away in the cupboard.

She shrugged, tossing it to the cabinet and opened the refrigerator. "You made my favorite! Lime *Jell-O* with mandarin oranges." Leah gave Darci a delighted look. "Did Peter call to tell you we were coming?"

Behind her, Darci heard the stomping of feet.

"Brrr, it's getting colder out there. Did I hear my name?"

"Mom made Lime *Jell-O*." Leah turned to Peter sporting a grin as she held up the glass dish.

"Hey." He glanced at Darci. "That's great."

"Close the fridge, Leah, you'll let out the cold." Darci

resumed her task.

"Wine?"

Darci closed her eyes and with a heavy sigh realized that she would have to face the music at some point. "I had—someone coming to dinner. There—it's done, I said it." She turned around hoping against hope there'd be no further discussion.

"That photographer fellow, by chance?" Peter's voice prompted her to turn around and face them a second time. She had the feeling of being thirteen and being interrogated by parents again.

"Yes, as a matter of fact. That photographer. His name is Tyler Landston." Her answer was quick, direct, and very adult, given how adolescent she felt at the moment. She tried to convey in her tone that there was no need to discuss the subject further. "He's unable to make it now anyway. It was very open and very flexible. No problem."

Still concern needled at the back of her mind and she glanced at the clock to note that ten minutes had passed since she talked to Maevey.

"Mom, we hope we haven't ruined any plans. Uncle Peter and I could go to a movie while you have dinner." Leah glanced at Peter, seeking his compliance.

Darci did not immediately see it. "It's okay, it was one of those things that if he got done with his aerial tour and *wanted* to he could stop by. Really, don't worry about it. I highly doubt he'll show." Darci's gaze followed Leah and Peter's as they looked at the feast sitting on the table waiting to be put away.

"You bought wine on the *off* chance you *might* have a dinner guest?" Peter picked up the bottle, glancing briefly at the label and then looked at Darci with a skepticism written allover his expression. "And no *Boones Farm* variety of wine at that."

"I happen to like a glass of wine now and again before bed. To help me relax." She plucked the bottle from his curious grasp and shoved it into the refrigerator.

Darci turned to catch the curious look from her daughter and the less-than-pleased look of Peter.

Using the sound of the crackling fire, she peered around Peter's frame filling the kitchen entry. "Oh, what a nice fire. You know it doesn't look very big, but the back is a glazed ceramic—like they use in pizza ovens?" Her gaze bounced from her daughter to Peter's, mirroring the instability of her thoughts.

She took a quick, deep breath and placed her hands with purpose on her hips, "Well, if you'll excuse me I'm going to go change into something more comfortable." She turned to her daughter. "Will you start the water for the pasta?"

Leah nodded, a smile tugging at the corner of her lip as she ducked to the bottom cabinet to get a pan.

Her last and only obstacle, she hoped, from this most humiliating scene was Peter. "Excuse me." She started past him, and he turned to the side forcing her to wedge herself between him and the doorjamb.

The scent of the smoking wood met her and she chose to keep her eyes averted from his.

"Is there anything you need me to do?" His voice was quiet as he shifted, causing her to brush against him as she squeezed through.

Flustered enough with concern for Tyler's safety and how she was going to manage to corral Peter for an entire weekend, Darci blurted out the first thing that came to her mind. "You could set the table?" She broke free of the doorway and glanced over her shoulder as she headed for her room.

"For how many?" he asked quietly.

"For three, of course." She picked up her coat where she'd dropped it earlier, hooking it on the antique hall tree near the front door. It was one of the few pieces of exquisite antique furniture that Matt and she had bought over the years. She'd sold much of her furniture when she moved to a smaller house and the rest of the pieces went into storage until Nathan and Leah had homes of their own.

Glancing out the bay window near the door, she noticed

Tyler's form, braced against the wind coming up the walk. The black turtleneck against his upturned collar of his leather jacket gave him a youthful, dangerous appeal. In his hand he carried a bottle of wine and her heart raced like wild horses, though she couldn't say if it was images of what might have been, or the disaster that was about to happen.

He rang the doorbell and she shot a startled look to Peter, now joined by Leah peering from the kitchen entry.

"Better make that four." The sarcasm though masked presumably for Leah's benefit was caught clearly by Darci.

She squared her shoulders and opened the door.

"You haven't had time to change?" Tyler opened the screen door and stepped in giving her a light peck on the cheek as he handed her the wine. "Your favorite, madam." He smiled having to admit to his self-proclaimed single's lifestyle that she was a welcome sight after a long day. It was as though the minute he walked through the door, he felt at home.

Presumptuous thought, since two strangers stood at the kitchen door giving him the once over.

"Tyler." Darci touched his elbow averting his gaze from the steely borderline glare of the tall man beside the young woman who was the spitting image of Darci. "This is my daughter, Leah and Peter Beck, a close friend of the family."

The tall blonde man with the polished and professional outward appearance made the first move in manner in which Tyler would have expected.

"Peter Beck." He reached out to shake hands, laughingly placing the towel in his other hand.

"Nice to meet you," Tyler replied with as fake a smile as he was certain was plastered to the Peter Beck's face.

"Hi, I'm Leah."

Tyler took the soft hand of the young woman and saw for the first time, the blend of the genes that he'd seen earlier in the photo on the mantle.

Her hair was her mother's, a dark chestnut, but where Darci's eyes were a rich golden honey color, Leah's were a striking hue of turquoise, like the color of a tempest sea.

"Tyler Landston, glad to meet you." He smiled cordially and then searched immediately for some excuse to disappear.

He faced Darci. "I came right from the airport." Her pallor was a bit pale, even for her. "I thought it was best to come straight here since I was running late."

The phone rang and Darci visibly reacted with a start. "Hello? Yes. Yes. No, there's no problem. I'm sure." Darci sighed unable to move from where she'd answered the phone. "Because he's here." She glanced his way, quickly averting her gaze.

There was no doubt that she'd been caught by surprise of her unexpected guests and that he needed to find a way to excuse himself for the evening.

"I'll call you tomorrow, bye." Darci hung up and turned to him with a smile.

Granted, her smile marginally quelled the awkwardness of the moment. He stepped toward the front door, reaching for the doorknob.

"May I speak to you for a moment?" She grabbed the elbow of his leather coat and ushered him down the hall and into her bedroom.

Just as he was getting comfortable with her choice, his vision whirled as she spun him from the room and across the hall to the bathroom.

Thankfully she left the bathroom door open.

"You didn't go back to the hotel to change?" she whispered as she backed him against the bathroom sink. Another time, he might find her "take charge" attitude rather alluring.

"I told you I came straight from the airport."

"You brought wine," she countered, making it seem like a challenge. Clearly the woman was dealing with issues that he knew nothing about—yet.

"Guilty as charged and I apologize, I should have called first, but the grocery store was right there and I thought, Tyler, you're being invited to a beautiful woman's home for dinner the least you can—" The panicked look in her gaze stilled his joke. "You're afraid. Of what?"

Whatever warm and toasty thoughts he had about their shared kiss evaporated, replaced quickly by the sensation of a small pool of water he'd sat down on. All in all, perhaps it was better that neither of them continued this dangerous pursuit of the chemistry between them. One or both of them could well get burnt.

"Look, I can solve this relatively easy. It's obvious that my presence here is uncomfortable for you." He held up his palms in defense.

She covered her forehead with her palm, offering him an apologetic look. "I had no clue they were coming."

Tyler grinned. "That much I figured out." At least he'd gotten a smile out of her.

"It's not you causing any problem." She looked at him then, *really* looking at him for the first time since he'd arrived. "Hi, I'm glad you're back on the ground."

His gut tightened and he suppressed the urge to yank her into his arms and kiss her senseless. If only the bathroom door had a lock.

"Mom?" Leah's quiet rap on the bathroom door silenced his current thoughts.

Darci drew the door open completely and mother and daughter stared at each other. For a brief, but odd moment, it was as though their roles were reversed.

"Hi."

She gave Tyler a shy glance.

"I'll leave. This is family time." He moved toward the door.

"No, please." Leah stood her ground blocking his exit. "Please we'd like you to stay for dinner."

"We?" Tyler's questioning gaze turned to Darci.

"We—meaning, Leah and me."

"And Uncle Peter."

"Uncle Peter?" Tyler's tone hinged on incredulous and he hoped only Darci caught it.

"Uh, the kids just sort of picked up on that when they were

young."

"Right, maybe we should do this another time." He headed toward the door giving Leah no alternative, but to move.

"Tyler." Darci's voice followed him into the hall. "Please, I'd like you to stay. You have to eat somewhere."

Cozy images of he and Darci sipping wine in front of the fireplace danced in his head. He faced her to explain he'd call her tomorrow.

"Landston, we'd be more than happy to have you dine with us."

That image vanished in an icy puff of smoke. Tyler turned around and scanned the giant Scandinavian with eyes the color of blue ice. Donned in a navy and white striped BBQ apron two sizes too small, he snapped his tongs. "Dinner is nearly ready. While you all have been—" He peered around Tyler. "Checking out the bathroom, I've been slaving over a hot broiler oven."

Tyler knew what he'd like to do with those tongs.

Darci appeared at his shoulder. "Let me take your coat." Her breath whispered near his cheek and he gained some satisfaction that Peter Beck's charismatic smile faded just a notch.

He shrugged out of his coat deciding that if Darci really wanted him to stay it might well be she wasn't one hundred per cent comfortable being around her "old family friend."

"I'll open the wine." Tyler slapped his hands together and caught Darci's smile from the corner of his eye.

Chapter Twelve

Darci pulled back the kitchen curtain unable to distinguish the outline of her tool shed in the back yard for the driving rain. Pellets of ice tapped a cadence against the glass urging her to turn her attention back to the radio's dial. The crackling pop static drowned out the sound of the easy listening music they'd had on most of dinner.

"Why don't we just turn it off, Darci. It's not like any of us are going anywhere." Peter looked at her from the dinner table, then his gaze rested on Tyler. "At least for a while." He chuckled. "If Landston can handle it, maybe I'll teach him a thing or two about your marble game over there."

Peter poured his second glass of wine and raised it in mock salute towards Tyler.

Darci slid into her seat and caught Tyler's quiet smile before returning to his meal.

The wind outside howled at the corners of the house, as though reflecting the tension around the table.

"So, Landston—"

"It's Tyler." Tyler didn't look up, but continued to stab at his salad.

"So, *Tyler*, tell me, where'd you get your Masters?"

Tyler paused, his fork midway to his mouth. "My Masters?"

"Sure, in photography. I assume you've attended the best—Columbia? Berkley?"

"The University of Nevada. Major in Communications." Tyler stuffed a piece of steak into his mouth.

"Hum…really? I didn't know they were well known for that. So, are you from Nevada originally?" Peter tipped back his glass and drained it, scrutinizing the empty glass in the reflective glow of the candle flame.

Darci had hoped the soft candle-glow ambience would soften the tension. She closed her eyes and kept quiet. If Peter continued to be rude to Tyler she would ask him to leave. She was certain the hotel had a spare room, if not the wicker couch on the front porch.

She picked up a bowl of crusty bread and handed it to Tyler. "Tyler is originally from Illinois."

Leah's gaze shot to Tyler. "Where in Illinois?"

The thought occurred to Darci that she'd never asked where his home was, or perhaps it was because at the time it seemed like a painful topic.

He shrugged as he buttered a piece of bread. "Nothing spectacular, just a smaller midwestern community."

"My dad came from a smaller town." Leah glanced at her mother and raised a brow.

Peter rested his elbows on the table, cradling the empty goblet in his hands. His gaze studied Tyler with all the precision of a panther about to go in for the kill. "Whereabouts in Illinois—*Landston*?" The emphasis on Tyler's last name was not a mere slip.

The air was heavy with an unknown animosity between the two men. Darci glanced from one to the other and considered tossing them both out on their keesters. Hoping to dispel some of the macho driven tension, she scooped up the bread bowl. "Anyone need more bread?" She smiled at Leah and patted her shoulder as she headed to the kitchen.

"A little place in southeastern Illinois. A hole in the wall really, Bradyville." He shrugged.

Darci's heart came to a halt, as her hand cemented to Leah's shoulder for support.

"Just—a—"

She could hear the hesitation in Tyler's voice.

"Place around fifteen, twenty thousand, maybe."

"*Bradyville*, Illinois?"

She turned to Peter as he repeated the town's name for her

147

benefit. There was little mistaking the smug look on his face as he leaned away from the table and hooked his arm over the back of the chair.

Tyler nodded glancing at Peter, only then aware that everyone in the room was staring at him. "Did I say something wrong?" He straightened in his chair, wiping his fingers on his napkin. His gaze scanned their faces, lighting on Darci's with a puzzled expression.

"Do you happen to remember a guy by the name of Matt Cunningham? Would have been about your age, I think." Peter gave Darci a hooded glance.

As much as she wanted to ease the obvious awkwardness of the moment, she was more than curious to hear Tyler's answer.

Tyler's brow furrowed, clearly he was searching his memory. Finally, he shook his head and shrugged. "Sorry, I can't remember that name." He faced Darci. "I'm sorry, I wish I'd known him."

"That's odd, Landston, since Matt was the town's pride and joy when he decided to go into medicine." Peter carefully set his glass on the table.

Peter's direct challenge bothered Darci. On the other hand, how was it possible she'd spent so much time with this man and had not known he'd grown up in the same town as her dead husband?

Tyler stood slowly as he quietly folded his napkin. "I don't know where this is heading, but it seems that my presence here this evening has created some undue tension." He faced Darci, holding out his hand to her. "Thank you—for inviting me." His smile was genuine, but his eyes reflected his discomfiture.

A thundering boom rattled the glass of the patio doors and the bowl leapt from Darci's hands into Tyler's.

The lights flickered once and then they were pitched into darkness, save the flickering glow of the candles on the table.

"Sounded like a transformer nearby." Peter rushed to Darci's side, touching her on the shoulder. "Have you got a weather radio?"

Her gaze locked to Tyler's. Still reeling from the recent discovery, she nodded. "On the shelf in the kitchen."

"I'll go get more wood for the fire." Leah pushed from the table and headed for the patio where Abe Fiskas had stacked a cord of wood in for the season.

Tyler placed the bowl carefully on the table. "Really, thanks for dinner." He chuckled quietly. "Give my thanks to the cook. Either way, I better go."

Darci's hand clung to the back of Leah's chair, her mind a network of confusion.

"Don't go."

The words tumbled out pf her mouth and she blinked as though said by someone else.

He held her gaze, the uncertainty plainly etched on the strong line of his clenched jaw.

"It's probably black as pitch out there." She grappled for any sensible means for excuse, unsure why she wanted him to stay, but not wanting him to leave. Maybe it was simply this new discovery made her want to know more about him. Then again, the truth might be that she didn't want to be stuck in a dark house with Peter Beck and that thought bothered her a great deal more.

"I'll help Leah, then." He scooted his chair to the table without discussion and walked to the patio doors, sliding them open. A sudden fierce wind took the curtains to flight, barreling through the living room and scattering the dinner napkins across the floor.

The frigid chill startled Darci from her reverie and her mind clicked to where she had stocked extra candles and flashlights.

Peter appeared from the dark kitchen with her radio in hand. "I'll try to get something here. Do you have a flashlight? I don't think this is going to help us much." He held up a small squeezable penlight attached to his key chain.

"In the linen closet." She skirted past him, hoping the radio would occupy his time, but he followed her down the hall.

In the dim light of the fireplace, she found the drawer and dropped to her knees, fishing through the contents. She pulled out a flashlight and pressed the switch; glad to see it was working. Darci handed it up to Peter.

Leaning against the wall, Peter looked down at her as he took the light. "Interesting about your friend, Tyler, living in the same town as Matt."

The statement was said in a conversational enough tone, one meant generally as filler for awkward silences. Given that it were any other man except Peter, Darci would have taken it as just that. However, she'd known Peter a long time and on occasion Matt would remark of the jealous side of Peter. That too, was a private joke between she and Matt, as she never, herself detected any note that Peter was jealous of anything she and Matt had. Not until now.

"It's probable that they didn't know each other," Darci reasoned as she grabbed a box of wooden kitchen matches. Perhaps her paranoid frenzy to prepare for the upcoming winter had been a blessing in disguise. She handed the matches to Peter.

He flashed the beam of light into her eyes, before aiming it to the drawer as he knelt beside her. Lowering his voice to a conspiring whisper. " Sure, it's possible, but don't you think that somehow, somewhere he'd have run into Matt?"

"Tyler was a loner in school. He was very open with me about that. He wasn't a social kid, had some problems at home." She regretted telling him the confidences the minute they issued from her mouth, but she hoped it would serve to help Peter understand that in all probability Tyler and Matt's lives were at opposite ends of the spectrum. She stood, shutting the drawer with a little more force than necessary.

"A loner?"

"Lots of teenage boys are loners, Peter. It doesn't make him a liar, thief, or psychotic killer." She wanted to end this conversation quickly before Leah and Tyler returned. She hadn't told him yet that she'd invited Tyler to stay, better to break the news now.

"If the power doesn't come back on, I've invited Tyler to stay the night. At least we have heat from the fireplace." She shoved her shoulders back in an attempt to dissuade any argument he might toss back at her.

"Mom, you wouldn't believe it, you can't see a thing out there." Leah dropped an armload of wood in the empty box by the fireplace. Tyler followed close behind.

Peter sighed quietly and shook his head, his disappointment in her decision illuminated by the flashlight. "I don't think this is a good idea."

She shrugged, waltzing past Peter to seek out her odd array of candlesticks. It was entirely possible that Peter was right, still it felt pretty damn good to let him know that this was her turf and she would make the choices.

"I'll get a pillow and blanket, Tyler. If you don't mind sleeping on the couch." Darci lit several candles and then began the task of clearing the table.

"I'll help you, mom." Leah fairly leapt at the opportunity to assist in the clean up chore.

"Anything I can do, sweetheart?"

Darci bristled at Peter's remark, made out loud, no doubt, for Tyler's benefit. What had gotten into him lately? His input on their finances had always been impeccable, providing them a worry-free life insofar as finances go. He and Matt were forever coming up with yet a new way to invest their money. A tinge of guilt assaulted her as a single thought provoked by his recent behavior crossed her mind.

"Go get a room?" she muttered as she lit the squat kitchen candle in a jar. The scent of fresh baked cinnamon rolls wafted through the kitchen.

Beside her, Leah placed the dishes in the sink.

"I love that you're here." She pulled her daughter to her, relishing in the security of having her close. Right now, she and Nathan were the anchors in her life. They were the only people aside from herself that she could count on.

"When Uncle Peter called—" Leah muffled voice spoke

into Darci's shoulder.

"Peter called you?" Darci held her daughter at arm's length.

"Mom." Leah's brows knit with concern, "Uncle Peter has called Nate and I almost weekly since we started school."

At one time, this news would have been a welcome, but since the escapade with Nathan's deposit, Darci began to wonder if she shouldn't begin to draw some lines where Peter was concerned.

She hadn't thought much about it before now, but Peter had always had a penchant for bringing Leah and Nathan new toys when they were young. Rewarding them for good report cards and on occasion, he'd been very generous with monetary birthday gifts. Still, for she and Matt, not having siblings of their own, it was great to have the loving influence of "Uncle" Peter.

"Why?" Darci was truly curious what would prompt Peter to call her children now with such frequency, almost as though, since Matt's death, he'd assumed the role of their parent.

Leah shrugged. "To see how we were doing, I guess."

A cold chill crept up Darci's spine. "And what did he call about this last time?"

"He asked if I'd talked to you in a while. I guess he thought you sounded lonely."

Or maybe he thought she was not lonely enough?

"I told him that I hoped to get up here as soon as I could, but the drive is long for one person."

Darci, by now, had figured out the rest of the story and she wasn't happy that Peter had used Leah as a reason to come to the island. Still, it was wonderful to have her daughter with her now and as long as Tyler was around she was less concerned that Peter would try to force his advantage. It struck Darci that oddly she'd never felt the same unease when with Tyler—even alone.

She would need to find the privacy to talk with Tyler about this newfound discovery of growing up in the same town as Matt. Certain that there was no reason that Tyler would not be telling the truth. What possible reason would he have for not being absolutely straight with her?

"If you want to tell me where those blankets are, Darci, I'll get them myself." Tyler braced his hand against the doorway of the kitchen.

"They're in a trunk in my room." Darci let go of her daughter receiving a pat on the arm.

"I'll take care of this, go on get Mr. Landston set up."

Grateful for her daughter's offer, Darci pointed Tyler towards the bedrooms as she stepped past him. "It's through here." She scanned the living room, "Where's Peter?"

"Went on to bed. Said there wasn't much point in staying awake." Tyler followed her down the hallway to the bedroom.

Glad she'd picked up a candle from the dining room table, she cupped the flame as she walked. "I'm sorry about tonight," she whispered.

* * *

Peter sat in the middle of the bed, an odd figure hunched over the garish white light of his laptop. Surrounding him were mementos of Leah's childhood. A fluffy yellow dog won for her by her dad at a carnival, an antique doll, and a brown teddy bear, now with one eye missing, given to her on her eighth birthday by her "Uncle Peter."

He typed the email address of his good friend—good as long as he kept him satisfied with the means to continue his little sideline businesses in conjunction to his nine-to-five of hacking.

What he did with his talents was of little concern to Peter. It had served him well on more than one occasion, tapping into the Black Market for illegal drugs for example. Poor Matt, had he known, wouldn't have approved of his unorthodox means of obtaining special needs, but he was more than willing to risk his life for a long-shot cure. Peter shrugged. Hell, did the poor guy have much of a choice?

"Need you to find out all you can about a Tyler Landston. Graduate of University of Nevada, Las Vegas and hometown of Bradyville, Illinois, need prompt reply—next eight hours. Will

be waiting. Deposit made as per usual means with a little extra for expediency."

In the next room he heard voices and his teeth clenched in frustration. Their hushed conversation churned his gut, but as he gently closed his laptop, he reminded himself, it was only a temporary setback.

Tyler Landston could not be trusted, of that, he was certain. He'd find out about him and present the facts to Darci. That would convince her that his warnings to her were valid. Then maybe she would listen to him. Then maybe she would see that he'd always been there for her—watching and protecting her, from those who could bring her harm.

* * *

Tyler quietly closed the bedroom door, grateful for a moment alone with Darci.

Her gaze shot to his with a terrified start, the same look she'd had moments before at dinner. And while he could easily understand her shock—as was he—at finding out he and Matt came from the same town, he didn't understand her apprehension.

"Darci, tell me what's wrong? Why are you so jumpy?" He edged toward her, uncertain if she wanted him any closer by the peculiar look on her face.

Tyler was careful not to get too near her all evening. He'd sensed that his presence had not yet been explained to either her daughter and certainly not to Peter. Then again, Tyler himself was unsure he had an explanation of whatever relationship he had with Darci. Still, there was something he didn't care for about that guy, like the way he spoke to Darci as though they were married. By the same token, as independent as Darci appeared to be on the outside, he hadn't seen her stand up to him. Not that he pretended in this short time of knowing her to understand what kind of arrangement she had with other men in her life. Still, for whatever reason, Tyler didn't want to see that untrusting look in her eye when she looked at him.

"Well, Tyler, you've got to understand—"

Paranoia about Peter Beck broke through and he placed

his finger to his lips. "Please, keep your voice down," he whispered taking a step closer.

He didn't believe for one minute that Peter Beck had retired early. Chances are he had a glass to the wall right now, listening in. Tyler couldn't pinpoint what it was about Beck that bothered him most—lots of things did.

Darci sighed as she flipped open a wicker trunk filled with blankets, but she complied with his request, lowering her voice. Perhaps his assessment of Peter was not as far off kilter as he thought.

"Tyler, you grew up in the same town with Matt. Give me a break, that's a bit of a shock." She drew out a comforter and blanket, and then moved to the closet where she snagged a pillow from the shelf.

"Lots of people grew up in that town, Darci. Why is it so strange that I would?" He rested his hand on the dresser, giving it something to do rather than touch her.

She hesitated as she turned to him, clutching the linens to her body. It was a moment before she spoke.

"How'd you know I was here?" She boldly walked up to him, pushing gently against him, the folded blankets forming a barrier between them. The pillow found its way into his hand.

"I—I didn't. I was assigned to this project, if you'll recall. Why would I be looking for you? Darci, what is this all about?"

She studied his face, a myriad of emotions, like a kaleidoscope, shifting through her eyes. He'd made a living of looking at people's souls through the viewfinder of his camera. This woman's heart was extremely scattered.

Her shoulders slumped and she sighed. "It was just such a shock. I've had a really hard time lately, accepting Matt's death. It was so unexpected—so sudden." Her watery gaze lifted and held his in a silent plea for him to understand.

Her pain stirred the part of him that empathized with her feeling of loss—having no answers—never having a second chance to make things right, living with the regrets. That part of him had been shoved under the rug of his emotions when he received the note from one of his brothers, telling him that his parents had been killed by a drunk driver—two weeks after their funeral. They hadn't seen the need to contact him; their wishes—unknown to him—had been for cremation.

At the time, he had only his employers around him, strangers really, who knew little of the past he kept closely guarded, but accepted him and all his secrets, without conditions.

Staring down at Darci's face, seeing the questions, the abandonment in her eyes, brought all of those memories to a crystal clear realization. He wished now that he'd had someone to simply hold him—someone who could understand that type of loss.

With great care, he gently pried the blankets from her grasp and dropped them to the floor. Opening his arms, he allowed her to follow her heart.

And she did.

Tyler closed his arms around her, embracing the loss of *his* past. "If it's of any consolation, I left Bradyville a long time ago. I hardly knew anyone there."

Her arms clamped around his waist as she buried her face in his chest, letting go her suffering in the form of silent tears.

He cradled the back of her head like a child, her tears soaking the front of his sweater. Resting his chin to the top of her head, he prayed no one would come through that door—especially Peter.

Suddenly, she pulled away from him, leaving his arms empty, and his heart on the verge of something he didn't fully understand.

"I'm sorry." She swiped the back of her hands over her face and reached for a tissue on the nightstand by her bed.

He wanted to tell her he understood; wanted to tell her that he didn't mind her mascara, now dotted over the front of his shirt—it was black anyway. He wanted to tell her that he'd welcome her into his arms anytime—for any reason, in a heartbeat.

Still unsure his emotions weren't terrifically careening out of control, he reeled those thoughts quickly back to the safety of silence.

"I'll take these out to the living room." He picked up his bedding for the night.

"Tyler?"

Her voice stayed his hand to the doorknob, knowing that at this emotional moment he needed to be strong against the desires that had him wanting to lay her back on the bed and give comfort to the both of them.

"Thank you." She smiled and though wobbly, it caused him to return the smile, truly glad that he'd been there for her.

"I'll keep the fire going, " he whispered realizing the huskiness in his voice. Something in her expression seemed to challenge his words and though meant for the obvious reason, he could not help but ponder their double meaning.

A light tap came from the opposite side of the bedroom door. "Did you find the blankets?" Leah whispered from the other side.

Darci brushed past him, placing her hand over his on the doorknob.

He stepped back, releasing his grip as she swung open the door.

"I had to look around for them, but we have everything now." She clamped her hand to his arm, ushering him through the door. "Leah, will you see to Mr. Landston?"

Assuming he'd done his duty for this damsel's momentary distress, he nodded his goodnight to the two. "I can find the couch, thanks."

The soft glow of the fireplace illuminated the small living room. Tyler stared at his the loveseat-turned-bed for the night and wondered if he would sleep at all.

Chapter Thirteen

It'd been a long time since her daughter had shared a bed with her. A few times after the death of her father, Leah would wind up beside their bed in the middle of the night. The first time it scared Darci, but she grew to understand. She had also found comfort in Matt's scent still lingering on his pillow.

Darci stared up at the inky blackness that enveloped the room. If the entire evening had been less tension filled, she might be less riddled with concern and enjoying the simple company of her daughter more.

"Mom?" Leah whispered beside her. "Are you still awake?"

"I'm awake." Darci rubbed a finger over her eye, wishing she could sleep, but the memory of Tyler's arms holding her in a protective embrace rattled her to the core. How was it that she could sense his understanding so readily and not have ever felt Peter's?

"Do you remember that camping trip we took to Colorado and how dark it was in the woods after the fire died out?"

"You were supposed to be asleep by then, I believe."

"Yeah, that was something Nathan and I perfected—being able to pretend we were asleep."

Darci smiled at the memory of she and Matt attempting to make love in the double sleeping bag while trying to stay quiet. They ended up laughing nearly through the event—which, given their acrobatic maneuvers, is what they declared it from that moment on.

"It didn't appear you and dad were asleep either."

Shocked at her daughter's bluntness, Darci perched on her elbow and looked in the dark at where her daughter lay. At the moment very glad that she could not see her face. "How old were you then?"

"Twelve, thirteen, maybe."

"Leah Cunningham, tell me that you and your brother were not eavesdropping."

"I can *tell* you that if it makes you feel better." She giggled.

The sound of it lifted Darci's spirit and her lips in a smile. "I'll never be able to face your brother again."

"Oh, mom, he was pretty young. He didn't really get it."

"That's some compensation." Darci flopped back onto her pillow, throwing her forearm over her head.

"That's probably explains why Nathan refused to have me talk to him about the birds and bees." Darci chuckled, remembering her son plugging his ears and singing out loud as he rocked back and forth.

"I wouldn't worry too much about him, mom. He's got the jest of it now, I can assure you." She could hear the smile in Leah's voice.

"Is this stuff a mother really wants to hear about her children?"

"Probably not."

She reached over and tapped where she guessed her daughters nose would be. "Then don't. I just hope you are both wise when it comes to relationships."

"Ow…that was my eye."

"Sorry."

A comfortable silence fell between them and for a moment everything seemed right, the way it should be.

"Mom?"

"Yeah?" Darci sensed the playful banter was only a prequel to what was really on Leah's mind.

"Did you love dad?"

A stab of guilt precipitated by the weeks' events with Tyler sliced across her heart. "What a silly question, of course I did."

"I always knew you loved dad the way kids think of it

between their parents, but I mean did you love him in a "stop-your-breath-make-your-heart-race-'til-death-do—"

"Us part," Darci finished the sentence for her daughter.

"I'm sorry, Mom."

Darci swallowed the lump in her throat and turned to her daughter. If Darci was experiencing her own brand of confusion and questions about Tyler Landston popping up out of nowhere in her life, why wouldn't she expect her daughter to also be struggling with questions of her own?

Darci brushed Leah's hair from her forehead as she'd done a million times when she was unable to sleep as a child. "I loved your father. Whatever definition you want to give it. We had our moments of bliss, moments of anger, moments of contentment, some of struggle." She paused at the realization dawning in her mind. "But that's what real love is, Leah. There is life beyond that initial euphoric stage, where love takes root and becomes as real and normal to your existence as breathing." Darci cradled her head in the crook of her arm pondering what she'd just told her daughter.

"Do you think it's possible that you could love another man like that?"

"Are you concerned about that, Leah?" She heard her quiet sigh.

"I think you are too young to live the rest of your life alone."

It wasn't what Darci expected to hear. "I—I'm not alone, I have you and Nathan."

"Mom, you know what I mean." Leah cleared her throat. "What do you think of Mr. Landston?"

"Leah, what are you trying to do?" She rolled to her back and stared at the dark ceiling.

"I saw the way he looked at you, Mom," Leah replied.

"You're awfully astute these days."

"Mom, I plan to teach kindergarten. I'm being trained to keep my eye on everything around me."

"Ah, I see." Darci smiled trying to pass off the jittery sensation in her stomach. *Had Tyler been looking her?* "What do *you* think of Mr. Landston?"

"Aside from the obvious fact that he's incredibly hot?" Leah chuckled.

Darci laughed quietly remembering Tyler's reference to her the night of the pasta incident. "Notice any other redeeming qualities, oh wise one?"

"Well...he has good taste."

"In?"

"Women."

"And you know this *how*?"

"He was staring at you more than once tonight, mom and don't think I didn't notice you'd been crying when you were supposed to be getting blankets."

Darci lay still, silently reprimanding herself for not giving her daughter enough credit in noticing the world around her. She was more than astute, perhaps she was right on target, and that's what made Darci so uncomfortable.

"The fact that you were standing close when you opened the door, and the major dark spot on the front of Tyler's shirt is kind of a no-brainer that he was holding you mom. And I'm thinking, you might not have hated that so much?"

"That's none of your business."

"I think the guy likes you, mom."

"So how's school?" Darci searched for a way to steer away from this topic, not liking that out of control feeling skittering through her system.

"Mom." Leah's tone was serious, peppered liberally with reprimand.

"What?"

"I'm not finished."

"That's what I was afraid of."

"Tyler Landston is an attractive guy, mom. He's interesting, talented—"

"Hot and interesting." Darci recapped her daughter's view of their dinner guest. The same one she reminded herself that kissed you, not once, but twice now. And no, you didn't hate that very much either, she admitted mentally.

"Relationships have started on a lot less, mom."

"I'll keep that in mind." She grinned. It was more than a little odd to feel as though their roles had been reversed. "Well, I wouldn't go planning any weddings just yet." Darci didn't hide the comic sarcasm in her voice.

"Promise." Leah responded grabbing her mother's hand, giving it a squeeze. "Just one more thing."

Darci returned the squeeze. "What's that?"

"Uncle Peter does not like Mr. Landston."

So her daughter had picked up that as well. The tension created as the two men silently circled each other was part of the reason Darci couldn't sleep.

"I noticed that."

"What I can't figure out is why." Leah's question had already run through Darci's mind more than once that night. Unfortunately the only answer she could come with was one she didn't want to have to face.

Darci patted her daughter's leg. "Let's try to get some sleep and stop worrying about things tonight. More often, than not, these things work themselves out."

* * *

Tyler lay on the loveseat couch, his calves resting over it's curved arm. Being this close to the roaring fireplace had kept him warm, even as the temperature in the house dropped with the weather outside.

He slipped the comforter over his bare shoulder. His usual preference in sleeping attire consisted of a pair of long knit pants and nothing more. Tonight he'd stripped down to his jeans and socks and after performing more than a dozen pretzel-like contortions, finally ended up flopping on his back and hanging his legs over the sofa arm.

He stared at the fire unable to erase how Darci felt snuggled next to him. He'd known instinctively what she needed and his arms somehow felt incredibly "right" around her.

Tyler chuckled at how hokey the thought was—*"felt right?"* Tyler had never "felt right" with another woman in his entire life. Not like this.

His eyes grew dry as he gazed stupefied at the flames and he averted his face to blink moisture back into them. Remembering the sensation of Darci's tears soaking through the fabric, he also recalled the icy chill that remained when she backed away.

Perched on the coffee table was his cell phone and checking his watch, he picked up the phone.

Quietly clearing his throat, he listened as the phone rang.

"Hello?"

"Hey Jer."

"Hey man, how you doin'?"

"I'm okay, can I speak to Daphne?"

"Sure, hang on."

A moment clicked by and in the background Tyler could hear the sound of laughter. He grinned, some things never changed and somehow he found a measure of comfort in that.

"Tyler, my darling. How are you?"

She sounded as young as always, Tyler's grin stayed on his face thinking of how she was probably dressed in one of her outlandish sequined velour outfits.

"I'm okay. We're having an ice storm up here." He hesitated, "Would much rather be there right now, but I'm staying with a friend."

"Oh, I see. I hope its nothing dreadfully serious."

"Nah, its not terrible. I'm sacked out in front of a fireplace." He turned his attention to the fire picturing the bright yellow and orange neon lights of the Vegas strip.

"Not your usual sleeping arrangements, darling. Is she pretty?"

The woman had a penchant for wanting him to get married and settle down. He thought he'd tease her a bit. "Not as pretty as you." Tyler's grin waned as her raspy voice crackled over the line.

"Oh Tyler, you make me laugh. Listen darling, I've got guests this evening, and you know how that is. I really must scoot back to them. And listen Mr., we need to have a long chat you and I—very soon."

Tyler sat up, her request sending up a red flag in his mind. "You're okay? You need anything?"

"Tyler I'll call you tomorrow. I'm fine. You go now and enjoy that friend of yours. Love and kisses, darling."

"Love to you, too." Tyler spoke quietly into the phone.

* * *

His back pressed against the shadows of the hallway, Peter kept one eye on Darci's closed bedroom door as he listened to the one-sided conversation going on in the living room.

He knew his gut about Landston was right. From the first moment he saw the leather jacket and Hollywood bad boy good looks.

He edged back to his room, glad the call of nature had brought him into the hallway at just the right time. Then again, Peter smiled; maybe fate was giving him the break he needed to plead his case with Darci.

* * *

Tyler placed the phone on the table, his thoughts now troubled by his conversation with Daphne. He went back over the dialogue trying to remember hearing any signs of the disease affecting her voice. At least if her coughing was controlled, it meant she was taking her medication.

On occasion, she'd been known to hide it and say she took it, then when caught she would look at him, begging him with her adoring eyes to understand. She told him that she didn't like the goofy way it made her act.

Tyler teased her that she didn't need medication to act goofy and she would laugh, but always resigned to taking it.

He sat upright on the couch, resting his elbows on his knees. Clasping his hands, his memory wandered back in time, wishing the media had been more kind to her. He was young and resilient, but Daphne—Daphne didn't deserve the mud slinging created by the rumors and the too-eager media looking for a hot story.

If she didn't call tomorrow, he'd make sure to call her back and have that chat.

His gaze hung on the shadows dancing on the wall, and followed to the mantle heavily laden with framed photos. As he scanned the faces, he noted some with Darci alone, some with her children, some with Matt and the two kids. And it clicked with a quiet realization, that in all of those pictures—not one included old friend, Peter Beck.

His stomach growled and laying his hand over it, he stood and headed for the dark kitchen. Having had his dinner interrupted by the storm, he realized that he was hungry. From someplace in the back of the refrigerator, a small plastic bowl full of lime *Jell-O* called to him.

Chapter Fourteen

Darci lay awake, listening to Leah's gentle snoring. It was not a matter she would bring up later. Leah would deny it vehemently.

The occasional crack of a tree limb splintering in the still of the night kept Darci's nerves on edge. No more so, however, than the thought of Tyler Landston sleeping on her couch.

Darci raked her hand through her hair and sighed as she stared into the inky blackness. There had been tension between Tyler and Peter, she'd sensed it and even more so after she suggested Tyler spend the night. Peter had grown silent and sullen, eventually as Tyler indicated, gone to bed. She had no intention of hurting Peter or to appear ungrateful for all he'd done for their family, but she wasn't attracted to him in the way she was beginning to suspect he might be to her.

With Tyler's arms holding her earlier as she sobbed, she sensed the peace of being in another person's embrace. For so long, she'd been tending to the needs of others, while neglecting her own needs as a woman.

In his arms came unexpected emotions she'd thought long since forgotten, challenging her to take what she needed—if only for the moment.

Darci's throat went dry. A glass of wine might help since there could be no tea, without heating water.

Careful not to stir Leah's slumber, she slipped out of bed and pulled on her blue and white flannel robe in lieu of the rich, black velveteen robe that Leah had given her for her birthday. It was lovely and warm, and on occasion she'd worn it, but the style simply wasn't as comfortable and secure as her flannel robe.

She straightened the sash, tugging it at her waist before gently opening the door. If she did run into Tyler—and she assumed she wouldn't—she didn't want him to think that she was trying to—well, actively seek his attention.

Tiptoeing out into the hallway, she glanced at Peter's bedroom door and found it shut tight. Grateful, she pulled her door shut hoping he was as sound of a sleeper as Leah. Pausing a moment, she listened and relaxed, Peter's snoring was worse than Leah's

From the end of the hall, she could see the waning flicker of the fireplace, but from her vantage point she couldn't see if Tyler was sleeping. She crept to the back of the couch and peeked over the high back edge.

"Looking for someone?"

She whirled toward the low-timbered voice coming from the darkness of the kitchen.

He appeared sporting only a pair of jeans, white socks, and a wicked grin. As he leaned against the doorjamb, he crossed his arms over his bare chest.

Forcing her heart to slow, Darci fumbled with the tie on her robe, cinching it so tight she had trouble catching her breath.

She waltzed past him, pausing long enough for him to turn to the side and allow her through the narrow passage. She'd not commented on his question.

"I got hungry, I hope you don't mind."

His voice under most other circumstances over the past few days did not affect her in the same way as it did at this moment. She'd been laying in her room, trying to abandon her feelings to moments of whimsy and nothing more. Still, faced with them, here in the darkness, she was afraid to speak for fear her voice would reveal just how nervous she was.

"Um." The odd sound emitted from her throat and she licked her lips as she grappled for the cabinet door handles. What she really needed was a glass of water—or was it wine?

"I didn't have the chance to tell you earlier, but I'm a big fan of lime *Jell-o* and mandarin oranges."

She detected his grin as he spoke. "Is there any left?" She grabbed onto the conversation hoping it would lead then to ordinary, everyday conversation.

"I've got the bowl on the table—sorry, creature of habit. I guess I wasn't planning on any being left. How's that for the guest helping himself to the hostess' graciousness? Still, I would be happy to share."

She heard the gentle sound of the kitchen chair scoot quietly over the linoleum floor and she knew he had pulled out a chair for her.

Considering she had two options, one—to run hell bent for election back to her room and hide under the covers, or, two, sit down—she chose the least noisy of the two.

In the darkness, her other senses kicked into overtime, and as he passed behind her to his chair, she caught the scent of his cologne mixed with the warmth of his skin.

She shut her eyes, trying to regain her perspective on this situation.

"Here, you can use this, I swear I have no communicable diseases."

Her thoughts leapt immediately to the two heady kisses they'd shared. Thoughts of making an issue of not using his spoon seemed absurd. Thinking of that, she spoke, "Did the stain come out of your sweater?" She realized they hadn't spoken about the incident that had led them to the night on her front porch. She also realized the question sounded a bit out of left field, making her nervousness all the more obvious.

If he noticed, he was kind enough not to comment. "Yep, good as new and I understand your cousin let the guy sleep all through the night. Here, try this."

He picked up her hand and lifted it midair to meet where he held the spoon. "The handle is here—"

Her fingers searched for the handle and then she heard the gentle plop of the gelatin dropping to the table.

"You going to eat that?"

He chuckled, the sound warm and rich, just as she remembered it over the phone the first night she'd heard it. She grinned. How comfortable she was sitting here in the dark with him as she realized that neither had offered to light a candle.

"Let's try this again."

There was a brief pause, and then his fingertips gently touched her chin, drawing her face to his.

"Open your mouth."

Mesmerized, she did as she was instructed and the cool metal of the spoon slid over her dry lips. Tangy and sweet, the taste of lime burst on her tongue as juicy mandarin oranges squished between her teeth."

"Isn't that great?"

"Um...." She worked at swallowing the wiggly dessert, acutely aware that technically *Jell-O* should travel easier down one's throat.

"More?"

"Maybe one more, I'm watching my weight." A short giddy laugh emitted from her and his sexy chuckle joined in.

"Okay, open up for me."

She wanted to desperately.

Unprepared for how his simple statement would affect her, Darci's eyes flew open wide and she was glad he couldn't see the shock of surprise on her face. The *Jell-O* hit her closed lips and slipped down her chin.

Instinct pushed her hand under her chin, trying to save the disaster from reaching her lap. She wound up with part in her hand and part down the front of her robe.

She laughed quietly at the absurdity of the situation. She'd taken his ordinary statement and blown it clean out of proportion.

"I missed, didn't I? Damn, sorry about that. Where do you keep paper towels?" He started up from the table.

She grabbed his arm. "It's okay, I'll get it. It was my fault, I didn't open my mouth fast enough." Her voice was visibly nervous.

His fingers wrapped around her wrist, turning her palm to his mouth and his tongue relieved her of the gelatin in her hand. A lingering kiss to her palm left her breathless.

He tugged her slowly back into his lap and his hand cupped her chin. Darci stilled, her mind keen on what might come next.

"Let me help." His mouth touched the shallow crevice beneath her bottom lip, the tip of his tongue gently lining her lower lip, grazing the edge of her mouth.

Darci closed her eyes to the erotic sensation of his nibbling kisses along the curve of her jaw. He hadn't come close to her mouth and her lips tingled.

"You taste fabulous." His warm breath fanned across her cheek.

"Who knew that Lime *Jell-O* was an aphrodisiac?" she whispered.

"Want more?"

The query, she knew had nothing at all to do with *Jell-O* and she craved his offer more than anything else she could imagine at that moment. "Yes."

He took the bowl, holding it between them and dipped the spoon into the gelatin, scooping out a generous portion. Keeping his dark gaze to hers, he drew his teeth over half the serving and turned it to her.

Darci stared mesmerized trying to equate the tingling between her thighs to the gelatin being offered to her. She opened her mouth and he placed the spoon over her lips, drawing it with slow, sensual deliberation from her mouth.

"More?" His voice was but a whisper from her face. She could barely breathe. Ready to eat the whole bowl from his hands if he wanted her to.

He dipped his finger to the side of the dish, where the gelatin had turned to liquid. "It reminds me of you."

"*Jell-O*?" She barely got the word out.

"Sweet." His finger gently swept across her lower lip, followed by his mouth tasting after it.

"Just a little cool." He trailed the same finger down her throat just above the top of her gown and followed with the feather light touch of his tongue. "But refreshing. Tell me how much more you want, Darci"

His breath was hot against her skin and she giggled at how intoxicated she felt. "I'm suddenly very hungry." She held her palm to his warm cheek, hanging on to his gaze, hoping nothing would stop him.

He stood lifting her to sit on the table in front of him, gently parting her legs to stand between them. "This is not about *Jell-O*, Darci."

"I know." Her heart was about to climb through her chest.

He kissed her then, fully capturing her mouth as his hands plunged into her hair, holding her face to his.

* * *

It was something he dreamt of doing ever since he'd seen her in the lobby. Finding the passionate woman behind those amber colored eyes, having the freedom to explore the questions that had built up in his mind.

Cautiously, her hands perched at his waist, slid fully around him, drawing him against her, making them both fully aware of his arousal.

She turned her face to the side. "Tyler," she whispered, "what if someone wakes up?"

He grinned, smoothing his palms over the gentle curve of her shoulders. The thought of Peter Beck finding them in a passionate lip-lock gave him a certain amount of enjoyment. "Is Leah a light sleeper?" His fingers itched to tear off her robe, to touch the woman beneath.

"She snores, she sleeps so hard, but don't say that I told you."

"Your secret's safe with me." He tugged at her robe sash. "How could you breath with this so tight?"

"I didn't want you to think I was seducing you."

Tyler smiled as he parted the robe bending forward he nuzzled the warmth of her neck.

Tipping her head to accommodate his kisses, her sighs drove him on.

He lifted her hair, brushing the robe off one shoulder as his lips roamed over her soft, warm flesh. "You taste sweet, like lime *Jell-O*"

171

She grinned, her emotions tossed between giddy and desire every time his mouth touched her flesh. "That's because you slathered me with it."

He stopped, hovering over her with an evil grin. "What a fabulous thought."

His mouth found hers and he took his fill of what she was offering him.

Suddenly she sat up licking her properly ravaged lips, kicking in a fierce hunger inside him.

"What about Peter?"

"I'm not interested in a *ménage a' trois*, Darci." Her body responded to his exploration, pushing him lower, desiring to hear that catch in her breath again.

He tugged the lace strap of her gown down her arm until it caught at the crook of her elbow.

"Do you want Peter to find out?" Not that it mattered to him at the moment, nothing was going to interrupt what they had going, short of Darci herself.

"I don't care, just don't stop." She sighed as she curled her fingers in his hair.

He cupped her breast in his palm, pushing it from its confines revealing to his hungry mouth the sheer bliss of her hardened nipple.

Before he could sample her sweetness, her hands tugged at his shoulders until he stood facing her, both of them labored in their breathing.

"Do you want me to stop?" He knew his tone was not as gentle as perhaps it should have been with her, but he realized that he wanted to be buried deep in this woman—to feel her strength, her warmth, to give her the same in return.

Her answer came when she grabbed his face, kissing him with such ferocity that he had to grasp the edge of the table to keep from toppling over.

That was all the incentive he needed. He pressed her back flat against the table as they delighted in exploring each other. His fingers tugged fistfuls of her cotton gown, bunching it around her hips until he could feel her flesh against his. Hers traveled across his bare chest, kneading, seeking satisfaction—both for him and for her.

Tyler's brain raced with the danger of being caught and how they would explain, and at the same time, he wasn't sure if either of them could stop.

He brushed her robe apart seeking the warm, sweet flesh he knew awaited him. Reeling in a fierce desire to satiate what he wanted to do, he deliberately slowed his pace, determined to bring her as much pleasure as she was offering him. "Come here." He pulled her upright and his breath caught at the sight of her hair drooped over one eye and her gown dipped to reveal her beautiful body.

He needed to feel her against him, reaching out behind he found the chair and sat down drawing her straddled across his lap.

Cupping her in both his hands, he satisfied his burning need ravaging her mouth as he drew her pebbled nubs through his fingers, driving them both to the brink of oblivion. Unable to resist any longer his mouth followed suit, the scent of her skin and the taste of Lime *Jell-O* assaulting his senses.

She clung to his neck, bowing her body to accommodate him. "I breast fed both children."

Her statement lodged someplace in his brain, far removed from the bliss he was experiencing. He blurted out the first thing that entered his mind. "I'm jealous." His hands molded against the gentle curve of her back, sliding over her satin underwear. Urged by her soft sigh he continued his savory quest to remove all residue of where the gelatin had disappeared down the front of her gown.

"What I mean," she gasped, "is they aren't as perky as they used to be. Oh God—"

He grinned, purposely drawing her peaked bud gently through his teeth. Here he was about to burst from his jeans with desire and all she could do was apologize for not having perky breasts. In his experience, the variety he'd seen were of the synthetic means, she had no idea, what a turn on this was for him.

Sensing she needed more time to get used to a man again, he splayed his fingers over her backside, drawing her closer, hoping she could feel what she did to him.

"Do you have any idea, woman, how incredibly sexy you are?" He held her gaze, his hand gently brushing over the warm apex between her legs.

She kissed his mouth, gently brushing her body against his hand and then she dropped her forehead to his chin.

Tyler felt the first drop of wetness on his chest and he imagined it sizzling on contact. "Darci, honey. Look at me."

She did and he wrapped his arms around her, his gaze searching the darkness over her shoulder. "I'm going to say something here and I want you to tell me to back off if you don't want to talk about it." He stroked her hair, carnal desire still coursing through his blood, but greater still, the desire that she want this as much as him. What was more of a shock to him was that at that moment, he desperately wanted to know that it was *him*, and no conception of anyone else, that she wanted to be with.

She nodded as she pressed her cheek against his shoulder, its warmth giving him the courage to continue.

"Do you think Matt would want you to be happy?"

"Of course he would."

She'd answered that easy enough.

"And are you happy at this moment?" He gently pushed her from his chest, brushing the hair from her temple. As he waited, it occurred to him that in an odd twist, her answer was paramount to his own happiness.

"I'm happier than I've been in a long time, I'm afraid I'm just—just—afraid."

She sniffed.

"I understand, Darci. I do, and we can take things slower if you want." He kissed her softly, wiping the wet streaks on he cheeks from her recent tears. "I'm glad then. I have no regrets about this, I hope you don't."

Tyler pulled her close, slipping her gown strap back over her shoulder and carefully pulled her robe back in place. As much as he wanted her physically something foreign gnawed at his gut and he wasn't sure he had it in him to give her what she deserved. What she'd come to know from Matt. "I can't make you promises, Darci." He kissed her again, more reserved this time, but he could taste the remnant of lime on her lips.

Her arms snaked around his neck and in the span of a heartbeat her mouth, loving his in abandon, shook him to the core. The open trust she displayed intoxicated his senses—or what was left of them.

"I'm not looking for promises," she whispered capturing his mouth as she pulled his hand over her breast.

Had he been better prepared, he'd have taken her right there in the middle of the kitchen.

"Someone in here?" A bright beam of light followed the voice and Tyler stood, stepping quickly from Darci and turning to the counter as though he was searching for a glass. He turned on the faucet.

From the corner of his eye, he saw Darci clutch her robe shut as she reached beside her for the bowl of *Jell-O*—left on the table—what seemed like days ago.

"I couldn't sleep." Her voice was softly strained, laced with guilt.

Damn Peter Beck. The high-powered beam swung to light on Tyler and he half-turned, shielding the glare to his eyes with his arm. "Could you turn that thing away from my face?"

Immediately, the beam traveled to the ceiling casting the small kitchen in an eerie light. Peter stood blocking the only exit to the rest of the house. The alternative was the door to the backyard.

"I couldn't seem to either. I thought I heard a noise and well, I wasn't sure how sound of a sleeper you were, Landston." His tone was cold, deadly soft. "Apparently, I don't have to wonder about that."

Darci slipped quietly in to a nearby chair, hugging her robe around her. "Are you hungry, Peter? We were—just raiding the frig." Darci picked up the spoon and it slipped from her fingers as it clattered to the floor.

Anyone with half a brain could cut what was left of the sexual tension in the room with a butter knife. Tyler hoped Peter would be a gentleman and offer to go back to bed and not ask any questions.

Instead, he sat down across from Darci, balancing the light on end like a candlestick. "Actually, now that you mention it. Yes, I think I could go for some of that *Jell-O*." He grabbed the bowl, and then looked from Tyler to Darci. "Anyone have another spoon?"

Chapter Fifteen

It was deathly quiet. Darci eyes pulled open, the gray light of day piercing her vision as she struggled to see her alarm clock. Frowning, the memory of the storm and all that transpired in the wee hours of morning came rushing back to her in a flood. She swung her legs over the bed, realizing she was alone and blinked to clear her head as she searched for her clothes.

How she was going to face Tyler this morning was nothing compared to Peter. And what if Peter had already mentioned something to Leah?

Darci ruffled through her dresser, snagging a white turtleneck. She tugged off her gown, the material brushing over her sore nipples reminding her of Tyler's pleasuring. Her cheeks warmed and only then did she realize that the air was damp and cold still.

Slipping on her jeans, she finished dressing and quickly ran a pick through her hair hoping that the transformer would be fixed today and life could go on in a normal fashion—whatever that was for her at present.

Stepping into the quiet hallway, she felt a wave of warm air and realized that the core of the house stayed warm from the fireplace when the doors were shut. She treaded carefully down the hall, wondering if she was the only one awake. Peering over the back of the couch, she expected to see Tyler still dozing.

"They've gone out." Peter smiled at her as he looked up from the book in his hand.

Darci stepped back, for a moment her gut cautioning her about being alone with him, but realizing in the next instant that she was probably letting her imagination run away with her.

Peter sat up. "I've been keeping wood on the fire. It kicks out quite a bit of heat."

"Where did Tyler go and where's Leah?" Darci stepped to the patio doors, staring out at the brilliant glare of a gray light against the ice-covered trees. Brilliant, it seemed to her, considering she'd only dozed after finally retiring for the night. She'd left Tyler and Peter at the table discussing some inane topic that she knew Tyler brought up to sway the focus off of what Peter walked in on.

"Tyler decided to go check out the damage. Said something about wanting to get some pictures. I was not happy that Leah volunteered to go with him." Peter walked behind her, a cold chill swept around her in with his presence. She rubbed her arms to ward off the feeling.

"Why is that?" What Darci wouldn't give to put her hands around a warm cup of coffee.

"I found out some information on your boy that I think you might find interesting." Peter fished out a cold bagel from the sack left on the table presumably from an earlier breakfast. *Had Tyler and Leah had breakfast together?*

"Mr. Landston, Peter, is *not* my *boy*." She crossed her arms over her chest and sat down in the chair at her computer desk, averting her eyes from Peter's.

"That's not what it looked like to me, " he muttered under his breath as he raised the bagel to his mouth, tearing off a hunk.

Perturbed by his recent intrusion into her personal life and those of her children and more than a little embarrassed at being caught, she clenched her teeth and stared at the dark screen, wishing for a way to send him off the island without Leah.

Her mind shifting back to his statement she asked, "So, what's this information?" If he was going to be here, she wanted to steer away from the kitchen incident. She'd spent most of the night awake, her body humming from Tyler's touch. It still did.

"Well, it seems—" Peter sat in one of the wingback chairs near the fireplace and stretched out his long legs on the ottoman. He picked up a small yellow ledger pad on the arm of the chair and crossed his ankles appearing all too smug in his comfort.

Darci sensed what he had to say was designed to paint a bleak picture of Tyler. She waited with as much patience as her weary brain could muster.

"Have you ever heard of a man by the name of Antonio DeMarco?" Peter gave her a side-glance, and then held up the pad narrowing his gaze as though studying what he wrote. "Powerful man. Reputedly involved in a Vegas syndicate— gambling, extortion, and mob-related activities. A very wealthy man."

Though her stomach muscles tightened not wanting to hear anymore she had to know. "So what does this have to do with Ty—Mr. Landston?"

"It's seems Mr. DeMarco was Landston's former employer." Peter cast an uninterested look her way, "Apparently their personal photographer."

Darci held his gaze determined to believe that Tyler Landston had no secrets—none of illegal variety anyway.

"Former, you said?" She kept calm. If Peter were using this information to deface Tyler's reputation to his own advantage, she wouldn't allow it.

"Seems there's good reason he wouldn't have known Matt."

Darci considered whether to ask him to leave now or wait until he was finished.

"I'm sure that he and Matt didn't run in the same circles. Landston apparently has a record and did some time in juvenile detention."

"I knew he had a troubled past, Peter. People can change." Darci stood, hugging her arms as she walked past him to the patio doors. She leaned her forehead to the cool glass.

"Right, it's really not important, but here's something you may want to ask Mr. Landston about."

Would the man stop at nothing to gain her favor? She straightened her shoulders and stared at the brown vine-covered trellis in the backyard. Next year spring, it would be filled with bright purple clematis blooms.

"There was an accident a few years back. The media reported the case and of course with DeMarco's high profile there was speculation." Peter tossed the pad on the corner of the coffee table and walked to the fireplace. He bent down, using the poker to idly stir the burning embers. "That Tyler might have had something to do with the accident."

"That's absurd. He's not the type." Darci shivered; maybe she needed a sweater.

"Well, its just that allegedly Landston had been keeping company with Demarco's widow, Daphne DeMarco these past three years." He placed the fireplace utensil in its holder and tucked his hands in his front pockets of his slacks. His gaze stayed on the fire as he spoke. "The rumor was she was keeping him—in exchange—" He looked at her with an arched brow. "For being her companion."

The blood drained from Darci's face, her fingers pinching the flesh of her upper arms.

"Why—" Darci had difficulty getting past the constriction in her throat. "What would make him leave all that?" She hesitated as she considered a very real alternative. "Or has he left? Peter where did you get this information and how do you know its reputable?"

Peter shrugged. "She apparently pulled some strings to get him in with his current employer."

Peter rested his elbow on the mantle as he looked at Darci. "Maybe he's run out of money and somehow is choosing to play on a widow's fragile emotions?"

"Oh Peter, please. This is really going too far—" Her hand sliced through the air as if negating everything she'd just heard as improbable and untrue. She would've been able to tell if what had happened between them wasn't real. Wouldn't she?

"Besides, why would he need my money? I'm sure he makes a descent living." She didn't want for Peter to be right in any of this.

"Look Darci, you know—"

She felt his presence close behind her, even before his fingers closed over her shoulders.

Gently he kneaded the tight muscles under his fingertips. "You know that I would never do or say anything to purposely upset you, but as a friend and as your consultant regarding your future investments, I feel you need to have all the facts to make sound and rational choices."

Heat radiated from his body, still warm from the fireplace. "A woman who has been through one of the most traumatic episodes of her life can be very vulnerable. And while I hate to say it, honey, there *are* men out there that would take advantage of that."

But that doesn't include you, does it? Darci kept her body slightly forward so as not to rest against Peter.

"I just want you to be careful. I don't want you to get hurt."

His face appeared intimately close over her shoulder, close enough she could feel the breath on her cheek. His hand touched her jaw, turning her face to meet his gaze. "You believe that about me, don't you, Darci?" His gaze darkened, dropping briefly to her mouth.

The front door slammed behind them.

"Hi—Mom." Leah stopped mid-sentence and her brows rose under her pink and orange striped stocking hat.

Behind her, Tyler stood perfectly still, his cheeks a blaze of red from the frigid temperatures outside. If he had questions—his eyes, as cold as they were dark—did not reveal them.

Peter took a step back and tucked his hands in his pockets, glancing to the ground with a bashful stance. As though the tables had been turned and they'd been caught. She wanted to kick him in the shin.

"We were just talking." It sounded completely ludicrous

given what they'd walked in on, but still she needed to say it.

"Thanks for walking with me, Leah. It was great to meet you. Good luck at school."

Tyler showed no hint of any concern about what the situation implied. Darci wasn't sure what to make of that.

In a gesture, much more bold than she'd expected, Tyler approached Peter and stuck out his hand. "Nice to meet you, Beck. Have a safe trip home." His gaze stayed on Peter, not once looking at Darci.

Peter laughed in a good-natured way. "Am I leaving?" He glanced at Darci.

"Just in case I don't see you before you go." He nodded and pushed his glasses up the bridge of his nose.

"Tyler—" Darci took a step, but Tyler was already halfway to the front door.

He spoke over his shoulder. "Thank you for dinner, Darci and for the use of your couch. I need to go check out my rental and see if the power's on yet."

"Tyler—" she repeated his name, but too late as the door snapped shut with a firm resolve in his wake.

A heavy silence followed as Darci stared at the door, her thoughts grappling with the last tumultuous twenty-four hours of her life.

* * *

"Dammit." Tyler lost his footing twice on the ice-covered sidewalk, grabbing the fence before he could plummet to the ground. There'd been numerous other occasions in his life when he'd been fooled by a woman's wiles, but he thought she was different.

He shifted his camera bag and tugged his gloves over his hands as he headed down the block to his own place. Hell, he couldn't even call that *home.*

The island was eerily quite for midday. The sky, gray and filling with dark clouds gave warning of more bad weather on the way. By evening, there was the real possibility they'd have more of that god-forsaken ice. Perfect.

He thought of Darci's home, the warmth of the fireplace

and the touches that made even a stranger feel welcome. He guessed at this point that was the category he fit best into.

"This is stupid," Tyler muttered, a quiet reprimand. It had completely thrown him off to walk in on them, as they were about to kiss—not that she couldn't bloody well kiss anyone she wanted as far as he was concerned.

He wrestled with the front door lock, iced over from exposure and shoved open the door, letting it bang against the wall as he strode inside.

The more he tried to brush off his frustration the worse he felt about it. "She said she wasn't looking for promises and you told her you couldn't give her any." He spoke through clenched teeth as he peeled off his coat and slung it across the room. Only then aware that he could see his breath. *Damn island.*

His cell phone rang from somewhere nearby and he realized that it was still in the pocket of his parka.

He scrambled over the sofa and retrieving his coat, snatched the phone from the depths of his pocket.

"Hello?" Part of him hoped it might be Darci; then again, they hadn't gotten far enough yet for him to give her his cell number.

"Tyler?"

Her voice was weak, maybe only bad connection. He shifted the phone to his other ear. "Daphne? I can barely hear you, sweetheart. Can you speak up, we have a weak connection."

The line crackled and her voice cut in. "This damn medicine they give me has me so doped up at times I sound like I'm on a three day drunk without the fun." Her weak laughter echoed on the line.

Tyler smiled, but concern prickled his intuition. "Is everything okay, Daph?"

"Well sure honey, if you consider what the years of chain smoking and hosting parties does to a body." She laughed again, ending it in a coughing fit—one he recognized immediately.

There was something she wasn't sharing with him. Over

the years he'd become her confidant. She and her late husband, Antonio DeMarco had taken in a struggling college kid a long time ago estranged from his true family, and filled with dreams of seeing the world through his camera lens.

Her silence spoke to him what he feared—Daphne's emphysema was finally catching up to her.

"You aren't smoking, you promised me." His voice was tender as he remembered how she'd already lost so much weight and looked so frail last time he'd seen her. Her addiction had whittled much of her body away, but gratefully, not her spunk.

"Nope." She breathed in deep and he knew she was getting a hit off her oxygen tank.

"You sounded so much better last night, I hoped—" *God, why did things like this have to happen?*

He'd made the promise to Antonio during what became his tenure as the DeMarco's private photographer that should anything happen to him, he would keep an eye on Daphne and make sure she took care of herself. That was in the early stages of the disease.

Two years later, when a suspicious car accident claimed the famous Vegas business tycoon, rumors and accusations spread like wild fire. Though the ruling of the investigation rendered that it was an accident, much damage had already begun to tarnish Tyler's reputation. And that was too much for Daphne to live with. So she got him the interview, and lovingly, sent him packing.

"It was always tough to get anything past you." Her voice softened. "Even your thirty-fifth birthday when I spent weeks planning for that Vegas showgirl to pop out of your cake— what are you doing, but standing at the table with a bottle of champagne and a can of whipped cream."

Tyler chuckled, a lump forming in his throat. Daphne was one of that rare bread of women, left in this world. Fiercely, loyal to Antonio, she was the soft strength in his life, but she loved life and rarely missed the chance to live it.

"That was a great birthday." Tyler remembered the

shocked look on Daphne's face when he grabbed the woman and slung her over his shoulder, yelling as he left that he was having his cake alone.

"Yes it was. We've had a few good times, haven't we, hon?"

She coughed heavily into the phone and though she pulled the phone away, he could tell the episodes were getting worse.

"Look, enough about this. If my guess is right, you probably have that friend of yours waiting for you." She sighed. "Dammit, I hate to interrupt."

"You haven't—" Tyler sighed. "Daphne, what can I do for you?"

"I need you to come home for a few days. There are some loose ends I need to tie up and they simply cannot be done over the phone."

Home. The thought struck him that in many ways the DeMarco's had given him all the benefits of being a son. He also knew she would never ask him to leave his work unless it was vital.

"I'll leave as soon as I'm able. It may take me a couple of days, but as soon as I can get a flight. Will that—" he started to say, "be enough time," but cut himself off to reword his sentence," work for you?"

"That will work fine, darling. It will wonderful to see you. Be a dear and bring me some pictures?"

Tyler nodded uttering a "yeah" through the lump in his throat. He swiped at the tears welled in his eyes. Sometimes life could be a real bitch.

"I will. You take care of that cough and don't give the doctors a bad time."

"Only the cute ones."

Tyler grinned, knowing that even now, Daphne's heart was steadfast to Antonio's memory. "Is Jer around?"

"You miss that big brute? Oh fine, he'll mope around here an hour after he talks to you and be totally useless to me, don't fill his head with any ideas." Her voice grew soft. "I'll see you soon."

He said something then he could only remember ever saying to his mother the last time they spoke, for what little good it did. "I love you."

Tyler heard a sniff. "You crazy kid, hurry and get your butt out here. This old lady misses you."

It was more than his mother had said and he knew it was Daphne's way of telling him she loved him, too.

A new voice, much deeper and gruff came on the line. "Ty?"

The three hundred pound bodyguard had eventually become the brother Tyler never really had.

"How is she?" Tyler knew he wouldn't candy-coat matters.

"Not good, not good at all, buddy. You comin' soon?"

"Dammit." Tyler gritted his teeth, his eyes stinging.

"Yeah, I know, man. See you soon, right?"

"I'll be there." The line went dead and Tyler dropped the phone on the dining room table.

There'd been at one point, just after their picnic tour of the island, the fleeting thought that Darci would have really liked Daphne. Now it looked like Providence was about to change all of that—snatching from him, the two women that had ever meant anything to him.

Chapter Sixteen

Tyler studied the thermostat, turning the dial up to eighty in hopes that the heater would simply kick on. Hesitating, listening for some telltale sign that he would be able to stay in his own bed tonight, Tyler tapped his fingers to the wall, then flipped off the automatic heat and headed with a flashlight to the basement to find the circuit box. With any luck, maybe a blown transmitter just tripped the circuit breaker. And if that didn't work, there was always hope that by noon, they'd have the transmitter fixed. Then again, luck hadn't been a real pal to him so far today.

He stepped gingerly down the steep wooden steps to the cement floor below. The dark, musty scent assaulted him as did the intense chill and he shivered hoping that no north woods creatures had managed to get in from the cold.

Searching the wall, he found the box and his mouth dropped open at what the flashlight revealed. "What kind of idiot puts a lock on a circuit box?" He closed his eyes and tore off his glasses. *Could this day get any worse?*

"The kind that go away for the entire winter."

He turned toward the voice coming down the dark stairwell and wished like hell she hadn't come. His gut tightened not knowing what to expect from her, much less what to expect from him.

"They must have forgotten to take it off before they left. Mine was the same way when I first moved in."

She walked slowly toward him and his breathing hitched. Nothing more than the cold, no doubt.

"If you let me borrow that a second, I'll see if they left the key in the same spot as mine."

He chose not to respond for fear of what might come out of his mouth. There were a great many questions and some of them frustrating as they performed on the merry-go-round of his mind. He handed her the flashlight and stepped aside.

"I wanted to be sure your heat was on." She moved closer to the wall, aiming the beam of light upwards scanning the floor rafters just above the breaker box.

A sarcastic smile played on his lips. Had she asked him that question last night, he'd have answered without question, yes, his heat had been turned on. Not that it mattered now. Maybe in a way, she was doing him a favor, really. This way he wouldn't become involved in a potentially sticky situation that he'd just have to sever in a couple of months.

Besides, Peter was probably better for Darci, if he could get over the domineering attitude. Still, he had the whole package—close to her kids, financial advisor, even his pushy behavior could be loosely construed as concern for her, and her family.

"Here it is, just like mine." She turned, dangling the key from a piece of grosgrain ribbon discolored with time. She held out the key. "I'll hold the flashlight if you like."

He nodded his agreement and after unlocking the small metal door, he methodically flipped through each switch, pausing at each one, hoping to hear some sign of normalcy in the house's response.

Much to his dismay, however in complete accordance to how his life was going lately—nothing worked.

"Well, it looks like I'll need to find a room." He dropped the key over the edge of the breaker box, his grin felt as shallow as the rest of him.

"You know you're welcome." She hesitated briefly. "To stay at my house. I at least have the fireplace."

"Is *he* going to be there?" It shouldn't have popped out like that, but Tyler's every nerve felt precariously close to the surface of his skin.

The light bounced back from the low ceiling above them, casting Darci's expression in a hazy light. He watched the slim column of her throat swallow before she answered. "Nothing happened."

He gave a short laugh. "I think that even Uncle Peter knows better than to maul you in front of your daughter."

"He wasn't mauling me." The tone in her voice was clearly defensive and it irked his frustration all the more.

Tyler raised his hand as he nodded. "A simple difference in definitions as far as I can see."

"Then you don't see very far." She whirled toward the stairs taking the flashlight with her.

He stepped forward and grabbed her coat sleeve, spinning her to face him. The flashlight clattered to the floor, immersing them in darkness save the swatch of daylight at the top of the stairs.

"What do you mean, I can't see very far. I have eyes, Darci and what was going on between you two doesn't take a rocket scientist to figure out." His confusion riddled him with questions, the greatest being why he should be jealous?

"Hey, but you said you weren't looking for promises. I just didn't think that what you were looking to be played by a guy like Peter Beck?"

"Played?—Played?" Her tone was as cold as the cement walls surrounding them. "Here I thought I was coming over here to see how *you* were doing. Afraid you'd misconstrued what you'd walked in on. Afraid of what *you* might think. You know, why do *you* even care?"

"I thought you came to check my heat." He'd caught her there, though it did nothing to erase the memory of Peter's face that close to hers.

An icy silence fell between them, giving a moment to diffuse his angry thoughts, making him realize the validity of her question—why did he care?

Then Darci spoke, "Do you think that what happened last night meant so little to me? Do you think I just fall into the arms of the nearest man available?"

Tyler's lips pursed as he lowered his gaze to the dark as pitch floor.

"Do you think that it was so easy for me to open myself to another person as a woman again?"

His brow furrowed, perhaps it was true that he'd manufactured more of the situation than was there. That still gave him no claim her. They'd both made it perfectly clear to each other, that they were not interested in the long term.

"You 're right, Darci. Why should I care?" Tyler stood with his hands clamped to his sides. He could hear the gentle rhythm of her breathing in the stillness.

Whether it was the need to finish what he'd started, or to prove to himself she'd always choose him over someone like Peter Beck, or hell, maybe for the simple release of the tension pent up inside him—all he knew is he wanted her.

"You have no reason to care. You have your solitary life and you're happy with it. I've just begun to live a solitary life and I'm still trying to figure out if it's too much of a risk to be happy again."

Tyler rubbed a hand over his forehead, his gut churning in a mix of desire and frustration. "What do you want from me, Darci?" He sighed.

"I want you to kiss me."

* * *

If what Peter had told her was true, Darci was more than a fool, or she was blatantly playing with fire.

"I don't think you know what you want."

Darci sensed his presence as he stepped toward her. He was right, she wasn't at all sure what she wanted, or that what she wanted was wise, prudent, acceptable behavior. She had no reason to give him explanations, but she wanted him to understand. Even if it meant nothing to him, she wanted him to know. "Tyler, what you saw wasn't what it appeared. Peter was—" Maybe deep down she *was* looking for more.

"So he wasn't going to kiss you."

He hadn't touched her yet every nerve in her body crackled at his proximity. Her mind spun with answers and questions, logic and reason, fear of wanting him, and fear that he didn't want her back. "I didn't want *him* to kiss me."

There was nothing gentle in his embrace as he closed the gap between them. His hand grabbed her chin holding her face up as his mouth connected with a fierce hunger to hers.

Darci knew what was happening would not last forever, but what had that notion taught her? Perhaps it was better to take your moments of happiness and pleasure—no matter how fleeting—when you had the chance.

Her hands clutching for equilibrium, grabbed fists of his sweater, as his mouth shifted over hers, tasting, plunging, taking with abandon what she offered to him.

"Too many clothes—" He worked at her coat, ripping down the zipper and pushed his hands inside, encircling her waist.

His kisses, frantic, yet passionate trailed her jaw as he cupped her bottom pulling her flush with his body. "See what you do to me, Darci." His strangled whisper sizzled against her neck.

She wanted more, unable and not wanting to stop the desire that raced like a runaway train inside her. She slid her hands beneath his sweater, his warm smooth flesh sparking to mind how he looked in the kitchen last night—all tousled and sexy.

"Darci, I could do this right here, but its not going to be like this." He grabbed her hand and stumbled once trying to find his way to the stairs. Catching himself, he chuckled as he brought her around ahead of him and backed her to the wall.

She was out of control as his mouth ground down on hers and she clamped her arms around his neck, abandoning herself to the chaos.

Tugging her to the top of the stairs, Tyler pulled her into the shadowed hallway, shucking her coat over her shoulders and tugging his own sweater over his head. His hands touched the hem of her sweater, his brief gaze offering her one last chance of escape, before they went any further.

Darci could see the puffs of cold air in their labored breathing, but her body did not feel the chill in the heatless house. She raised her arms, closing her eyes as his kisses, beginning at her navel, left a path of fire to the valley between her breasts. He held her hands still encased in the sweater over her head as he pleasured them both, teasing her with his teeth through the sheer lace of her bra.

Everything she'd accepted as ordinary, as mundane, he magically turned to erotic and sensual. Her body delighted at his every touch, celebrated every sensation that he was making her feel. God, just to *feel* again was exhilarating.

She was only marginally aware of their clothes being discarded as he steered her towards the bedroom, a shoe being pried from her foot, her jeans landing atop his dresser, her mind a slave to every sense, except logic.

His bed was unmade; the sheets askew as if he'd just climbed out of them and the thought of her reckless behavior gave her a thrilling shiver. Like the quivering ascension to the top of a roller coasters crest, her heart pounded against her chest in anticipation.

He backed her to the bed, her knees buckling as she fell with him to the crumpled sheets.

"I want to take my time, but I swear, Darci, I want to be inside you. It's like I've waited forever for this. God, how weird is that?"

She touched his face, amazed at his open admission.

"You did lock the front door?" Propped on his side, he worked down her plain cotton panties around her hips, his heated gaze causing her to believe she 'd been dressed in the sexiest thing that *Victoria's Secret* had to offer.

"I did." She swallowed, dropping her gaze to his hand sliding up over her hip, dipping with measured slowness to the warmth between her legs.

Instinctively she turned toward him, capturing his mouth as his fingers gently coaxed, inviting her to forget her fears, the pain of her past, and give over to sensual pleasure. Tears formed at the corner of her eyes, squeezed shut as she set herself free from the abstinence of feeling.

He kissed her, delving into her mouth as she gently bucked against him, her need for more driving her over the edge. A soft gasp caught in her throat, cut off by his mouth moaning against hers.

"I'll be right back." Tyler kissed her gently before edging off the bed. He yanked open his nightstand with one hand as he pushed out of his jeans with the other.

Rolling to her back, Darci's heart stopped as he sheathed himself, glancing at her in the process. He smiled folding his glasses, placing them carefully on the nightstand.

There'd never been anyone but Matt in her life, at least to this degree of intimacy. She was grateful for the protection he offered her. As she raised her arms to welcome him, she held his gaze—afraid to close her eyes for fear she would picture Matt and yet at the same time petrified that she wouldn't.

"Honey, relax." Tyler's gentle voice broke through as he brushed the hair from her forehead, as though he could detect her unease. "You look terrified."

"I want to, it's—" She swallowed, searching for how to explain what was going on inside her. Tears pricked at the back of her eyes.

"If you're not ready—"

Tyler pushed away, bracing himself above her and a frigid rush of cold air sandwiched between them.

"No, it's not that." She cupped his face, timid suddenly with touching another man's face—*wanting* another man with such fierce desire. It was something she never anticipated happening to her again. His eyes were gentle, filled with intense desire—and it was for *her*.

He turned her hand and softly kissed her palm. "I'm not Matt."

She nodded and tears leaked from her eyes, spilling past her temples as she forced a smile. It was the greatest fear she'd come face to face with—that and the fact that she knew she was not the type to give her heart, or her body to just any man. Despite what Peter had told her, despite Tyler's profession of being a wandering bachelor, Darci realized that somewhere along the way, she'd started to fall in love with him.

Darci reached for him then, wanting to share this moment

in time. "I think this works better if you're a little closer." She tugged his face to hers and his body covered hers with its delicious warmth.

"You feel wonderful," he whispered against her mouth, trailing slow kisses over her jaw, near her ear. "Are you sure about this?"

Her fears ebbed with the flow of their passion and she gently rolled her palms over his shoulders, relishing his sinewy strength. Her body thrummed acutely aware, of how magnificently his body meshed with hers. "I'm sure."

He kissed her softly, conveying to her that he understood.

All else was lost as her body responded to his. The ancient pitch and roll of rapturous sensation washed over emotions that she'd not allowed to touch her since her last afternoon with Matt.

"Darci, look at me," Tyler's voice whispered; his voice muffled by the escalating roar in her mind.

She opened her eyes and was captured by his gaze—dark and determined as the strength she felt coursing through his body.

Out of control as an untamed stormy sea, waves of ecstasy slammed through her body as she cupped his face in her hands—afraid to let go—afraid if she did, he too, would disappear from her arms. "Don't let go," she whispered through the desperate dryness in her throat

He buried his face in the curve of her neck as his body surged against hers in quest of his own release. "I'm here, Darci. I'm here, sweetheart."

* * *

Peter stamped the icy slush from his shoes, his thoughts disturbed greatly by his recent walk. He'd accompanied Leah to the hotel where she said she wanted to see if Maevey needed help in case staff couldn't get to work. He'd gone ahead and had a sandwich though his stomach churned with the idea that Darci had gone to check on Tyler.

That was well over an hour or better. He'd considered knocking on Landston's door on his way back to Darci's, was even standing at the door with his fist raised, when he heard a woman's voice inside—a woman in the throes of pleasure.

Maybe it was wrong, but he'd wanted to break down the door and rescue her from the man she was giving herself to. Someone who couldn't love her, as he did, who had no background with her, wasn't there when her kids were born, at backyard barbeques, or at Nathan's First Communion.

Instead, he clenched his fists and moved closer to the window at the side of the house where the sounds grew clearer. Unable to tear himself away, his heart constricted as he listened to the sound of Darci's quiet moans. It should be *him* in there with her—*him*—bringing her body to a height of ecstasy—*with his.*

He leaned his forehead to the frigid vinyl siding, his stomach nauseous and he thought for a moment he would throw up. Rubbing his thigh, he fought for control of the thoughts of passion and hate swirling in his mind. Confusion licked at his groin as he thought of her beneath him, her sweet body hitching to meet his thrusts, her hands clutching his buttocks as she came to him.

He stuffed his leather-covered hand in his mouth and shuddered as the image in his mind matched what he was doing to his body. Slumping against the house, he gasped for air as he stared at the hedge surrounding the house. He blinked, wanting to cry out in frustration. How long before she realized that he was the best thing that had ever happened to her? With Matt gone, it opened a window of hope that she would finally see *him*—instead of someone that was Matt's second hand man. No longer would he have to be slated as the best friend, but as the viable man that had watched out for her, sacrificed for her, and quietly desired her all these years. When would his unrequited affections be returned?

Turning off his emotions, as he'd become a master of, he adjusted his pants and stepped away from the house, quietly watching to be sure he was not seen as he hurried up the sidewalk.

Peter threw his gloves on the couch, inspecting the angry

red marks on the tender flesh of his hand, shaking it in the air, wishing he had a drink. Removed now from the situation, he was able to think more clearly and as he prepared to change his stained clothes, he decided he could let her have her little fling. Landston would be moving on eventually, he wasn't the stay around type—maybe he should be grateful that he'd resurrected Darci's sexual appetite. It would make it that much easier for him, once he found the opportunity to be alone with her.

Peter smiled as he wadded his pants up and stuffed them in the bottom of his suitcase. He glanced at his reflection in the dresser mirror, nude except for his red silk underwear. He flexed his arm and grinned at himself. "You won't be able to resist me for long, darlin'."

Chapter Seventeen

Tyler awoke with a start, blinking as he realized that Darci slept peacefully in the crook of his arm. Her body snuggled to his took his memory back to a few...minutes? Hours? How long had they dozed under the warmth of the down comforter? Stretching his free arm to the nightstand, he picked up his watch and saw that it was nearly four in the afternoon.

"What time is it?" She whispered with grogginess, her warm breath wafting across his bare flesh.

He pulled in his arm and turned to her, tucking her fully into his embrace. Somewhere inside, it occurred to him that he'd waited his entire life for this moment. Given time, there was hope that she would want him for more than just her pleasure. Until then, he'd give her that, if that was what she needed.

"It's almost four." He held her maybe a little tighter afraid she would bolt out of bed, but thankfully, she didn't.

"I suppose Leah will be wondering about me." Her fingers touched his mouth trailing down his flesh, splaying her palm against his chest.

"What about Peter?" He hadn't really wanted to ask, but his curiosity won out.

"What about him?"

Her gaze lifted to his and he was lost.

"I forgot how wonderful making love was. Thank you for reminding me." She smiled as she raked her fingers through the hair at his temple.

"Give me a few minutes and I'll make sure you won't forget." He grinned, but it dissolved as he watched her face

197

pale. "Darci, sweetheart, are you okay? What is it?"

She closed her eyes as if erasing whatever thought had popped into her head. "I'm all right."

Her fingertips touched his mouth. "You have a sexy mouth."

She grinned again, her eyes bright, and he knew she was fighting off her private demons. God help him, he wanted to make her forget every man she'd ever known, even her dear husband, but he couldn't tell her that, not now, and maybe not ever. The thought of committing again, of sacrificing her heart to love again, was one of her greatest fears. She wasn't the type to jump between the sheets with anyone, and that knowledge, though private for now was incentive to be patient. He'd give her time to realize that that she needn't be afraid of losing him.

Tyler chose to find another means of convey his intentions. "You know, one of these days, I'd love to take some photos of you."

Her leg slid over his thigh as she pushed her body from the mattress. "Really? My mother warned me about guys like you."

Enjoying the change of attitude to playful, Tyler went along, his heart tripping that this woman wanted him as much as he wanted her. "She steered you away from dating photographers?" He grinned as she climbed on top of him. "It was that damn rumor about long lenses, wasn't it?"

Bracing her palms to his chest, she smiled easing down over him, her fingers flexing like a contented feline. "I think there may be some truth to that rumor."

His body moving inside her felt so natural, like they'd been together for years, knowing what to give and take in their love-making.

A quiet moan emitted from her throat as her heat contracted around him. His fingers dug into soft the flesh of her thighs as the heat, coiled tight in his gut, threatened to set him on fire. He held her amber gaze unable prevent his heart from wanting to claim this woman as his own—and then he realized hadn't used any protection.

"Oh God, Darci. We can't—" He lifted her as he twisted sideways on the mattress, releasing their union. Her shocked expression faced his.

"Tyler?"

"No protection." He squeezed his eyes shut. *Dammit.*

"There's more then, right?" She flipped to her other side, and he heard the drawer open, but he already knew the answer.

"I only had three, I'm sorry, Darci." He sat up running his hand through his hair and over the back of his neck.

Tyler opened his eyes and caught sight of his erection standing as proud as the Washington monument—the unfortunate prerogative of a photographer's vivid imagination.

"You understand, don't you that I was protecting you. I should have stopped you earlier, but I wasn't thinking."

"Three? Did we use three already?"

Visibly dazed, she pushed upright beside him and brushed her hair over her shoulder. "Okay, well, okay—yes, I—uh, appreciate that, really. Its not like I need to take any chances with getting pregnant at my age, right?" She laughed nervously.

At that point, Tyler mentally bludgeoned himself, vowing to keep a case on hand from now on. His only hope now that he'd ever need them with her again.

She glanced at his engorgement as if speculating how they could get back the ambiance of the moment, but Tyler knew it was lost—at least for now.

"It's okay, you know, maybe it's a sign. I need to get home and break it to Peter and Leah that you'll be staying with us until your power is back on." She eased off the bed, searching for her clothes strewn carelessly around the room.

Break it to them? Hell, he probably deserved that remark after what he'd just done. Tyler sat up, bracing on one hand as he watched her collect each item, hurriedly slipping them on.

She'd grown quiet as she methodically gathered her clothes, even though she smiled when she caught his eye.

"So?" She slipped her sweater over her head. "I'll see you

later at the house?"

Had he forgotten to tell her he was leaving for a few days?

"Uh...I might have forgotten to mention something." He slid the sheet over his lap, already his faux pas made too public.

"You forgot you had a wife?" She snapped her jeans and stepped into her chukka boots.

"Me?" He chuckled. "No, not me."

"Odd notion."

"Right. Right—" Tyler scratched the back of his neck, noting the monument to his sexual prowess now resembled the Leaning Tower of Pisa.

"What then?" She seemed preoccupied with twisting her hair into the clip she so often wore. The same one that made the springy tendrils of hair bounce against her sweet neck.

She glanced up and held his gaze.

"I have to leave for a few days."

Something he couldn't discern flashed briefly in her gorgeous, and totally readable eyes.

"I, uh, have to fly to Vegas—on business." For all intents and purposes, it was the truth. He planned on settling business matters with Daphne and getting back here as fast as he could to see about building on the foundation they'd recently started.

"Vegas?"

Her face showed nothing more than a pleasant expression, but he sensed something was definitely wrong. Perhaps she thought he wasn't coming back?

"Darci, honey, I'll be back."

She nodded as she shrugged into her jacket and tugged a stocking hat over her ears. "Well, then." She spread her arms out to her sides, and let them drop against her hips. "*You* have a great trip."

He sensed strongly she didn't really mean that.

An overly happy smile was plastered on her face as she tossed her muffler around her neck and stormed out the door.

Leaving him alone and wondering what had just transpired between them.

* * *

Leah turned as Darci slammed the front door.

"I was getting ready to walk down and see if you got lost." Her smile revealed that she was teasing her mother about the length of time she'd been gone.

"Mr. Landston has no heat."

Peter leaned forward from his spot in the chair beside the fireplace. "Shall we set up the couch again?" He didn't look at her, but Darci wondered if he could hear her anger. It killed her to think that Peter might have been right. Probably was, given Tyler's blatant admission that he had "*business*" in Vegas.

"No, Mr. Landston has to go away for a few days, he won't be needing the heat in his house."

Peter stood then, glancing at Leah as he picked up the picture of Matt and Darci and the kids. "Has to go away on business?"

Darci hung her coat and scarf on the hall tree. She glanced at the reflection in the small mirror, and saw Peter watching her closely, waiting for her reply.

"Yes, Peter. He has to go to Vegas on business." There she'd said it and it was done. Peter could declare himself winner in whatever macho-driven charade he'd been displaying for her and her family.

"Will he be coming for dinner?" Leah's tone was more hopeful than the expression on her face.

Darci straightened her sweater. "No, he won't. Now I think I need a glass of that wine."

Peter bowed slightly and headed to the kitchen. "Your wish is my command."

Leah's gaze followed Peter until he was out of sight, and then she turned to Darci. "He's broken up," she whispered, an evil grin on her face. It quickly dissolved as she walked over and enveloped Darci in a warm hug.

"You okay?"

Darci hugged her daughter tight, finding comfort and strength in their embrace. She would not cry. "I've been through worse."

"I am woman, hear me roar, eh?" Leah pulled back, still holding her at arms length.

Darci sighed. "Close enough."

"Wine for everyone?"

Peter returned with a tray and three glasses, his smile just a little too polished, a little too much on the giddy side for Darci. Still, she accepted his hospitality graciously.

"To family."

Peter raised his glass. "I'll drink to that."

* * *

Darci returned to work at the hotel the next day after seeing Peter and Leah off at the dock. There'd been several phone messages left on her new answering machine that Peter and Leah brought as a "house warming " gift. Collectively, they'd decided to ignore them, much to Peter's unmitigated joy and Leah's apprehensive looks.

Most were from Tyler, asking to speak with her before he left on a red-eye commuter flight from the island airport. Around ten that night, the messages stopped and Darci dressed for bed toying with the idea of just going down there and facing him straight on and ask him about the woman in Vegas. She knew though, that she could be tempted to stay with him, that he could tell her whatever he wanted to lure her once again into his bed and she couldn't risk that. This time if she was going to lose someone, it would be on her terms and not theirs

Two days later, as she brought in more wood for the fire, a knock sounded on the door. Peeking through the curtained window, she saw Abe Fiskas and his horse drawn dray stationed outside of her house.

"Hi Abe," she commented as she opened the door and peered towards the street. "What's this?" Darci searched her memory—the electricity had been restored yet she hadn't gotten around to calling Abe about her furnace yet. How did he know?

"Heard you had some furnace problems." He nodded his head toward the street. "A lot of this places need updated furnaces now with all them fancy rules and regulations they got slapped on homeowners these days."

"So, you're just out scouting the neighborhood to see who needs one?" She grinned and leaned against the doorframe.

Abe's raspy cackle of a laugh followed as he spit a wad of chew into her would-be rose bushes.

Darci cringed, but tried not to let her face show it as he turned back to her.

She chocked it up as a habit from his early days on the Lakes.

"That young fella, the one with the camera. He said you needed one of these."

"He did, huh?" She folded her arms debating whether to tell Abe he made a mistake, or go ahead and accept Abe's help since he was here. Heaven knows when she'd get back to him.

"Okay, Abe, come on in, but I need to know what this is going to run me." She pushed open the door for him as he shuffled in. How the bow-backed man was able to haul his equipment from house to house was beyond her. Still, she thought as she watched him maneuver the dolly toward the stairs that people who appear fragile could often times possess the greatest strength.

"Can I help you with guiding that, Abe?" She hurried to the door.

"Thanks, Ms Cunningham, you go on down and guide her down the stairs. I can usually hang on to her pretty good."

"Great." Darci squeezed between furnace and the wall. "What did you say this was going to cost me?" She waited until she was in front of the dolly. "Okay, Abe."

"I didn't."

"Excuse me, did you say you didn't, as in you aren't going to tell me?"

"No, I didn't." The dolly bumped down one step at a time, the thick rubber tires landing with a defiant thud.

Darci held the front of the furnace, hoping the orange colored tether strap was secure enough to manage the vibrations.

"Because—"

The furnace bounced down three more steps and Darci pushed against it to balance the precarious steep angle.

Two steps.

"It's paid for." The words rushed out of Abe's mouth as he fought to hang on to the furnace. The furnace teetered on its wheels before Abe brought it upright.

"Whew, I'm getting' too old for this. You'd think with all our technology they'd come up with something smaller to heat our homes with." He yanked a dirty bandana from his pocket and mopped his forehead beaded with sweat.

Darci rested her hands on her hips, eyeing the monstrosity in front of her. It might have been her hearing, but she could've sworn he said this was already paid for.

"Abe? What did you just say?"

He glanced at her, his furry gray brows raised on his forehead like some flesh and blood "Muppet."

"Paid for." He tugged a piece of folded paper from the pocket of his coveralls. "See here?"

Darci took the paper from his hand and unfolded it, wondering if perhaps the staff at the hotel were trying to make up for the jokes they'd had at her expense. Her gaze scanned the scribbled data and her brows raised at the cost, making her think that she might've waited if—

Her eyes zeroed in on the signature at the bottom of the page. "Tyler Landston?"

"That's what I told you." He blew into the same handkerchief, brushing the ratty cloth under his bulbous nose.

"You said he told you I needed one." Darci rattled the paper in her hand.

"Well now, Darci. If a gentleman is thoughtful enough to want his—" He glanced away as though unsure what to call her. "Anyway. It's a fine and noble gesture. Besides, he said he'd leave you a note that I'd be comin'." Abe shrugged. "Seems a bit odd though, you not knowin'."

He pushed his hands back into his heavy work gloves. "I'll just get 'er outta the way, then."

Darci reached out and clamped her hand on his forearm. "That's okay, Abe. Go ahead. I'll take care of this." She waved the paper at him.

He shrugged. "I'll get started, right away."

> *Darci,*
>
> *I'd hoped to be here when Abe delivered the furnace. I tried to contact you, but had no luck. I hope that when I return, we can talk about what's happened between us. Until then, stay warm and please keep the "fire burning."*
>
> *Tyler*

Short and to the point, the brief note had virtually no tone of commitment. Darci reread the note, forcing herself not to read more between the lines. She'd found the envelope stuck in the ice on the porch, where it must have fallen from the door.

Downstairs, Abe clattered noisily with installing her new furnace, as she neatly folded the letter, returning it to its envelope. She sat down with the bill from Abe in front of her on the desk and pulled open her checkbook. Carefully she wrote out the exact amount of the furnace and then neatly printed out Tyler's name as recipient.

Peter kept telling her she had to take hold of her finances and protect herself from those who might take advantage of her. Maybe it was time she listened to him, in that regard. Darci folded the check and placed it in an envelope, she'd ask Abe to deliver it to Tyler's home. Maybe it was time to take a look at those papers and see what Peter had to say about future investments.

Chapter Eighteen

Tyler peered through his dark glasses at the woman on the other side of the luxurious cement pool. You wouldn't know by looking at her that the woman was going to die. And that's just the way Daphne handled her life—as long as he'd known her. She was in charge of what she wanted and how things were going to be and a tough old broad at almost eighty years old.

He grinned as he slid open the patio door and stepped into the warm sun. A shiver ran through him as his body reacted to the change in the weather.

"Darling."

Her wrinkled hand flew in the air as though she was greeting him from some cruise ship about to sail. He could give her that. He raised his hand and waved back with enthusiasm. "How's my girl?"

Reaching her side, he bent down and she wrapped her spindly arms around his neck, planting a dry kiss to his cheek. He knew later, he'd have to rub off the *Revlon Fire Engine* red that she impressed upon his cheek.

"You look dreadful." She patted the lounge chaise beside her. "Sit down and tell me why you look like hell."

That was the one thing Tyler generally admired about her, she cut straight to the chase. "I caught the first flight I could get, I haven't had any sleep, except on the plane, and it's been an interesting last couple of days." He stretched out in the lounger, allowing his muscles to relax under the suns rays. "You know you shouldn't be out here too long."

"Why not? The damn ultra-violet rays can't make matters much worse now, can they?"

Tyler sighed. She had a point, unfortunately. "I'm sorry, old habit of trying to tell you what to do."

"You come by it naturally." She smiled, her red lipstick framing her million-dollar smile.

He leaned over and gave her a lingering peck on the cheek. Her skin—as always—scented with Shalimar.

"Did you bring your friend with you?"

Daphne peered around his shoulder as if expecting to find someone standing there. He almost hated to disappoint her. He had a feeling she and Darci would get along well.

She adjusted her too large-for-her-face sunglasses down her nose to make her point.

"Not this trip."

"Hum…well, *that* doesn't sound good, but we can get to that later. Have you eaten?"

Before he could answer, she'd picked up a tiny silver bell and jingled it delicately. The contrast of her talon-like red fingernails in contrast to the miniature handle brought a smile to Tyler's lips.

A middle aged woman appeared from the house, dressed in a melon-colored maid's uniform, complete with starched white apron and cap. Tyler stared at the woman, wondering if he'd gone through a time warp back to the forties.

"Don't stare, Tyler. One, it isn't polite and two, the doctor insisted that I couldn't run about like I used to."

"We'll start with shrimp cocktail and please remove the dreadful shells on the end. And what to drink? Tyler? A Bloody Mary or are you ready for martinis?"

Tyler grinned and glanced at the woman waiting patiently as though she was tolerating Daphne's movie starlet spiel. "Orange juice—straight."

Daphne cast a long-suffering gaze to the sky. "Oh, fine, make that two orange juices."

The woman left as quietly as she'd appeared.

"What a god-awful combination, shrimp and orange juice, ugh." She held her frail hand to her throat and stuck out the tip of her pink tongue.

"I forgot what a stitch you can be." Tyler chuckled as he situated himself in the chair beside her.

"Okay, enough about me. Tell me what *you've* been up to." She turned, resting on her hip, her hands clasped in her lap as though awaiting a wonderful gift.

Her hair once dark, was now completely white, kept that way no doubt by her weekly rinse. Still, in her black Capri pants and crisp white cotton blouse she was the epitome of the glamorous Hollywood forties.

Tyler sighed, wondering where to start. "It's a helluva lot warmer here in October than it is there."

She nodded, her glasses dropping a bit on her nose with the gesture. Her bright blue eyes, now hazy with age and the consequences of her ill health peered at him over her black frames.

"I've managed to collect a number of pictures, though. Rented out a place from a guy on the island, so I've been able to develop my pictures. It's really beautiful and probably more so in the spring and summer, I imagine."

The woman returned with a tray that she placed on the table between them.

"Thank you, that will be all for now." Daphne gestured to the large crystal bowl full of succulent pink shrimp and a small dish of hot sauce, surrounded in a bed of chipped ice. "Eat darling and tell me more."

He shirked off his jacket the warmth of the afternoon beginning to melt the chill he'd retained through the flight there. He emitted a content sigh as he snagged a delicate prawn and scooped up some sauce.

"Tyler." Daphne's ruby lips pursed in agitation and his guess was it had little to do with his eating habits.

He licked his fingers, waiting for her to ask what she really wanted to ask and unsure if he could honestly give her any of the answers she was seeking.

"You look like you're eating well. I've never known you to slough off any job, and we've established that it's warmer in Vegas than in Michigan this time of year."

Enjoying the fact that she even cared about his private life, he grinned, leaning back in the chair. "Yep, I guess since everything's covered, its time for a nap then."

"Like hell."

He sat up, swinging his legs over the side of the lounger. His grin intact, he removed his prescription sunglasses and replaced them with his regular pair. "What do you want to know?" He knew, full well, she was fishing to find out more about his "friend."

"Tell me about this friend of yours? Is she pretty? Is she settled? And for God sakes, tell me she's not a model." Her lips puckered over the straw as she sipped from her tall, frosty juice.

"Oh, I didn't you were interested in my love life."

"Hum…this one must be a keeper." She tapped her nail to the glass as she peered at him.

"Why do you say that?" He helped himself to another shrimp.

"Because you're keeping so private about it. If you recall, the other women you've dated have usually been swimming naked in the pool at this stage."

Tyler cringed. She was probably right. "Well, she's not like other women I've known." His tone sobered as he realized the truth of his words.

"Ah ha! Now we're getting somewhere." She grinned and then lurched forward as she began to cough, its fierceness racking her frail body.

Tyler moved to her side and covered her hands, holding the towel to her mouth. He watched helplessly, wondering if he should call an ambulance, but her spasms slowly subsided and she seemed to wave the fit away.

"Such a nuisance I've become." She gasped for breath, clawing at the oxygen mask sitting atop a portable tank, tucked behind her chaise.

He handed the clear plastic mask to her, flipping a small switch as she covered her mouth and nose and eased back to rest her head against the back of the chair.

"No, Daphne. You're sick and I'm sorry for getting you agitated." He folded his arms around her. "I want you to know everything about her. God, I wanted you to meet her—I wanted—I wish we'd been in a better place in our relationship where I could have brought her here."

"Okay, okay, Sparky. I'm not keeling over just yet. Not before I hear everything about this woman that has your shorts in an obvious twist."

Tyler blinked, and started to laugh. Even in the face of death, she showed no thought to herself. What a gutsy woman she was and how much like Darci in that respect.

* * *

More than a week since he'd left and Darci still hadn't heard from him. In all truth, she had only herself to blame. She'd made it clear by not returning his calls that she didn't want to speak to him. Yet, he'd left her the furnace. What was she supposed to make of that?

Instead she chose to pour herself into her writing, dispelling the demons she tried to ignore. When her thoughts would wander to Tyler she simply took long, invigorating walks in the icy chill. The towns main street businesses were already in preparation to close for the winter, leaving the island all the more quiet and desolate as each day passed. Not hearing from him allowed her to move through the familiar stages of loss yet again and convince her heart that it wasn't affected.

She sat in the park across from the marina, reflecting on the past couple of weeks. With a sad smile, she mused at what a good storyline it would be for a book—if it had not been her life.

"Move on, Darci," she muttered, "it's going to be a long winter as it is." Shifting on the bench, she scrunched down, burying her nose in the warmth of her muffler. The kids would be up for Thanksgiving and that's what she could focus on now—that, and her writing.

Darci stood, renewed in mind as she stuffed her hands deep into her coat pockets. She'd made her choice. As she walked the empty street toward home she became more determined with each step.

Leah called later that evening. "Hey mom, how's the book? Had any inspiration?"

Darci frowned as she stirred one hand in the kitchen sink, frothing with bubbles. "No—have you been talking to Maevey again?"

"Mom, I'm pretty good at being able to figure out that "I'm miserable" tone in your voice. Give me a break." She paused. "He hasn't called, has he?"

"Leah, there was nothing ever really solid in that very brief relationship. We both satisfied a need for company at a particular time." Her heart cringed at the untruth of her words. "Besides, I have no intention on putting my life on hold for him or any other man. And if you think about it, he travels and I'm not interested in being his entertainment when he comes to port."

"Uh, huh, that's understandable."

Darci pressed on, her fervor to convince her daughter she was doing fine waving as a herald before her. "It's not as though I expected anything to come of it. There were no commitments of any kind—I mean, he was absolutely sweet and seemed very sincere—" Her memory flashed back to their shared afternoon and the passion in the way he'd kissed her. "Then you think when a guy kisses *like that*—you know, your emotions run away with you and you think—"

Leah cleared her throat. "A little too much information."

"You know, he sent me a furnace. What kind of guy sends a furnace to someone he barely knows." Her cheeks warmed as her body responded to her memories. Blinking away the thought, she continued. "Wouldn't you think that would at least warrant a phone call or something? You know—did you get it installed? Is it working?" Her voice cracked with agitation.

"A furnace?"

Darci reeled in her angst and realized she'd been rambling at her poor daughter. Her daughter who probably thought god-knows what about her wayward mother at the moment—so much for all those discussions about being careful at college. "Are you still there?" Oddly, she'd hoped for a second that perhaps they'd been disconnected and Leah had missed the greater share of her litany.

She picked up the dishcloth and dropped to her knees, attacking a faded green splotch under her kitchen table.

"You have to admit…that's original," Leah finally offered.

"Well, maybe it was his version of a goodbye gift. More out of guilt—" She snapped her mouth shut, clenching her teeth at letting that slip.

"Guilt? About what?" Leah asked.

Darci heard a gentle gasp on the other end and cringed.

"Oh—*guilt*," Leah repeated solemnly.

The spot, hardened since the time it fell to the floor that fateful night, finally budged under her stressful rubbing. Darci tossed the dishcloth in the sink as she pulled herself up right. "I need to move on. There is a box of papers here that I've got to wade through. Some of these things I've just put off, not wanting to face them, but I think its time I did. Uncle Peter is calling almost daily to ask if I have any questions and I can't answer him. He's getting concerned about diversifying investments before the end of the tax year."

"Yeah, he's pretty handy with those finances."

"Yes, he is, but maybe I feel as though I've been in a fog, whereas before I always left these things to your father and he had complete faith in Peter's choices." She paused, wanting to find a way to explain her point without tarnishing Peter's reputation in Leah's eyes.

"Well, it's about time."

Her daughter's somber response surprised her. "You have an opinion about this?" Darci waited with newfound interest, wondering why Leah had never said anything before now.

"Well, you have to remember that the Nathan and I are pretty close to the age when we will receive that trust that dad and Uncle Peter set up a long time ago."

"I'd almost forgotten." Darci rubbed her palm over her forehead as though she was awaking from a deep sleep. What else had she allowed to slip by in this past year and a half? Particularly in light of their financial future resting in Peter's hands? The thought gave her more cause for concern.

Odd that in all the years Matt was alive she'd not questioned their ventures. In a sense, she'd taken for granted that Matt kept his eyes on their security. And there had been an ample life insurance settlement after his death. Enough to cover their debts, take care of the house mortgage, and start both children in college. The sale of the house and some furniture had made her move to the island possible.

Not wishing to burden Leah any further with her concerns, she opted to change the subject. "Hey, are you guys still planning on coming up the Tuesday before Thanksgiving? And you're traveling together, right? You know how the weather could be at that point."

There was a brief pause. "Yeah, I'll check with Nate again to be sure we're on the same page. Listen mom, I have class in ten minutes and I need to walk across campus."

Darci clutched the receiver with both hands, thinking that Thanksgiving was an awfully long time away. "Sure, honey, I'll talk to you later. Have a great week and I love you." Darci hurried with her mother's litany knowing her daughter was already putting on her coat.

There was a muffled sound and then Leah's voice returned. "I love you too and hey, Mom? Don't worry, everything is going to work out fine."

* * *

Maevey was cautious of using the "T" word around her "much-too-solemn-as-of-late" cousin. Sitting with her at dinner one night, she decided to jump in and get her feet wet.

"So?" Maevey paused as she played, twirling her angel hair pasta around the tip of her fork. She glanced across the kitchen table eyeing Darci's response. When none came, she waded in a little deeper.

"Apparently, you've not heard from one Mr. Landston?" she asked casually.

"Why would you say that?" Darci did not meet her gaze,

instead lifting a chunk of breadstick to her mouth; she bit off a dainty piece.

Thinking perhaps she should have worn her wader boots, Maevey sloshed into the conversation unsure at what point she would lose her footing.

"Well, you haven't mentioned him. I guess I thought things between the two of you—were—good, or at least getting there."

Darci shrugged as she picked up her wineglass. " I guess maybe we were both mistaken about Mr. Landston, then."

Her gaze flashed briefly to Maevey's before she took a swallow. There was pain in those eyes and it pierced her heart to the core, but if her cousin chose to face it as a challenge, then she would stand by her. *Damn the man.*

Still, she could not forget the look on both of their faces that day in the lobby when they first met. A believer that fate had a lyrical way of working things out, she smiled and decided to drop the subject—for now.

*C*hapter *N*ineteen

Tyler shoved his arms into his sweatshirt as he groped in the dark for the doorknob. He'd heard the tinkling of the silver bell in the distant corner of his blissful dream of Darci; her gauzy sheer nightgown fluttering around her curves as she stood by his bed.

"I heard the coughing and then the bell." Jerry met him in the black hallway as they both headed toward the dim path of light emitting under the door of Daphne's bedroom.

He pushed open the door calling to her as he peered through the rose-colored light inside.

She was seated upright in her bed, her satin comforter swirling in a great purple sea around her small body. Her lavender tailored pajamas hung on her now scrawny shoulders and she resembled the ragamuffin look of a scarecrow.

Daphne jiggled the near empty goblet in her hand, trying to break free the ice chips solidified in the bottom.

"Daphne? What are you doing? Trying to give us all heart failure." Tyler plopped down at the foot of the mattress, closing his eyes in relief as he leaned against one of the four massive mahogany bedposts.

The periodic nightly occurrences were happening now with greater frequency. Tyler wondered if it was the fear of being alone when the end finally came.

"As you can see." She held her glass out showing evidence of her dilemma. "I have no water." The fine line of a faded eyebrow arched still with great authority.

Tyler smiled as he rubbed his hands over his face, attempting to jumpstart his brain.

Jerry walked past him and smiled as he took the glass

from Daphne, and then he reached for the pitcher. "You two sit tight, I'll go get us all three something to drink."

Tyler appreciated that the hulk of a bodyguard had stayed on after Antonio's passing. Though his body was this side of Mount Olympus, his heart was as gentle as a rose petal.

Daphne adjusted the thin plastic tubing trailing from the tank to her pert nose. She'd gone from occasional tokes of oxygen since Tyler's arrival to the need to wear it full time now. That was less than two weeks ago.

Awake now, Tyler rubbed the sand from his eyes, a stray image of Darci popping into his mind and quickly dissipating. "Okay, what shall we discuss this evening—oh wait, it's 2:30 in the morning. Make that what shall we discuss this morning madam and may I say that you look ravishing for this hour."

Her gaze followed him to the window as he cranked it open and took a breath of the cool desert air, something before this moment, he'd always taken for granted.

"Tyler, there's something I wish to speak with you about." She had that business-like tone in her voice.

"Well, this sounds like trouble. Are you sure you shouldn't be getting some rest?" He turned, giving her a sleepy smile.

She fluffed the down comforter with agitated persistence. "I've too much on my mind to rest."

Tyler nodded as he returned to the foot of the bed. "I can see that, sorry. So what is it that's on your mind that I can help you with so you'll be able to rest?"

She patted the covers, her way of ordering him to sit. "Darci Cunningham."

Tyler hesitated mid-air, before seating himself on the bed.

Jerry returned at that moment bringing a fresh tray of water and two extra glasses filled with orange juice. He handed one to Tyler.

"If you'll not be needing me, I think I'll let you all greet the dawn. Me? I need some shut eye."

"Night." Tyler raised his glass to his burly friend. What would happen to Jerry when Daphne was—?

"Tyler?"

Her voice interrupted his thoughts and he was just as glad.

"There are two things I'd like to know." She held up her wrinkled hand, accented by her glamorous nails. The diamond ring given to her on her wedding day slid loose in a complete circle around her thin finger. "Do you love this woman and have you slept with her?"

Tyler pushed down the swallow of orange juice surprised by her question. "Please, don't hold back, ask me anything." He grinned, taking another drink. The icy juice cooled the parched dryness in his throat. He'd forgotten in his time living in Chicago how the desert climate could do that to a person.

He glanced at Daphne, her face completely somber. "*This*—is really what's on your mind?" His gaze narrowed to a frown.

"Of course not, these are but the steps to my other concerns."

"Ah...okay." It came out as more of a yawn than an acknowledgment.

"You're stalling."

"You're right." He gave a snorted laugh.

"Tyler, this is important."

"Daphne. How is whether I slept with her or not of any importance to you?" He wasn't sure if it was sorrow or anger that flashed in her pale blue eyes.

"Because—" Her thin lips parched looking without benefit of lipstick, pressed in a tight line. "I need to know that you're happy."

He knew her reasons for asking and it bothered him. Yes, he could tell her what she wanted to hear, hell, maybe what he wanted desperately to believe as well. Yet circumstances being what they were, he couldn't lie to her. "I wish it was that simple, Daph." Tyler rubbed at his eye aware of a dull ache between his brows.

Her brief intake of air bolted him upright, his attention wholly on her face. His shoulders slumped in relief.

Unaware of the havoc she'd brought to his senses, she

reached into the drawer of her nightstand and withdrew a think white envelope.

His brows puckered as the hairs on the back of his neck stood on end. Tyler had a feeling that this was part of the "loose ends" she talked about needing to tie up. "What's this?" Already suspecting its contents, he accepted the envelope from her bony grasp.

"It's a copy of my will."

Tyler's gaze stay glued to the folds of paper in his hand. All that she was of material wealth while on the face of this earth, he now held in the palm of his hand. No envelope could encase what she was worth in his heart.

In an attempt to keep things light, he asked, "What would you like me to do with this?" He flipped it over in his hand, seeing it was not sealed.

"The original is sealed and is with my lawyer." She sipped from her water goblet. "I'll save you the time and mystery, Tyler. I've left you a tidy sum and if I may be so bold as to suggest what you should do with this?"

"Do I have a choice?" he remarked, encompassing both the gesture and the suggestion.

"You always have choices, darling."

"Your suggestion?" He held up the envelope, unable to believe he was having this conversation at this hour.

"That you use it to open that dream gallery of yours somewhere that you'll be inspired and content, for however long God intends to put up with you."

He wanted to laugh at her last remark, but the solid lump in his throat prevented him from doing so. His eyes welled and he squeezed his eyes tight. "Daphne, I can't—"

"Well, I'm sorry, what's done is done and you wouldn't want to break an old woman's heart now would you?"

He shook his head no.

"Listen here young man, there will be no discussing this, except for me to say this. I've been around long enough to know that the heart is a fragile thing. Even as much as we both know how much it can endure, we both know that it needs to love and be loved."

She patted his leg and smiled wearily.

"If you believe even just suspect that you've found love, don't ignore it. The outcome remains to be seen of course, but if you never pursue what your heart is whispering, you may never know the happiness that may be in store for you."

Tyler bowed his head, covering his eyes with his hand, squeezing his temples to keep from falling apart in front of her—this frail woman who exceeded the bravery of any man he'd ever known.

"I only ask that you promise me that you will pursue this, or at least until you know absolutely one way or another if this is your destiny."

Tyler cleared his throat unable to speak instead nodding his response.

"Good. Now please take your rear end, cute as it is, out of here. God knows I can use all the beauty sleep I can get." She settled herself snug under the comforter, her white hair a stark contrast to the deep concord grape-colored pillowcase.

Tyler swiftly brushed his eyes and stood, determined that she would see the man she'd raised him to become. He walked to her side and she smiled up at him, reaching her hand to his face.

"You are the son I could never have." A tear slid from the corner of her eye. "Be happy. Get married and have children, so you can understand how much I love you. I'm very proud of having had that chance and to see what a wonderful man you've become."

She caressed his cheek, now streaked with tears.

"Someone special deserves all that you have to offer, Tyler. Don't be afraid to love."

Tyler grasped her hand, fighting back the flood of tears threatening his control. He pressed his wet lips to her palm and returned it to his cheek, willing all the strength inside of him to her weakened body. A glimpse of truth illuminated his thoughts and he realized at this moment what a mother's unconditional love really was. "Sleep well, Mom. I'll see you—," he whispered as her eyes drifted shut and her hand went limp.

* * *

Sweat beaded on Peter's forehead as he stared at the computer screen. The figures of his once foolproof plan reflected precisely the opposite—he had a problem. His problem, of course, was Darci's procrastination.

He was sure they'd connected that last day his was on the island and he'd silently thanked Tyler Landston for revealing so easily his true intentions. In retrospect, he hadn't really done any more than plant the seeds of doubt in Darci's mind and then gratefully, Tyler himself, had taken care of the rest.

Still, a problem existed. His funds were dissolving before his eyes, a result of his stopgap measures to appease greedy informants for the investments he brokered between his clients on the black market.

Peter's jaw muscle clenched in frustration as he thought of the substantial amount of his own finances had been used, unable to touch Matt's portion, other than what had already been invested. At least until Darci signed over power of attorney to continue the investment plan they'd started long ago. Naturally, he'd only let Matt in on the investments that were, according to Matt, reputable. Peter figured what he didn't know wouldn't kill him.

He laughed aloud at the startling irony of his thoughts—then again, maybe it had.

It pissed him off though that the going rate to keep an informant happy these days exceeded what he'd started out paying. There was something wrong with this world when you couldn't relay on a well-paid, crooked informant to give sound advice.

Already Peter had received a certified letter from a client in Milano, requesting status of a certain venture involving rare Egyptian artifacts, discovered on a dig a year ago. His informant had told him that they were being shipped to museums in the states, but that some could—for a price—become conveniently lost and "may" show up on the black market.

His client, eager to have them for his personal collection, contacted Peter to make arrangements with the informants contact. That was nearly six months ago. Had the contact been a more reliable source, the commission alone would have given Peter the freedom he needed to pull into fluid cash flow. As it was, not only was the information a hoax, but also both the contact and the informant disappeared conveniently off the face of the earth, leaving Peter to explain it all to his Italian client.

His client was now anxious for news of the intended arrival of his precious purchases and if he told him the truth, no doubt he could well end up as fish food.

Thus far he'd been able to appease him, by saying there had been problems with the shipment, substandard quality that he was seeing to personally, as he worked another contact to obtain a few artifacts from another arena that might be a better lure for his client.

Either way, he was in desperate need of being able to work freely with Matt's portion of the money. He'd have to call Darci again and stress the importance of signing over to him the freedom to continue his investment opportunities.

Before now, he'd hoped that the gentle reminders would be enough, and that given his long time relationship to Matt, Darci, and her family she would trusted him to continue to take care of them. Reluctantly, he'd also hoped that she would return the sincere affection he'd shown her repeatedly.

Peter grabbed the short, stubby glass next to his computer and took a large swallow of *Maker's Mark* perfectly chilled over exactly three ice cubes. He breathed in deep, allowing its potent slow burn to penetrate his scattered thoughts.

Perhaps he'd been approaching this dilemma from the wrong angle. If Darci was not responding to his gentle advances, then maybe it was time for him to take off the kid gloves and show her the powerful man beneath the quiet exterior.

Peter smiled. Of course, why hadn't the thought occurred to him sooner? He'd taken her lack of response as a rejection, when maybe all Darci really wanted was something totally different that her late husband. She was a tease and as he pondered it the whole scenario crystallized in his mind. She'd even used that afternoon tryst with Landston to make him jealous. It all made perfect sense now. Darci secretly wanted him to aggressively hunt her down and claim her.

The whiskey warmed Peter's body along with the sensual satisfaction of his recent epiphany.

He picked up the phone. It was a Thursday night, and barely past midnight. The phone rang once. She should be home.

"Yeah?" a sleepy feminine voice answered.

"Hey sugar, daddy's lonely. Come take care of me." Peter opened the patio door to his fifteenth story balcony, the cold air slapping his face with a delicious icy tingle.

"You sure call at the damnedest times," she murmured with a throaty chuckle.

Peter frowned. Vixen—she liked to be called—was to keep herself for him on certain nights. They'd had that arrangement for years. The fact that he'd given her a plush penthouse apartment just below the standard of his own, had her nose done to a greater perfection, and had her hair dyed, you think would have solidified their agreement.

"You're busy?" His gut tightened. He'd had enough go wrong today, he needed to be the one appeased for a change.

"No baby, I can come shortly, hopefully, though, *you'll* take longer." She purred into the receiver. Her sultry southern accent—the only aspect keeping her from being Darci's exact physical double—slid over him like a warm breeze.

"I'll see you soon, then." He started to replace the receiver and remembered his request—something a little different than their usual time together. "Vixen?" Peter's voice was urgent.

"Yes, darlin'?"

Thankfully she was still on the line. Peter's tension subsided. "Wear something wild. I'm up for a hunt tonight." He grinned feeling his game plan begin to firm up in his mind and in his lap.

"Leopard print, okay?"

Peter grinned. "Perfect."

Chapter Twenty

"I'll be heading over to St. Ignace this evening and I'll be back first thing Monday morning. Why don't you let me pick up your costume for the Halloween Party Monday night?" Maevey made another check on the inventory list. "I'm going to have to order more glasses before spring. Where do they disappear to, do you think?"

Darci counted out the spoons in her hands before answering. "I've watched people slip them in their purse, or coat pocket. They get carried outside, or upstairs." Darci shrugged.

Maevey picked up one of the glasses, holding it up to inspect it in the florescent kitchen lighting. "They're nothing but plain glasses." She shook her head as though in disbelief. "Hey, you are still going to the costume party, right?"

Darci stopped counting the utensils in her hand. "I haven't thought about it much, Maevey. I'm not sure I feel up to a party right now." She rolled her shoulders to ease some of the tension she'd been carrying there since Tyler left. Almost two weeks had passed, and still no word from him. When he left, he'd claimed it was only for a couple of days and while she tried desperately not to think of him, everywhere she turned on the island it seemed, they'd spent a moment there, together.

"It will be good for you to get out, you've been like a hermit working on your book or down here helping me close up."

Darci gave her cousin a side glance, "You're the one that's been bugging me about this book, remember?"

"Well, sure I want you to finish it, but you need to allow yourself some down time as well." Maevey handed her a glass of wine left over from the lunch. "Besides." She smiled. "Did you forget that you promised to help me set up the tables and decorate?"

Her promise to that had slipped her mind amidst the other chaos swirling inside her. Darci' sighed. "Okay, I'll go, but if I *have* to wear a costume, I want something absolutely stunning. Something royal and lavish that will make heads turn when I walk into a room. Something befitting a—"

"Queen?" Maevey teased.

"Author." Darci corrected with the arch of her brow, followed by a grin.

Maevey smiled in return. "Now that sounds like my cousin. I'll get you the best. You'll be the center of attention."

"Drop-dead gorgeous would be enough."

"But of course, dear cousin." Maevey's laughter lifted Darci's spirit. Now if she could go home and not find Peter's voice on her answering machine, her spirit would do summersaults.

There were no blinking lights when she got home. Nothing. Here it was, a Friday night, the beginning of the weekend and nothing even from Nathan or Leah.

Darci hung up her coat, breathing a sigh of relief that neither were there any messages from Peter or from Tyler. Sauntering towards the kitchen, she paused to snap on her stereo, the soothing strains of the Celtic music, as always, giving peace to her soul.

As she fixed herself dinner, she picked up the phone and dialed Leah's number. The fact that Maevey was gone for the weekend spawned the need to touch base with family. The recorded message of Leah's answering machine clicked on and she listened with a soft smile to her daughter's effervescent voice, "Hi, I'm not home right now, but if you'll leave your name and number, I'll get back to you as soon as possible."

Darci waited for the tone. "Hi Honey, it's mom. Calling on a Friday night and I figured you were out. Just letting you know that I'm around if you need anything." She replaced the receiver, her hand poised on the hard plastic, warm beneath her hand. She picked it up again and dialed Nathan's number.

A click signaled someone had picked up, there was a pause, and then her son's laughter emitted on the message.

"You little turd." Darci cast a long-suffering glance to the ceiling and listened to her son, mischievous as her cousin, Maevey.

"Guess you were probably hoping this was me, but you'll have to get in line and wait your turn. Leave the pertinent info at the beep. Have a good one."

"Nathan." Darci's tone was firm, though she tried not to smile. "This is your mother checking in. Nothing important. Just how long is this waiting line?" She chuckled and hung up, her gaze landing on a box tucked in the corner of her living room.

With a resigned sigh, she picked up her microwave Chinese dinner and headed to her desk. Maybe tonight would be as good a time to force herself to go through these papers. Knowing Peter would be elated at the progress, she placed her meal at the edge of her desk and scooted the box to her feet.

The contents inside, she knew were varied. Much of it, she'd simply stuffed in the box when moving, promising herself that one day she would go through them. Peter's reference to some of the investment papers were tucked amongst insurance forms, funeral receipts, and medical reports of Matt's death and unable to deal with any of them at the time, she'd put them away until later.

Darci unfolded the cardboard flaps, slicing her finger on the razor thin edge of the packing tape. "Dammit." She pushed from the chair and walked quickly to the kitchen nursing her finger to her lips as she found where she stored band-aids. She marveled how easily the pain subsided with the simple fabric covering, and as she returned to the desk, she knew that the pain inside that box would not be so easily soothed.

She plopped back into her desk chair and stared hard at the box. Maybe she'd feel more up to dealing with it after she ate. After all, she had the whole weekend ahead of her with nothing but time on her hands. She picked up the heavy plastic bowl and propped her feet to the box, lifting a forkful of rice to her mouth.

* * *

"Mr. Landston, how would you best describe your relationship to the deceased?"

The microphone shoved under Tyler's nose and he pulled back to avoid getting swiped with it. The crowd of media camped out side the church, swarmed he and Jerry as they fought through the mass toward the waiting limousine.

"No comment." He tossed haphazardly over his shoulder as Jerry's massive arm cut off the persistent reporter.

Tyler reached the door and crawled in the back, grateful for the tinted windows.

Jerry pulled the door shut after him and turned to Tyler. "Must be a slow news day." His grin, weary, reflected the emotional wear from fighting off the thrill seekers trying to get into the estate for an exclusive on the famous widow's death.

Tyler rubbed his eyes wishing that he were anyplace but there. "You know, you'd think that there would be more respect for the dead and for their families and friends." Tyler turned to the blinking camera bulbs, knowing that all they would get is a roll of black window. He looked away disgusted with the whole media circus.

"Daphne wasn't just any lady Ty, I don't have to tell you that." Jerry chuckled, swinging his gaze to Tyler's. "How many people can say they had foreign dignitaries attend their funeral service?"

Tyler shrugged. Daphne had known one thing about him. He was beginning to grow less and less enthused about the high profile of fame. Perhaps opening a gallery/studio idea was something he should give serious consideration to. Now only one problem remained—where would he feel most comfortable, away from the fast lane of the metropolitan life?

"Oh, hey. I just about forgot—" Jerry pulled out a small manila envelope from the inside of his jacket. " I wasn't sure when you'd be heading out and I know Daphne would want you to stay as long as you want, but she asked me to give this to you, in the event—" He cut off his own sentence and looked at the package in his hand.

"Thanks." Tyler took the envelope. "What are you going to do now?"

The limousine cruised through the streets, teaming with vacationers and sightseers, all unaware of the passing of one of the town's most influential women.

Jerry shrugged. "I don't know for sure. I always wanted to go to cooking school, you know—become a chef."

"Get outta here, are you serious?" Tyler grinned finding the image of the hulk in a white cap and apron an oddity if nothing else.

"That or be a teacher. I'm good with kids you know. Think it's too late to go back to school?" He cracked the knuckles of his huge hands.

"I think you could manage to do about anything." Tyler's gaze rested on the man's hands, picturing them trying to tie a small child's shoelace. Damned if it wasn't a clear and gentle picture.

"Thanks, that's…um, good to know, Ty." Jerry glanced out side, and then returned his attention to Tyler. "You think I'd make a good cover model then?" He gave Tyler a cheesy smile.

Tyler checked over the massive square jaw of the man, a nose that had been broken on more than one occasion, and the scars donning one eyebrow and the outer corner of his lip.

"I'd say you have all the ear markings of a hero on a romance cover, Jer." Tyler slapped a hand to his shoulder and the gentle giant smiled.

* * *

The wind rattled against her window, causing Darci to get up and stoke the fireplace with another piece of wood. She returned to her desk and sat down, her gaze scanning the small piles of papers stacked neatly on its surface. It had taken her the better part of the last two hours to put them in some semblance of order. She took a sip of her second cup of tea, picking up the stack of files labeled "Investments" and curled one leg under her as she settled herself on the loveseat facing the fireplace. For a brief moment, the image of Tyler in only his jeans standing in the glow of the fire captured her thoughts and she wished things could be different for them.

Brushing those fanciful thoughts aside, she knew that if she didn't tackle the issue in front of her, that she would forever be dependent on Peter for her financial choices. It was time to learn all that she could about what Matt had invested in. The change of heart about how her finances were going to be handled, she had a feeling, wasn't going to make Peter very happy. Still, she had no intention of simply signing over Matt's share of the investment profit to Peter, even if the two of them had at one time, verbally agreed on what to do with them.

Darci opened the top file and began to read, trying to decipher the spreadsheet jargon that only someone with the background and love for facts and figures could truly understand. A dozen sheets later, her mind was a jumble with assets and deficits, projections and market ratios. She flipped the next ledger sheet and found sandwiched between the spreadsheets a faded yellow carbon paper.

Curious, she worked the adhered paper, pressed from being under stacks of files for so long apart from the spreadsheet. Clearly it did not belong as part of the package.

Her brows knit as she glanced at the header notation, between duel hole punches—"*Preliminary Report of Investigation By Medical Examiner.*"

Her gaze scanned the chart carefully picking out each word, somehow it bringing her closer to Matt's final moments on earth. It had all happened so fast, there hadn't been time to think in the days that followed. All she knew was that Peter had been there and gratefully picked up the shattered pieces of her life.

He'd insisted on taking care of the formality of the autopsy. She needed to concentrate on the children and family coming in for the service. The report was a simple formality to determine exact cause of death and Peter said he would bring the findings to her.

Her mind flashed back to the day Peter had called her with the report. "I wanted to tell you in person, honey, but I've got a flight leaving in an hour. You know how lines are now. I'm on my way to the airport."

There was a rattling of papers. "The report indicates he died of a complications."

"Complications?" Darci blinked. "Complications from what?"

"It goes on to indicate that the heart attack was the cause of death. That's probably what they call complications. Maybe it was a genetic thing—stress."

A crackling followed in the receiver. "I'm sorry, sweetheart. My connection is getting bad. I'll send this to you with some other things the minute I get home. Right now, you concentrate on you and the kids, okay? Take care, love."

Though she couldn't recall the age of Matt's parents, it seemed to her they'd always been in good health before they were killed in a tragic holiday car accident.

"Take care of yourself for now, Darci. Rest and I'll take care of the rest. Matt asked me to."

"When did he ask—?"

The odd statement made that day struck a cord in her head and she grabbed the file, tossing aside the spreadsheets, in search of any other papers that might have inadvertently been stuffed in the file. She couldn't remember that Peter ever mentioned the actual report again, or if he'd sent it.

Comments that Peter made, his possessive attitude, his constant attempts—though done with a benevolent intent—of trying to secure a greater foothold in her life and the lives of her children played in Darci's head.

An odd niggling fingered the back of her neck as she read the faded report. Her eyes narrowed, searching between the lines to find something she might have missed in her grief. At the bottom in small print she read the words of a stranger's handwriting.

"Probable cause of death: 1) congestive heart failure 2)

Due To: genetic complications, 3) Due to: complications of previous diagnosis"

Her brain froze and she forced herself to reread the scribbled notes once again. As far as she knew Matt had been in perfect health. He wasn't even taking his allergy medication at the time.

As if spawned by the myriad of question assaulting her brain, the phone rang, once, twice, and a third time before she could command her body to answer it.

"How's my girl?"

"Peter?" His voice sounded alien to her. Someone that had walked beside her all these years, yet suddenly was a stranger. She drew a blank, unsure whether to approach him with the newly discovered information. Information he'd neglected to mention.

There was a short laugh on the other end of the line. "Well, I trust it's a bit early for that Landston fellow to be calling you "his girl—"

Darci swallowed. "Was Matt on any medications that I wasn't aware of?"

"Darci, come on." His voice had a curious tone.

"Just answer me, Peter."

"No, not that I'm aware of." His answer was brief and succinct. "Why?"

"Do you remember calling me on your way to the airport with the autopsy findings?"

"It's been a while, but yeah, vaguely." His familiar tolerant sigh emitted over the receiver.

"Do you remember that you told me something about complications?" She picked up the paper; squinting to be sure she was getting every word correct.

"Is that what I said?"

"I have the report here."

"Okay." The sound of him clearing his throat signaled that she definitely had his full attention.

"It says that it was congestive heart failure."

"Right, we've been over this, Darci. It was signed before

the funeral home came to get Matt—before he was—"

"Cremated, I know." Darci's back straightened with the chill that went up her spine.

"It's what you guys wanted."

"I'm not disputing that." Darci took a deep breath, feeling as though she was being pulled into a current of knowledge that she didn't want to hear.

"What's this all about, Darci? What's got you upset tonight?" His voice was gentle.

"The report also indicates a second probable reason other than genetic complications."

"Really?" Peter sounded unconcerned. "I hate to be hard nose about this, Darci, but at some point you have to just accept that Matt died of heart failure and he's gone." There was a pause. "And I don't think he'd want you to be suffering like this. I think he'd want you to move on with your life, Darci."

"That's what I'm trying to do!" The tension building inside exploded with her words. "The report also indicates a second possibility, Peter. One that you failed to mention when you called about the report."

The silent tension hung thick across the miles of phone line.

"What are you saying?"

"This report indicates Matt could have died from complications of a previous diagnosis." She dropped the file to the floor and stared into the flickering flames. "What does that mean, Peter? What diagnosis is this person talking about?"

Peter's sigh was her answer. He'd kept something from her, perhaps something vital in her understanding why Matt died so suddenly.

"We need to talk and this can't be done over the phone." His voice was somber, punctuated with another sigh.

Her mind clicked into place, intuition forming a clear picture in her head. "I'm sorry Peter. It's just that I came across this report and all of the memories came flooding back and—" She choked back a fake sob, hoping it was good enough to convince him. She needed time to find out what was going on, but first she needed to contact her lawyer and freeze anything that was available for Peter to touch as a result of his partnerships with Matt.

There was a brief silence before he spoke. "It's understandable, honey. But as I've told you many times, your ol' Pete is here and I'm making sure that you and the kids are in good hands."

Darci clutched the phone with both hands, amazed at the sudden gentle turn in his attitude. She eased herself into a chair and pulled her thoughts together.

"Are you getting any writing done?" He laughed, a bit too exuberant for their previous conversation. "Leah tells me that you're considering writing a romance novel?"

She wanted to throttle her daughter.

When she didn't respond, Peter pushed on. "I think that's just about the best idea you've had in ages. It's time to move on, Darci."

Uncomfortable as to where the conversation might be heading, she quickly changed the subject. "I'll check over these papers, Peter and try to have them to you by the end of the month."

"By the end of the week would be better."

A red warning flag popped up in Darci's brain. As though jolted awake from a long sleep, Peter's actions began to clarify in her mind. He was hurting for money, and that, she guessed, was the bottom line of why he was pressing to have these papers signed.

If she was going to find out what he was up to, she was going to have to confront him face-to-face. "I have an idea. Why don't you come up for the Harvest party the community is having here on Monday night? You could come up for the party and afterwards we can talk about these papers."

"You're inviting me up there?"

"Well, yeah, if you can work it into your schedule." She tried to keep her voice light as chills ran over her arms.

He gave a short laugh. "Sweetheart, I'll make the time.

What time is this party?"

"It starts at eight at the community center. I'll have to meet you there, I'm helping Maevey with preparations."

"I'm looking forward to it. See you Monday night."

"Me too." Darci lied then added. "Drive safe." She hung up and looked at the stack of insurance papers on her desk. She had just two days to find out what this other diagnosis was.

Chapter Twenty-One

Tyler's gaze scanned the massive office once the heart beat of Antonio DeMarco's business empire. In accordance to Daphne and Antonio's wishes, if Tyler chose not to live in the estate and the adjoining acreage then it was up to him to give it to his choice of charity. With the inheritance they'd left him, he had no need of the money that could be driven from a sale.

Being executor to their will was yet another unexpected surprise affecting Tyler's sleep as of late.

The subtle creak of the leather Executive chair gave as he leaned back and placed his stocking feet on the huge chrome and smoked glass office desk. These past few days, his life had taken a drastic if not confusing turnaround, and now decisions he could no longer avoid with travel, were presenting themselves at his feet—*or under them.*

He lifted his feet to the floor and tucked his hands in his pockets as he walked the parameter of the room surveying in pictures the highlighted moments of the man and woman whose lives had influenced him most.

Tyler chuckled as he withdrew his hand and picked up a silver framed picture of the three of them, taken on his graduation day from college. He found it odd, yet in a way justifiable that his coloring so closely resembled theirs.

The muscle of his jaw clenched, a ping of loss coming unexpectedly as he returned the frame to its designated place. He took a deep breath, once more surveying the room and thought about his most recent decision.

It was only one of many facing him at the moment, but it felt right and he felt sure that Antonio and Daphne would have agreed.

He picked up the picture again and smiled tucking it under his arm as he returned to the desk and picked up the phone to dial the representative of the Nevada Network for Homeless Teens.

* * *

"I think they'd be happy with your choice, Ty."

Tyler and Jerry sat in the large formal dining room, finishing the last meal either would have in the stately mansion before it became a home for runaway and homeless teens.

"You know, there's a lot of kids out there, who just need to know somebody cares, Jer." Tyler bit off a piece of garlic bread, and took a swallow of iced tea.

The scant staff had been given generous severance pay and all that remained was Jerry and Tyler.

"You know, I'm having a hard time thinking about moving back to Colorado." Jerry chuckled as he poked at his filet as though checking for doneness.

"You're going to be great out there in that Chef's school, its one of the best, I hear."

"Yeah and I have you to thank for that. Without you giving me that loan—"

Tyler waved away Jerry's stumbling gratitude. "It's not so innocent as it looks, Jer. You get done out there, I might need you to start up a little restaurant enterprise I've been thinking about." Tyler grinned.

Jerry sat back and smiled. "I'll do that, man. You going back to the island?" He twirled the long neck of his *Samuel Adams* between his fingers.

It was one of the questions Tyler had successfully managed to avoid over the past few days. "I guess, probably. I need to finish this project and then decide what to do."

Jerry nodded as though he understood. "You have a chance to look at those papers I gave you?"

Tyler's brows knit, his mind replaying the enormous amount of paperwork he'd been through in the last forty-eight hours.

"That envelope I gave you after the funeral?" Jerry

reminded him.

"Oh." Tyler pushed from the table and headed to the front hall closet where his dress overcoat hung. He reached into the large inside pocket and pulled out a folded manila envelope, still slightly damp from the rain the day of the funeral.

As he returned to the dining room, he tugged the papers from the softened packet. He glanced over what appeared to be a handful of faded faxes, but what stopped him in his tracks was the name that appeared at the top of one—Peter Beck.

He stood at the entrance of the dining room reading the information on the top page. "Damn." His mind tried to comprehend what he was reading. If a mere tenth of what was printed on these papers were true, this guy had every one snowed.

"Interesting guy." Jerry glanced at Tyler as he worked at cutting his steak.

"You read these?" Tyler came around the edge of the table and sat down, still in shock, by what small part hc'd read.

"Daphne suggested that you might need some help with this guy. Sounds like some piece 'a work."

Tyler smoothed out the papers, as he continued to read about Peter Beck's enterprising lifestyle.

"Money laundering, black market, stolen artifacts—" Tyler's gaze met Jerry's. "This guy is pond scum."

The rancid thought that Darci would find anything of redeeming value in this guy made his stomach turn. Then again, there was the possibility she didn't know.

Tyler blinked realizing that in all probability she knew nothing of this side of Peter. He'd all along played up the "Uncle Peter" scenario and the wise and prudent investor to her and most likely her deceased husband as well—perhaps for a good many years.

His gaze fell to a hefty six-digit figure paid out to a John Smith, whose business card was printed on the fax—Dade County Medical Examiners.

"Holy mother of—"

"What?" Jerry leaned over the table trying to read the

papers.

"What kind of investment would a guy make to a medical examiner?" Tyler looked at Jerry meeting his solemn gaze.

"One he needed help from."

"Jesus," Tyler muttered as he pressed his fingers to his forehead, trying to sort through the barrage of possibilities swirling in his mind. There was always the hope that Darci knew nothing at all about this. Then again, if she did, her life could be in danger from this low-life.

Tyler dug into his wallet; flipping through cards until he found the slip of paper he'd jotted Darci's number on. He grabbed his cellular phone and began dialing praying that she would be home on a Sunday night. Halfway through, he paused, changing his mind.

"What's the matter?" Jerry sat poised on the edge of his seat as though awaiting Tyler's next move.

"I've got to get back there. She's not going to talk to me now over the phone, much less believe anything I'm telling her." Tyler rubbed his hand over his mouth in frustration. Too many questions raced through his brain. Was he going to walk into some love-triangle murder case? Or would he be the one to have to break it to her that she should have Peter investigated for the possible murder of her husband?

"You care about this woman?"

Jerry's question posed yet another unexpected thought that caused his brain to come to a screeching halt.

"I think I love her." Tyler snorted out a laugh, attempting to catch his breath, wondering how such a thing was possible in the short time they'd been together. This new information added a fresh list of questions already plaguing his mind. Ones that needed to be answered and only one woman could help him find those answers.

"I'm heading to the airport. Maybe I can catch a late night flight." Tyler folded the papers and grabbed the envelope off the table.

"You sure you don't need my help on this one."

"The woman is barely five foot five, Jer, I think I can

handle this one. Besides, Beck won't be on the island. You'll make sure that Tony and Daph's personal belongings are boxed up and stored though and I'll get them as soon as I can."

"Got it. You know where to find me, if you need me."

"Causing havoc in Colorado." Tyler called over his shoulder. He didn't have to look to know the giant was grinning.

* * *

With a well-practiced overhand throw, Peter tossed the unopened box of condoms in his suitcase. "Two points! He scores!" He laughed quietly at the prospect of making that a reality with Darci on this little trip.

Peter looked over his selections that he'd carefully laid out on the bed. He'd wanted to find just the right combination of sweaters and slacks to appeal to Darci and because this was going to be a couple of very special days he'd gone out and splurged on new cologne and a box of prophylactics guaranteed to please even the most discriminating woman.

Yes indeed, this was the beginning of a new relationship for him and Darci and he wanted it to be something she could look forward to for a very long time.

He glanced at the pair of handcuffs Vixen had left behind a couple of days ago. He picked them up and with a grin, tossed them into his suitcase.

The six-hour drive to the island was going to be hard tomorrow. Peter took a deep breath and let it out purposefully slow. "I've been patient this long, Darci. I can manage a little longer to give you the very best of my love."

He picked up a framed eight by ten picture from his bedside table—a blow-up of the three of them in college— Matt's presence conveniently removed by a pair of scissors. "Sorry buddy, but that cancer was going to get you sooner, than later. I know you'd want only what was best for your lovely wife and kids." He smiled with a content sigh. "And that—old buddy—happens to be me."

* * *

Darci had spent the better part of Saturday and Sunday

trying to track down the whereabouts of a Dr. Ronald Stillman. She'd found his name in an insurance report, and had she not been looking for something specific, she would've easily dismissed the report as routine.

The form itself appeared to be the type used by insurance companies when a policy is being considered. It was at the bottom of the third page that her heart stopped when she read the words—*pancreatic cancer*.

Adding fuel to the already smoldering questions she wanted to confront Peter with, she forced herself past the shock, and concentrated on tracking down this doctor to first find out some information.

"I'm sorry, Dr. Stillman retired a year ago. He no longer practices from this clinic." The office assistant on the other end of the line sounded as though she was tired of answering to the doctor's whereabouts.

"Is there any way I can reach him?" Darci tried not to allow the pleading in her mind to reach as far as her voice.

"I don't—please hold."

The line went dead and Darci thought for a moment she'd been entirely cut off.

"Hello? This is the office manager, may I help you?"

Relieved and hopeful that the woman on the phone was perhaps more seasoned in such matters, Darci explained. "I'm looking for a Dr. Stillman. He once treated my husband for—" She forced the words past her breaking heart. "Pancreatic cancer. I just wanted to touch base and thank him." Darci winced at the lie, hoping it would be enough to sway the woman to help her. This day and age, clinics were very cautious about submitting any sort of information over the phone.

"You can check directory assistance, they can give you his home number." Her tone was business-like.

Darci bit her lip. The phone number was unlisted, which is why she'd been forced to go back to the clinic to try again. "Look, I'm calling from out of town, all I wanted to do was thank him. Is there any way you can give me his number?"

There was a sigh and then silence for a moment.

"You tell him that you got the number from here and I'll deny it."

Darci gave a quite sigh of relief. "I won't mention it."

She gave her the number and Darci hung up. Now the only thing standing between her and the truth was a telephone number.

Darci cleared her throat as the phone rang, pulling back the curtain as she waited. The clouds over-head were dark and ominous, full of blustery wind gusts, and spackles of rain.

"Hello?" the man on the other end answered with a sleepy voice.

"Dr. Stillman?"

"Yes, and how may I ask did you get this number?"

"Uh, a friend—of a friend." Her lie was less convincing than she'd like and he knew it.

"Damn office," he muttered.

"Dr. Stillman, I won't take up much of your time. This is Darci Cunningham and I'm calling long distance. I'm hoping you'll help me with some answers to a couple of questions I have. It's most disturbing as I'm sure you'll agree when you hear me out."

"I'll do what I can, Ms. Cunningham."

"I'm hoping that you might remember my husband—a doctor, by the name of Matthew Cunningham?"

There was a strange silence and she heard him swallow.

"I often helped out at the clinic before I retired completely, mostly working with the residents and new doctors."

"I'm sure they found that helpful." Darci prayed that he would tell her what he knew. She had a feeling he had more to say.

He cleared his throat. "There was a small team of doctors interested in alternative forms of cancer treatments. You know the type that are just on the verge of a break through, tested perhaps in other countries, but not yet approved by the FDA."

"Yes." Darci chewed on her nail, before pressing on.

"Was Matt a part of this team?"

"Yes, he was and a damn good doctor."

"Yes, he was." Darci bit her lip to keep her composure. "I understand that had also contracted a form of cancer."

"Well, of course, you would know that he'd been recently diagnosed with pancreatic cancer. Unfortunately, when I saw him just before he volunteered for his treatment—"

"Treatment?"

"He told me that he'd obtained a drug from overseas and that he intended to try it. Of course, we all hoped that it would work."

"You were with him, then—during this treatment?" Darci's head felt as though it was floating somewhere between reality and fantasy. She sat down to simply ground herself.

"No, they preferred that I leave once I set up the IV drip. Your husband, in particular, asked that I leave. With him being a doctor and his friend there, he preferred that if anyone found out that he didn't want my reputation tarnished."

"Tarnished, how?" The questions rolled out of her mind like a ticker tape.

"Well, to be frank, Ms. Cunningham, drugs like this are only available for a very high price and in this country would only be attainable through someone with a connection to the black market."

Darci let that part soak into her being. *Matt involved with the black market? Why would Matt use himself as a guinea pig—?* "Um, Dr. Stillman. May I ask why Matt would choose this over other, more standard treatments?"

There was a heavy sigh. "Ms. Cunningham, your husband's prognosis was—um, very limited. Pancreatic cancer is a very lethal type of cancer. With little to no early signs, it can spread quickly, and unfortunately we still do not possess the level of treatments in this country to deal with this particular disease once it invades strategic areas of the body—as was the case of your husband. There was little chance of his survival using any of the known standard treatments. I will say that your husband was a very brave man to try something so radical. I can't say how or where he obtained this medication, but I can say, he must have had some connections in very high places."

There was another pause as she tried to assimilate what she was hearing. Whitney Houston's voice on the radio belting out "*I Will Always Love You*" floated through what little bit of reality Darci clung to.

"Ms. Cunningham? Pardon me for asking, but you act as though you weren't entirely aware of your husband's condition."

"He was my husband for twenty-two years." She heard the words and yet was detached emotionally from them, unable yet to accept what she was hearing. Maybe this was a nightmare and soon she would wake up and everything would make sense again.

"Perhaps he didn't wish to worry you with all the details."

Darci stared out the window unable to comprehend what Matt must have suffered, mentally and physically. Dr. Stillman's voice broke her from her reverie.

"I'm truly sorry for your loss. If there are any other questions you have, I'm afraid I won't be able to help. As far as any records go, your husband's treatment, or my involvement with them is non-existent. It was for the safety of all of us, you understand." There was a pause. "I know your husband must have cared a great deal about you to have gone to such measures to try to preserve his life."

His words, intended to comfort, served only to deepen the emptiness inside her.

"Thank you, Dr. Stillman."

"Good luck, Ms. Cunningham."

"Yes, thank you."

She placed the receiver in the cradle, her gaze redirected to the flames flickering in the fireplace. It was hard enough to digest that Matt had cancer. He'd looked in perfect health the last time—Darci fisted her hand to her mouth, squeezing back her tears.

She picked up the carbon report of the medical examiner

and frowned at the diagnosis. How long had Peter known about Matt's condition? Was he with him at the end? Why hadn't he told her what happened that night other than Matt had collapsed from a heart attack?

Sour bile rose in her throat and she covered her mouth, running towards the bathroom, stubbing her toe on the couch as she stumbled past it. She dropped to her knees on the cold tile flooring and hung her head over the porcelain bowl retching her insides over and over until her ribs ached.

Laying her cheek in the crook of her arm, she sobbed for her loss, for the deception, and for Matt's pain.

Pulling herself to her feet, she splashed water over her face and refused to look at herself in the mirror. Tomorrow, Peter would be here and she would try finding closure in the answers he could give her.

She pressed her palms to the wall for support as she made her way to the bedroom. For now, all she wanted to do was sleep.

Chapter Twenty-Two

The screaming toddler wriggled free from his mother's arms, slithering to the floor where she left him clutching at her calves in his torment. "I want to go *hooome*."

The woman glanced up catching Tyler's gaze and on her face was painted the frustration of everyone stuffed inside the now too small airport waiting area.

Long lines of travelers caught in the flight delays pushed toward the food vendors and bookstands, searching for some respite to their forced detainment. Fog all along the eastern coast was creating bottleneck problems with connections in most Midwestern major cities, including Chicago.

Tyler had managed to get a red-eye flight to O'Hare, but was now stuck in the restless mass of humanity; all wishing they could be somewhere else.

He glanced at his watch for the hundredth time, hoping for a window of opportunity to present itself.

"You the guy that called about a charter?" A man, not much younger than Tyler with a heavy black beard, stood in front of Tyler, his jaw working diligently on the wad of pink bubble gum in his mouth.

"Uh, yeah, that's me. They said it could be a few more hours." Tyler stood to face the man.

He shrugged. " You can wait until it's completely clear, or if you want, there is a bit of a clearing happening right now, if you're willing to head out immediately."

Tyler grabbed his carry on and his backpack. "Let's go."

They walked side-by-side, dodging children and people talking on their cell phones.

"Where exactly north are we headed?" It was the first

words the man had spoken for the last ten minutes.

"Mackinac Island."

The man nodded, cinching up the zipper of his combat parka as he pointed Tyler to an exit door.

"I'm from up there. Well, St, Ignace. Zachary is my name. Call me Zach."

Tyler adjusted his luggage to shake the pilot's hand.

"You live on the island?" He held the door open against a fierce gust of wind.

"Not yet," Tyler answered, his apprehension accelerating as he peered across the airway tarp and studied the twin-engine plane.

Another gust of wind nearly tore Tyler's glasses from his face as they reached the plane.

Zach pushed an oversized pack into the cargo hold and took Tyler's large bag pushing it into the opening.

"I'll keep this." Tyler shifted his backpack over his shoulder.

The pilot manually drew down a short flight of stairs that lead into the belly of the plane. "Hope you ate. There aren't any stewardess's on this flight." He chuckled as he followed Tyler, pulling in the door behind him.

Tyler scanned the six passenger seats in front of him, all empty. "I'm fine—do I sit anywhere?"

"It's just you and me, bud." Zach peeled off his jacket, hanging it in a small closet just outside the pilot's cabin.

"You mind if I use my cell phone?"

"Wait til we clear the tower."

Tyler nodded, feeling the small plane shudder with a gust of wind. "You sure—"

"I'll get you where you need to go, Mr. Landston. Have a few years under my belt. Did some time in Desert Storm as a pilot."

"That makes me feel better," Tyler muttered quietly as he chose a seat up front, where he could see the back of Zach's head.

* * *

Shaking off the after effects of turbulence, Tyler dialed the hotel number he'd logged into this phone file.

"Thank you for calling the Iroquois hotel. We are currently unable to take your call at this time, but a representative will be happy to return your call as soon as possible. Please leave your name and number at the tone."

He waited for the beep and spoke, hoping that it would be Maevey that would answer the message. "Maevey, it's Tyler Landston. I'm on a charter headed to the island tonight. I need to talk to Darci about this guy, Peter Beck. If you get in call me on my cell phone 555-3494."

"You like the Doobie Brothers?" the pilot yelled over the drone of the twin engines.

They were high enough above the clouds that the sun shone in the late afternoon, giving a new and brighter slant to things. Tyler hoped that it was an omen to a brighter tomorrow as well.

"That's fine," Tyler yelled back and looked at his watch. He leaned back in his seat and shut his eyes as *Michael McDonald's* gravelly voice belted out "*Takin' It To The Street.*"

* * *

The nausea from the night before subsided after Darci rested, but she lay in bed until close to noon trying to find the energy to face what she would have to face this evening. The weariness in her body precipitated by the emotions still stirring inside her over the past few hours.

As she cocooned herself in the warm, security of the comforter her thoughts drifted, not to Matt, but to her surprise, to Tyler Landston.

In such a relatively short time, he'd been able to turn her heart inside out. He'd made her believe she could experience a love as complete as the one she'd already been lucky enough to have once in her lifetime.

A pang of guilt pushed her face into her pillow when she thought of all the people who never find that kind of love just once. Had she been wrong in what she perceived was happening between them? Was she so desperately lonely that she saw only what she wanted to see, despite the facts?

And the fact was, Tyler had gone to Las Vegas, presumably to the home of this former woman he'd been involved with. There had been no more phone calls or attempts to contact her and she could only blame herself in that regard. Still, if he'd thought the relationship was worth pursuing—

She sighed, tossing to her back. "Stop torturing yourself like this and move on. You have things to deal with Darci and you are going to need every ounce of energy to get through this day." Despite the willingness to believe she could forget Tyler Landston, she could not forget the passion in his eyes every time he'd looked at her.

The phone jangled Darci from her reverie and she reluctantly pulled her legs over the edge of the bed. She reached for the phone, dropping the receiver once, before getting better hold of it. "Hello?"

"Mom? Got your message, is everything all right?"

"Oh sure it is, honey. Maevey left for the mainland this weekend and I guess I got a pang of loneliness. Just checking in." Darci moved around the room as she spoke, straightening the bed and picking up dirty clothes she'd allowed to pile up on her reading chair.

"That's understandable. Halloween was always a big deal at our house if you'll remember." Leah chuckled quietly.

Unable to deal with talking about the past with what lie before her, Darci pressed on to deviate from the subject. "You'll be proud of me. I am going with Maevey to a costume party tonight."

"Really? That's wonderful!"

Her daughter seemed overjoyed to pounce on the fact that her mother had a social life.

"Uncle Peter is coming up." She let the words fall casually, unsure how Leah would react.

"Oh. That's nice—I think. Why?" If nothing else, Leah had developed her mother's ability to face things head on— sometimes with a stubborn bent.

"We've got some things to discuss; finances, investments,

248

that kind of thing."

"Is he staying at the house?"

Darci held out the receiver, mildly surprised by Leah's bold query.

"No, he'll stay at a hotel. There are some open through the season." *If he chooses to stay at all after I'm done with him.*

"Good." The lilt in Leah's voice meant only one thing. She was holding out hope that Tyler Landston was not yet totally out of the picture.

"Let's not go there, Leah." Darci glanced at the clock on her dresser. Maevey should have called by now. "Sweetheart, I've got to go. Maevey has my costume and I need to find out if she needs me to come by and get it."

"Okay, well tell Uncle Peter hi and have a great time." There was a pause. "But, not too great of a time."

"I hear you." Darci laughed. "Talk to you soon. Love you."

"Love you too, Mom."

Darci disconnected with Leah and immediately dialed the hotel, receiving the answering machine.

Listening patiently, Darci waited for the tone and spoke, "Maevey, wondering where the costumes are—"

A knock on the door pulled her attention from finishing her sentence. Perhaps that was Maevey now with the costumes; either that or it was Peter, arriving earlier than anticipated?

Placing the receiver in the charger, she peeked out the window to see Abe's delivery carriage pulling from her curb. The last time he visited her, he brought a furnace. What had he left her now?

She ran to the front door, tearing it open and screamed as a large bag tumbled into her arms. A note was stapled to where the hanger emerged and Darci turned it over to read it.

"I had some last minute alterations on my costume. Abe was returning to the island earlier and said he'd drop this off for me. It's the best I could find at this late date. I honestly think you'll be the hit of the party. Could you please meet Abe

at the center and help him with decorations? I'll be there as quickly as I can. Ta, Maevey."

Darci stuck the paper between her teeth and scanned the huge, opaque blue bag. "Ta?" Darci muttered as she sought to grip the bag in her arms as she kicked the front door shut.

"This is some hoop skirt for this dress." She walked sideways down the hallway and when she laid the bulging bag on her bed, it looked like a small domed tent atop her mattress.

There was little time to speculate how she was going to handle a hoop skirt. She had just enough time to take a quick shower and get into her costume before she walked to the center to meet Abe.

* * *

"Boy, this fog is really going to sock in the island tonight. We're lucky we got here when we did," Zach called over his shoulder to Tyler, much the same as he'd been for the last half hour. He had a feeling the seasoned pilot was aware of his apprehension of flying in such weather.

Tyler tried to block out the dark gray and white swirl outside his window; visions of old *Twilight Zone* episodes running through his brain. "I assume it will it get better then as we get lower?" There was a recognizable dryness in his throat.

"Oh yeah, there's a good probability, but you'll want to stay buckled, we're bound to hit some turbulence."

"Not a problem," Tyler lied as he tugged his seat belt tighter. To take his mind off the flight he pulled out his cell phone and tried to reach Maevey.

He glanced out the window, listening to the succession of rings and caught glimpses through the clouds of city lights still far below.

"Is that the island?" Tyler chewed at the inside corner of his lip, wondering if he should try Darci. With a quite chuckle, he reprimanded himself that for a guy who traveled most of his life, he sure as hell was jumpy about this flight.

Tyler swallowed hard as reality pierced his nerves. Perhaps it was because he never had someone so important waiting on the other end before.

"Hello?" A woman's voice, and not the machine, finally answered the hotel's phone.

"Maevey?" Tyler wasn't prepared with exactly what to say to her.

"Yes? May I ask who's calling?" Her tone was cautious. No doubt it would be, given the message he'd left earlier.

"It's Tyler—"

"We're on approach to the island, Mr. Landston. You'll have to cut that short."

"Where are you?"

"I'm heading to the island. Listen, Maevey, I need to talk to Darci about this Peter Beck. I thought maybe if you could—"

"Well that's handy since he'll be here this evening for our Community Harvest party."

"Peter Beck is there?" Tyler's brows knit in confusion. He tore off his glasses, pressing the bridge of his nose between his thumb and forefinger, trying to track his thoughts.

"Darci invited him up for the party and then she had some business to discuss with him about Matt's investments. Not that that's any concern of yours, mind you."

Tyler bolted upright in his chair, wincing as the secure belt stretched taut over his lap. "Maevey, you can't let her—"

"I'm sorry, Mr. Landston. You'll have to wait—" Zach reiterated.

Tyler held up his palm. "Just a second. Maevey, where is Peter staying?"

"I'm not sure that is any concern of yours either, Mr. Landston after the way you've treated my cousin."

"I don't mean it that way—I mean—I do care, but, dammit, listen to me carefully, Maevey. I don't have time to explain. You have to contact the authorities on the island and meet me—" Tyler frowned realizing he'd never really seen an officer the whole time he'd been there. "You have police there, don't you?"

"It's a historical town, not the dark ages." Her tone was dry.

Tyler raked his hand through his hair in frustration. In his gut, he knew Darci had found out something and was planning on confronting Peter alone.

"What is going on?" Maevey's voice was insistent.

"Mr. Landston." Zach's voice was equally insistent.

They hit an air pocket, jarring the plane enough to jumpstart Tyler into a quick and candid overview—just in case he didn't make it.

"I have information about Peter. He's involved in some very shady dealings and I am concerned for Darci's safety. Please do what I say? Where is Darci now?"

"At the community center probably."

"Meet me there and bring the police, I swear I will explain everything."

"Tyler, I—"

"Maevey, trust me. I wouldn't be up in this pea soup if what was down there wasn't extremely important to me."

Static crackled over the phone.

"Okay." And they were disconnected.

Chapter Twenty-Three

"Next year, I'm not sending Maevey for costumes." Darci spoke to herself as glanced own at the three-toed orange feet—a compliment to bright orange tights and rotund, yellow, feathered foam "Big Bird" body.

"Sure has been a hit with the kids." Abe Fiskas sidled up to the buffet table laden with an array of tempting potluck contributions from the winter community residents. He surveyed the harvest of selections, finally deciding on a powdered lemon bar.

Darci felt a tug on her tail feathers and peered behind her to find Bo-Peep.

"Watch the beak." Abe ducked to the side and laughed as he walked away.

"Sorry, Abe," she called out to him, and then looked down through the narrow opening beneath the foot-long beak and smiled. "Hi."

The miniature Bo Peep stared up at her with wide blue eyes; apparently mesmerized at seeing the great yellow bird up close and personal. "I know my "ABC's," do you want to hear?" There was a lilt of pride tucked into her request that Darci couldn't refuse.

She bent down to meet the child's gaze, lifting the beak so as to see her more clearly. "I'd love to hear your ABC's." Darci grinned as the little girl stepped back giving out an ear-piercing squeal.

"I don't talk to strangers!" The child slammed the heel of her foot down solidly on top of Darci's foam foot and ran through the crowd screaming for her mother.

She took a deep breath and straightened, grateful for the

three inch padding softening the blow.

"Looks like you're already making friends."

Startled, her gaze shot to the familiar voice.

"Whoa, careful with that thing." Peter ducked to the side as the great beak preceded her.

"When—" Darci's voice broke from the immediate constriction in her throat. She lifted the rubberized headpiece over her head and stared at the one man who could answer the question that had kept her awake for many nights.

How did my husband die?

He bent forward giving her a quick kiss. "Just got in. Had a delay because their best pilot was booked. That fog is rolling in." His smile was congenial as he poured a cup of punch, lifting to his lips as he scanned the crowd gathered on the town hall.

She wanted to ask if he'd checked in to one of the hotels open all winter on the island. "So, where's your costume?" Darci averted from his blue gaze as she realized her Freudian slip. She fought to quell the nervousness that bordered on her fears. Fear that the man who'd claimed to be "Uncle Peter" had another side to him—one that held a great many secrets.

"Darci, I'm not into Halloween." He snorted, "I thought you knew that." He glanced at her in surprise, an odd grin on his face.

She took a sip of punch as she watched him from the corner of his eye. His gaze kept wandering back to her, sending icy chills up her spine. Darci knew that to openly confront Peter was treading on thin ice, hopefully her decision to do so in the safety of the crowd gathered there tonight.

"Would you like to dance?"

He placed his cup on the table and took hers from her grasp at the same time.

This was how he'd always been. Take charge, telling you what he wanted and then moving forward, however, perhaps the dance floor would be the most public place to ask him her question. "Sure."

He scratched his chin as he looked down at her as though

evaluating how to put his arms around her. It was the first time Darci thanked Maevey for the blessed costume. Had things turned out differently, it might be Tyler there trying to decide how to put his arms around her. There'd been times—like now—she wished she'd had him to talk to...lean on.

"It's hard to put my arms around you." He chuckled as he groped at her waist.

She grabbed his hands. "Maybe we'll just hold hands and dance?" She offered him a grin as fake as the oversized bird feet stuck on the ends of her legs.

A moment of silence hung in between them, Peter glancing at the other couples moving to the slow dance in each other's arms. She sensed he was not happy with the outcome. Still, she forged ahead, better to get things out on the table and deal with them. That's how she'd always lived her life.

"Peter? I was hoping you'd be able to clarify a couple of questions since we last talked about Matt." She approached carefully, not sure how much information he knew and how much he may have been keeping from her.

"Darci, honey—let it go." His voice reflected his weariness in talking about the subject and that gave Darci pause for concern.

Yet the voice of the retired physician echoed in her ear. *"Your husband must have cared a great deal about you to have gone to such measures."*

If Peter really knew only what the report indicated then he needed to know what she'd discovered in order to help her find out what really happened to Matt.

He touched her cheek with his fingertips, a softness pervading his gaze. "I'm truly looking forward to this weekend, Darci. I was so glad when you asked me to come up. I mean, it will be nice for it to be—you know, just the two of us. I promise I'll answer any questions you have."

He placed a gentle kiss on her forehead and for a moment, she wished she believed him—she wanted to, but more than that, she wished it were Tyler she was dancing with. Darci lowered her face, not wanting to give him anymore incentive than what was already flitting through his head.

She swallowed. "Peter, I think I need to sit down. Do you—" She edged from his grasp. "Can we just—sit over here and talk?"

"Sure sweetheart. You go ahead and sit down. I'll get us some punch."

Her mind swirled with how to ask him what she needed to know. If he'd kept information from her, she wanted to know what and how much—and more so why? Were there other secrets that Matt was keeping from her as well?

Darci's stomach turned and she closed her eyes, pressing her clasped hands to her lips. She had to get control of her emotions.

"Here we go." He grinned as he handed her the Styrofoam cup, his expression as chipper as if they were on a prom date.

He eased into the chair beside her, leisurely placing his arm over her shoulder.

Darci straightened as best she could without appearing rude, as she sipped her punch.

"Do I make you uncomfortable?"

She stared at the cup grasped between her hands. "I just think that maybe you have the wrong idea about why I invited you up this weekend." Darci glanced at him.

His blonde brow arched on his tan face as he carefully pulled back his arm, resting it on the table. "Not ready yet to tread into a new relationship?"

Her cheeks warmed, remembering the passionate afternoon she and Tyler spent not more than two weeks ago. "I guess so, yeah."

A tight, discomforting lag in their conversation followed.

Peter's gaze held on the few couples still dancing to the record-playing local DJ at the other end of the floor.

Darci sat quietly sensing the tension radiating from his body next to hers. Her eyes searched for Maevey. She promised to be there when she talked to Peter—*where was she?*

"Why did you ask me here?" His focus stayed on the dancers, but she detected the rigid tone in his voice and it was different than the annoyed tone he normally took with her.

She sighed, deciding it was time to lay everything on the table. After all, it wasn't as though he was a jealous psycho. His advances toward her, in retrospect, had been harmless and his loyalty to her family—devout.

"Peter, I need to know what happened to Matt." She pressed her lips tight until her teeth pressed into the soft flesh as she fought the tears threatening spill forth.

"Darci, honey. I know your counselors said it would take time, but you really need to move on with your life. Leah and Nathan need you. *I*—need you."

She pushed what he was trying to tell her out of the way, her obsessive pursuit for the truth keeping her train of thought in line. "You and Matt went to play basketball that night, right?"

"Darci—"

"Peter, please," Darci snapped, crushing the cup in her hands. Bile rose in her throat, hoping he would not put off telling her the truth. She needed to know everything to have closure. If Matt had been living a lie—

"Just like every Friday night, you know that." Peter leaned against the table, his muscular forearms showing where he'd shoved his sweater to his elbows.

A deep red scar divided the silky blonde hair of his arm. Darci frowned, having not remembered seeing it before.

"What's this all about, Darci?" He studied her, his gaze dropping to his arm and he tugged down the sleeve.

"Did you have an accident?" Her eyes lifted meeting his.

"It's nothing, but I am concerned about that look in your eye. It's like—hell, it's like you don't *trust me*, or something." He grabbed her hand, twining his fingers through hers. "That's pretty strange after all these years, don't you think?"

Darci pressed on despite his obvious attempts at being evasive. "And you were with him when he had his heart attack?"

He played with her fingers, the way a lover would do. "Yes, as I've told you several times now. We were on our way home from the gym when Matt started having chest pain. We both kind of laughed it off as over exertion, you know?" He gave her a weak smile and she could see in his eyes that he was going back in his memory to that night.

"By the time I got him to the hospital, Matt was—" He stopped, pressing the back of his free hand over his mouth, his face contorted in anguish.

Torn between compassion and mistrust, Darci tentatively reached over and placed her hand on his forearm. "I know about the cancer."

His brows raised, as miraculously, his expression returned to normal. He turned to her, his eyes as clear as a winter's night. "What did you say?"

She tugged trying to free her hand from his iron-tight grip. "Peter, you're hurting me."

As though she'd thrown ice water in his lap, he released her with a start, brusquely rubbing his hands over his face.

"I'm sorry, Darci. It's just I haven't thought about this for a long time. Maybe I've tried to block it out because it hurt too much."

She took a deep breath, wishing no stone to be unturned now. "What have you tried to block out?" Darci glanced around aware they sat alone at the far end of the gymnasium.

"Darci, you have to believe I was doing what Matt wanted. He asked me to keep it quiet."

Cold fear grabbed her heart as she forced herself to speak. "What was it that Matt wanted kept quiet, Peter?"

She stood, clutching the edge of the table and he followed her movement. Her stomach churned and for a moment she thought she would be sick.

"I had to. I couldn't stand by and watch that god-damn disease eat him alive."

Her mind grappled with this new information. Then it was true that he had cancer and Peter knew about it, but why did they keep it from her and the children?

Darci edged toward the door, unsure if it was she or Peter on the verge of madness.

"Don't you see, sweetheart? I couldn't let that happen. It wasn't fair to Matt, or to you—especially to you and the kids, Darci. I couldn't bear to watch you suffer as Matt withered away into nothing."

Peter's icy gaze frosted as he spoke, his tone becoming more insistent. "I tried to get him to tell you about it, but he knew you would never approve of the experimental medicine that—we found."

Ringing in Darci's ears caused her to stumble. "Found?"

He stepped around the table, quickly embracing her. "You realize that I have loved you from the very first day I met you at school. You remember, Darci?" His nervous laugh accentuated the insanity of his words.

Frozen in place, Darci hoped that someone would see them. Her mind wanted to scream, but the desire to know once and for all the truth of what happened to her husband. "Peter?" She eased away from him so she could look into his face. His hands still held a tight grip of her arms. "What happened that night?"

He frowned as he studied her face, and then he closed his eyes and took a deep breath. "If I tell you, you must believe I did what I did—for you and for Matt." His gaze lifted to hers, pleading with her to accept the conditions.

She nodded and wondered if this was the face of death that Matt had seen before he—

"Matt found out about the cancer, not long before he—" Peter shut his eyes. "He asked me to keep it quiet, certain that together we could find a drug to help treat it." Peter cleared his throat, his grip on her arms digging into her flesh. "He said he didn't want to frighten you and the kids. So, we told you that we were going to play basketball, like always. Instead, we arranged for Matt's first treatment."

Darci averted her face from looking at him. Her stomach sickened with the suspicion of what he was about to tell her. Fear and confusion washed over her debilitating her from moving. "You're lying—" She spoke the words, her mind hazy with confusion. She just wanted to be away from him, she no longer wanted to hear the truth. "You used Matt for his money and when you saw the opportunity to have it all—" Tears escaped, sliding down her cheeks in torrents as she envisioned Matt in a bed with IV's hooked into his arms. Had he fought with Peter? Had he been strong enough?

She jerked from his grasp and swung her arm at him, but too fast, Peter locked his arms over hers.

"I knew you would think that. I knew you would never understand why I couldn't let him live as half a man—when I was able to give you everything."

"You killed him!" She spat out the words, her heart splintering into a million tiny shards.

"Oh honey, I know you're upset now, but in time, you'll see it was for the best. There was no hope for poor Matt. The doctors had already confirmed the disease had progressed. Simply turning up the drip only aided the eminent. He was much better off going that way than suffering the ravages of that disease. None of us wanted would have wanted Matt to suffer, would we?"

She felt the blood drain from her face, reality slipping away with her blood flow. "But the certificate said it was a heart attack." Her voice sounded weak even to her own ears.

Peter raked a free hand through his hair as he brought his face within inches of hers. "I had to. I did it for you." He kissed her forehead. "It was all for us, Darci. Everything I did, I did because of how I felt about you."

He pulled her against him as he stroked the back of her head like a limp rag doll. Darci's legs turned rubbery as the thought flitted through her mind that she was in the embrace of her husband's murderer.

* * *

"Let her go, Peter."

The giant of a man turned toward Tyler, his grasp held fast to one of Darci's arms. "Landston?" His gaze shot to Darci's, "Did *you* invite him here?"

"She didn't. Now let her go, it's over." Tyler glanced at Darci, her face tear-stained and ashen stared back at him, but he could see she was in shock. He'd hoped Maevey and the police would have already arrived, but when he walked through the doors to see Darci take a swing at Peter, he knew he couldn't wait.

"Stay out of this, Landston. You only used her like you have all the other women in your life. I won't let you do that. I won't let you seduce her into your bed again and treat her like your other whores." Peter jabbed his forefinger at Tyler, his voice rising in anger.

A crowd of townspeople began to filter to that end of the building, parents holding their children from getting to close.

"Peter, you're not well." Tyler attempted to calm the wild-eyed man with reason. "If you cooperate with the police, I'm sure that—" He took a step toward Darci, poised to snatch her away from him.

Peter took a step forward, placing himself between Tyler and Darci. "You don't know anything, Landston. You don't know that Darci wishes that it was me that afternoon."

Tyler paused, listening.

"Yeah, I heard the two of you. How you fed her your bull about being special—well she knows, Landston. She knows you're a fake, only after her money. I told her about you." He turned to Darci, his expression half-crazed. "Tell him Darci. Tell him that it's always been me you wanted. Matt was never the kind of man you really needed we both knew that, didn't wc? I should thank you for sticking it out with him as long as you did. The money he made was something at least, making it possible for me to invest and build for our future. I know that's what you did. You stayed with him for his money, so we could build our future together. Sweetheart, I want so much for us. I can give you everything now. There's no one now to stop us from being together. Don't you see—?"

"Beck." Tyler's gaze met Darci's, but her eyes glazed over as she stared at Peter. He doubted she could even hear him.

"Darci, tell this jerk that you want to be with me now. That we can finally be together like we've always dreamed it would be—just you and me. Oh Darci, I've dreamt of this moment forever." He dropped to his knees in front of her and clasped his hands around her waist, pressing his face against the rotund yellow belly of her costume. "I love you. I don't know how else I can prove it. I've taken care of everything, every detail, so that nothing can come between us now."

Tyler stayed where he was, afraid for Darci's safety. Clearly the man was teetering over the edge. He tried to get her attention with his eyes, but she'd shut out Peter's rantings moments before and had not come back to reality.

"Darci, walk over to me. The police are on their way and there are all these witnesses. He won't do anything stupid." Tyler took a step toward the pair, praying his hunch was right.

"No." Peter stood, his eyes wild with determination. "She won't go with you. I can't let her, you see. I've worked too long to make her see my feelings. Too many years, too much time watching as Matt took her to his bed, when it should have been me!" He pushed Darci protectively behind him again, like a fierce dog with its catch. "She should have carried *my* children, she should have been in *my* bed. Then none of this would have had to happen. I had no choice, but I do now and I won't let her go again."

His voice turned menacing as his gaze narrowed. "No one, least of all *you*, is going to take away what's rightfully *mine*."

"She's a human being, Beck. She has a free will." Tyler held out his hand in reason. *Where the hell were the police?*

"Let her go," a voice piped up from the crowd.

Tyler kept his eye on Peter as he inched closer to where he had Darci pinned behind him.

Peter acknowledged the crowd that had formed a cluster behind Tyler. "This man doesn't have her best interests in hand. He only wants to use her. Just like Matt, don't you see? Did he secure her future? No, *I did*. He trusted me with everything—except the one thing I wanted most."

Beck closed his eyes briefly. "If she knew he was sick, she would have tried to save him. I couldn't let her do that. I couldn't let her suffer trying to save a dying man. Just wasting more precious time."

He looked over the crowd, his voice weary now. "It was meant to be, you see?' He shrugged. "Matt was going to die anyway, I just helped it along. So she wouldn't suffer. So I could take care of her where Matt had failed. It's all so simple." Peter chuckled with an exhausted laugh.

He was weakening, the reality of what he'd done, what he'd confessed to the entire group of strangers was beginning to take its toll. Tyler didn't care much about his condition; the courts could decide what to do with him. He needed to get him away from Darci.

"Come on, Peter. Let's go sit down. I won't go near her, you have my word."

"No. No, she's not ready yet. She's not—ready."

"Let her go, Peter." Tyler touched his arm; certain that given his mental state the anger would be turned toward him. Then he hoped someone would grab Darci.

Peter's arm swung out grabbing Tyler's throat and his breathing halted as he clenched his teeth for the last bit of air in his lungs.

Two men from behind rushed forward grabbing Peter around the middle and struggled to pull him from the iron grip he had on Tyler's neck.

Tyler worked at Peter's fingers trying to loosen his hold as he kept his gaze locked to Peter. "Was this how it was, Peter?" He spoke through clenched teeth.

"You son-of-a—you couldn't know how hard it was for me to have to kill him." Peter's hold tightened and Tyler fought to save his breath.

Peter forgot about Darci as he focused on Tyler. He wrapped both hands around Tyler's neck.

"Jump him!"

Freed from her imprisonment, Darci blinked as though

just awakening. With a fierce look of determination she swung at Peter with her bright yellow wing, connecting with a resounding thwack to the side of his head. "*That's* for my husband."

Peter stumbled, caught off-guard by the blow, and it was enough for Tyler to duck forward, plowing into the man's side and take him and the bewildered man to the floor.

Chapter Twenty-Four

Tyler's fist connected with Peter's nose, splattering blood over his jacket as it broke.

Dazed, Peter Beck raised his arm to protective himself from the assault. "Get him off me. He's crazy."

A rush of adrenaline coursed through Tyler at his accusation. He didn't even know Matt, but he somehow wanted to vindicate what Matt could not.

"You son-of-a-bitch." Tyler slammed his fist into Peter's jaw. "What kind of game did you think you were playing with people's lives?"

Tyler glanced at his knuckles, split and oozing with blood—or maybe it was Beck's.

"You don't understand—"

"I understand what you've put this family though." Tyler pulled his arm back, readying to take out his frustration out on Beck's face again.

"Put your hands on your head and don't move!" A gruff, authoritative voice of a man banked off the walls of the wide-open room.

Tyler looked up and Beck's hands captured his throat again.

"Get up, both of you. Right now."

Tyler set his knee purposely in Beck's gut and pushed himself upright. He staggered and Abe caught his arm steadying him.

"Nobody move. Let's just all stay calm."

The lanky officer rushed cautiously forward, brushing Tyler's shoulder as he moved toward Peter. "Name?"

Tyler coughed as the air seeped back into his lungs. He

glanced at Darci who was focused on the officer with the gun in his hand. "Tyler Landston."

The policeman nodded and turned his attention to the other man pulling himself off the floor.

In a change faster than weather on the Straits, Peter grinned openly at the policeman, holding out his arm refusing help at getting up. "Officer, it was a minor disagreement, I assure you, and no one has been harmed." His hand covered his nose, the blood streaming down his hand as gravity took over.

The officer lowered his gun point blank at Peter's chest. "Keep those on your head."

"My nose—" Peter clamped his palms against the top of his head, his gaze narrowing on Tyler.

Another uniformed officer slipped between Darci and Peter, carefully distancing her from harm as he grabbed Peter's wrist and snapped on a set of cuffs.

"What the hell is this?" Peter bellowed, twisting toward the policeman behind him.

Tyler grabbed Peter's free arm, twisting it perhaps a bit too far behind Peter's back. "Game over, *Uncle Peter*." He pushed just once up on his arm, satisfied in seeing the large man wince.

The officer snapped on the other cuff and grabbed the crook of Peter's elbow, the second officer flanking his other side. "We'll take it from here." And with that, they hauled Peter, broken and bleeding, from the community center.

Maevey rushed forward awkwardly embracing Darci. "Are you all right? He didn't hurt you, did he? The man is a monster. He had us all believing he was someone else." She glanced at Tyler. "Why don't you let Mr. Landston take you home? I'm sure the police will need to speak with you, but I can bring them by later."

As he waited for Darci's decision, Tyler looked over his shoulder at the semi-circle formed around the chaos. Given things were generally quiet on the island, most appeared to be in shock at the spectacle that had just unfolded before them.

In an effort to restore some sense of normalcy, Tyler spread his arms as he walked toward the crowd, taking charge if for no other reason than he wanted to talk to Darci in private. "Everything is fine now. No one is hurt, and it would be best if we all continued with the celebration."

They stared at him in silence and then Abe grabbed Dolly from the mercantile and bellowed to the DJ, "Let's get some music started!" He glanced over his shoulder at Tyler and winked, his bushy white brow covering his eyelid.

Slowly a titter of conversation started, followed by a few couples making their way back to the dance floor. This was one hell of a way to introduce himself as a new resident of the island, Tyler thought. Now, there was only Darci to convince—

Tyler took a deep breath and glanced over his shoulder as Maevey appeared at his side. Her expression was one of concern.

"She's on her way home."

"By herself? Maevey, she shouldn't be alone." Tyler turned to leave only to have Maevey grab his arm.

"She's been through hell. Give her some time for it all to settle."

Tyler thought back over the past twenty-four hours—hell, the last thirty-nine years of his life. "I don't want to waste one more minute of time without her. Can you understand that?" He smiled at the total simplicity of his thoughts. To his utter surprise, Maevey grinned and the sparkle of life snapped in her gaze.

She nodded. "Then I guess you better go do what you must do. She'll not be difficult to find."

"Look for a short, angry, yellow bird," Tyler called as he backed toward the exit. "Oh, by the way, the pilot who brought me here—Zach, he says to tell you hi."

Maevey's brows arched and she smiled. "Really?"

Tyler shoved open the heavy wood doors of the community center and nearly fell down the short flight of newly refurbished steps. A brisk whoosh of autumn air caught his breath as he peered down the silent, mist-covered street. The shrouded phosphorescent glow of the lamplights cast an eerie reflection on the damp pavement.

In the distance, he heard the muffled sound of horses' hooves tapping against the street and a full moon surrounded by a hazy ring gave an ethereal aspect to the deserted street.

He lifted the collar of his jacket, shaking the hand that had pummeled Peter Beck's face. Even with the insistent stinging, it felt damn good.

He stepped up his pace as the fog drifted quickly in from the water, thickening around him. The rustle of dry leaves skittered across the sidewalk sending an unexpected chill up his spine. While he'd never been one for belief in the oddities of *All Hallows Eve*, he had to admit, that tonight would definitely go down as one of the more strange ways he's spent the holiday.

However, it was facing Darci that frightened him more.

* * *

The heavy mist saturated the feathers of Darci's costume causing it to weigh her down even more than her mental state was already accomplishing. She'd seen Peter's battered face from the back of the squad car as she left. How could she have been so close and not known what kind of man he really was? The grin he gave her as the squad car pulled away was—she closed her eyes, thinking she might get sick.

Unable to absorb everything she'd heard tonight, Darci's mind was void of emotion. She only knew that she wanted to be home, where she could be alone to sift through the pieces of her broken life.

The echo of her solitary footsteps on the wet pavement sounded like rubber flip flops on linoleum—the sound creating an even greater sense of loneliness.

One of the officers told her they'd need a statement tonight, but he'd be by in a few minutes, as soon as they got Peter back to the station. They were probably talking to Tyler now. She was grateful he'd shown up when he did and even though she knew his heart belonged to another woman, she was glad for his presence at that moment. Tomorrow she'd have to stop by and tell Abe thanks for his help as well.

"Darci!" Tyler's voice sliced through the night, the sound of his shoes slapping the pavement indicating that he was running.

She bit her lip as she hesitated beneath the hazy circle of the lamplight. He looked like heaven as he approached from the darkness with a wide grin on his face.

Rain speckled drops covered his glasses, his dark hair hung in damp curls at his neck, wet from the dewy night air.

He stopped a few feet in front of her as though unsure what to say.

"Have you ever heard the term "madder than a wet hen"?" His grin weakened as he studied her. "I'm so sorry—"

Darci's lip trembled and she took a deep breath to keep from running into his arms. "It's not your fault, Tyler. It's not your problem. Thank you. Thank you for your help. Now go on back—to wherever." Darci spread her arms wide, letting her wings drop against her sides. She turned to leave.

"Well, see that's the problem." He grabbed for her arm, instead winding up with a handful of feathers.

"The feathers." Her tone was icy, she knew, but she'd had about all she could take for one evening and it wasn't over yet. "This is going to cost me a fortune." She glanced at him with a sarcastic laugh.

"Sorry, so are you going to let me explain?" He walked at her side, trying with great difficulty to avoid stepping on her great bird feet.

"Tyler." She stopped, turning to face him directly. "I appreciate what you did back there, but don't feel like you owe me any explanation for anything else. I can find my own way home."

He planted his hands on his waist and looked away with a heavy, frustrated sigh. "You know, you can be a damn stubborn woman, sometimes." He pierced her with a look of frustration

Something akin to a fragile twig snapped inside of Darci

269

and she stepped forward like a giant yellow Phoenix rising from the ashes of her evening. One wing smacked his left arm as the other followed close behind to his right.

"I wasn't the one who left and never called."

"I called." He dodged her angry wings as best he could. "You didn't answer my calls." He grabbed her shoulders and pushed her gently back, distancing himself.

"I didn't want to talk to you." She turned abruptly and walked as quickly as her feet would carry her to the gate of her home. God she was tired.

"Talk to me now, Darci. Ask me anything you want and I'll tell you the truth."

She paused staring at him. "Can you get the latch?"

"Oh sure, sorry." Tyler followed her up the walk.

"Anything?" She clomped sideways up the steps and opened her screen door.

"Anything."

He stood behind her holding the screen.

"Can you get the door?" He offered.

As much as she hated to admit it, she couldn't maneuver the wingtips to allow her to put the key in the lock. "No." She hated to admit that she needed his assistance yet again this evening.

He had no expression as he took the key, unlocked the door and pushed it open waiting for her to enter first.

* * *

"Where did you go almost two and a half weeks ago?" Darci stumbled over the ottoman trying to reach the couch.

Tyler reached forward to grab her, but she had managed to awkwardly plop down on the small loveseat. "To Las Vegas, just like I told you." He fought not to smile when her costume billowed up in her face and she groaned.

"Here, let me help." Tyler sat across from her on the coffee table and lifted each foot, removing the gargantuan rubber-soled bird shoes. "Any more questions?"

"Can you help me out of this thing?" Her weary voice was muffled by the feathered costume near her face.

"Thought you'd never ask."

He pulled her upright, facing him and he wanted nothing more than to bend forward the few inches between them and satisfy his craving for her mouth.

"Did you go to see a woman?"

Her gaze narrowed as his lifted from her lips. "Yes."

She wriggled in the space between them, turning around to face away from him and he had to hold onto her to prevent from falling backwards

"There is a hook and then an invisible zipper."

"That's' an understatement. How'd you get into this thing?" When the only response was a brisk sniff, he decided that the best defense was a good offense. He would simply offer up everything about Daphne, and then she would see that she had the wrong idea, just like the tabloids.

"Daphne was a woman I lived with for a time. She and her husband were very good to me."

"I'll bet, " she muttered.

"Are you going to listen to me before you go making judgments?" Tyler found the hook, and began to slowly tug down the zipper so as not to ruffle any more of her feathers. "Interesting costume, by the way."

The soft corkscrew tendrils at the base of her neck called to him, begging to be lifted to kiss the warmth beneath.

"We're talking about you, Mr. Landston."

"Right. " Tyler replied, wondering if he was ever going to get her out of this costume or this suspicious frame of mind. "Daphne and Antonio DeMarco found me on a street corner, selling my pictures for food."

Her head tipped slightly and he had a feeling she was really listening. "They took me in, sent me to school, and in return, I became their personal photographer. That's why the tabloid reporters hated them so much. They offered pictures of their private lives taken by me, whom they trusted, to the press. The pictures in the tabloids could never make it to the big papers because mine were already there."

"They must have been well-to-do and being in Vegas, it

would naturally make people curious how they made their money."

Tyler nodded. "Antonio had connections, sure, but no more than any other successful business man. He made wise choices, good investments."

Tyler thought of Peter and knew that Darci was still in for quite a shock when she found out how Peter had squandered much of Matt's money and why he needed more. Thanks to Daphne's connections, Tyler probably knew more than the authorities, but with Peter in custody, public knowledge of his escapades was only a matter of time. If she let him, though, he'd be at her side the entire way, gladly giving up his studio if she found herself in financial trouble.

Tyler worked at the zipper. "Unfortunately, when you have that high of a profile, the media would rather twist the truth for the sake of a juicy story than simply report the truth. Antonio made good choices, and his money probably helped start up a great many businesses in Las Vegas, but that alone isn't newsworthy."

"Like the questionable way he died?"

Tyler's hands stilled. Obviously Peter had done his homework. "Yeah, like that." He wasn't going to leave anything out with her. If she wanted the truth, then she would hear it all, but it would be from *his* lips.

"I can't say what happened to Antonio. The courts finally ruled it as an accident, but honestly, I have my doubts. The man had some enemies, I'm certain of that. The media though, made a circus out of a descent man's death."

"So, the rumors that you and Daphne were lovers—isn't true?"

She glanced over her shoulder and caught his steady gaze.

He finished unzipping her and the costume split like a giant, foam overcoat put on backwards. "No." Tyler waited as she pulled her arms free of the costume and it fell onto the couch.

He cupped his hands over her shoulders, turning her to face him. "I don't see how you can do that." He studied her face, watching her swallow as she held his gaze.

"Do what?"

"I've never been turned on by helping someone out of a Big Bird costume before."

She blushed and a brief smile played on her lips as she averted her eyes from his.

"Is Daphne your lover?" She looked at him with a seriousness that would have been comical had she known Daphne. Of all people, Daphne would have found the humor in this.

He brushed his hand over her cheek, lifting her chin so she could not escape his gaze. "I loved her dearly, but Daphne died last week."

She opened her mouth to speak and he touched his finger to her lips. "Daphne was eighty years old. You would have loved her yourself had you known her. She had emphysema and Antonio asked that if anything were to happen to him, that I would make sure she was taken care of, until—that's why I had to rush back there."

The memory of he and Daphne's last conversation came vividly to mind. It was that discussion that made him question his feelings for Darci. If this was his chance, he didn't want to let her get away.

"I love you." The words spilled out without thinking. He'd never said the words to anyone with more sincerity and at the same time with so much fear of what the response might be.

Her eyes welled as she studied his face, her expression unsure if he was telling her the truth.

"I'm opening a studio here on the island." He grinned as he thought of Jerry. "And who knows, maybe a restaurant down the road. What do you think about that?"

He wanted to kiss her in the worst way—more than that, he wanted to ask her to marry him, but she had a lot to sort through emotionally, and the distinct possibility of seeing Peter in court. It was too much for now, but he'd wait forever if he had to. It was enough for now that she knew he planned to settle down and that he wanted to be with her.

"I thought I was crazy. I didn't think it was possible for me to feel the way I did—I mean, do. We haven't known each other very long."

Her fingers touched his face, tracing his mouth and it took all of his will power to patiently allow her to think things through. "Do you think it's possible you could *learn* to love me?"

A soft smile played on her lips as she gently shook her head. "Tyler, I come with an awful lot of baggage. Some of it I haven't even opened yet."

He swallowed. "I understand baggage, Darci, remember? Just answer my question."

"Could I learn to love you?"

He closed his eyes and nodded.

"I already do, but is that enough?"

"That's a good start," he whispered as his mouth touched her lips, the soft welcome of her response settling his wayfaring soul.

"I can see that things are going well over here." Maevey's voice came from the doorway, where she and a uniformed officer stood on the other side of the screen.

She opened it and stepped in. "One should learn to shut one's doors, even on a nearly deserted island."

The officer behind Maevey grinned. "I have just a few questions and then I'll be on my way."

Tyler put his arm around Darci and kissed her temple. "You want me to stay?"

"I'm not letting you out of my sight anytime soon."

She glanced up at him and he had a mental picture of the two of them entertaining family and friends right there in that house. "We've got time, officer." He squeezed her close. All that families were supposed to be and more, they would make together.

"We do, don't we?" She smiled and unashamed, kissed him again.

The Beginning

A Brief History of the Hotel Iroquois:

Originally built as a home in 1902, the Hotel Iroquois was purchased and converted to its present use by Samuel Poole in 1904. Mr. and Mrs. Sam McIntire became proprietors of the Hotel Iroquois in 1954.

The Carriage House Dining Room was added to the original, Victorian structure as an additional guest amenity. Since then, the McIntire family has continued to operate the 40 room and six suite deluxe hotel with all the gracious hospitality of yesteryear.

From the Carriage House Dining Room, guests enjoy a unique vantage point to view the 1895 Round Island Lighthouse. The lighthouse served as a beacon to Great Lakes ships that passed through the Straits of Mackinac - confluence of Lake Huron and Michigan.

The Hotel Iroquois is located on the Straits of Mackinac waterfront. Its peaceful lakeside setting is juxtaposed with the lively town of Mackinac just one block away. The Island's historical points of interest are within walking or bicycling distance of the hotel.

906-847-3321 (April-October)
616-247-5675 (November-April 18)

Request a Brochure
http://www.iroquoishotel.com/island.htm

Used with permission: McIntire Family/Nickel Design & LLH Graphics. © 2003 Hotel Iroquois.

Special Links:

Visit magnificent Mackinac Island at www.mackinac.com

Iroquois Hotel
www.iroquoisehotel.com

Island Bookstore
www.islandbookstore.com

The Mackinac IslandTown Crier
C/o The St. Ignace News
PO Box 277
St. Ignace, MI. 49781

Pamela Johnson lives in the heartland of America with her husband and four children. In her short four years of writing, she is multi-published in fiction and non-fiction novels, anthologies, poetry, short stories, and novellas. During her career she has been the recipient of several writing and reviewer awards and contest finalist nominations. Pamela is currently working on the next book in her Shores of Mackinac trilogy.

You can visit her on the web at
www.pamelajohnson.net

Pamela Johnson
Unfinished Dreams

2002 EPPIE Finalist
"A delightful story, full of charm and warmth!"
--Holly Jacobs, author of *I Waxed My Legs For This?*

Gabe Russell is a product of the land, where respect for the earth and family are one in the same. But life takes both from him, leaving only shattered dreams and a deathbed promise in its wake. Now the promise to his father is all he has, but even that is as tenuous as his hold on the house he calls home.

With her spirit nearly broken by an abusive ex-husband, Tess Graham is given another chance--a chance to reclaim her life and find happiness. But in doing so, she risks stealing the dreams of the one man she finds herself drawn to. How can she make things right without losing her own dreams in the process?

Unable to ignore the passion between them, Gabe and Tess seek the comfort of one another in a quest for fulfillment of the ultimate dream...Love

ISBN 1-59080-045-1

To order, visit our web catalog at
http://www.echelonpress.com/catalog/

PAMELA JOHNSON
White Eagle's Lady

2003 EPPIE Finalist
"Sure to leave a sigh on your heart."--Lora Kenton

Embarking on a journey to meet her father, Sarah Reynolds heads into the untamed lands of Georgia. She sets out, eager to take her new position as teacher for the white settlers who, according to her father, are living peacefully with the Cherokees on their land.

Rescued from certain death by a bold Cherokee warrior, Sarah is thrust into the turmoil of the forced emigration of his people. Injured in the attack, White Eagle fights to survive while Sarah learns the hard facts of life.

Thrown together by circumstances beyond their control, White Eagle and Sarah overcome betrayal and tragedy to find a love strong enough to bring nations together.

ISBN 159080-114-8

To order, visit our web catalog at
http://www.echelonpress.com/catalog/

Or ask your local bookseller!

Printed in the United States
1169200001B/52-126